"Are there still men out there who even want to spend a lifetime together?" Ally asked.

Deenie glanced over her shoulder pointedly. "One or two."

Ally followed her gaze.

Ben. Crouching down to put a tiny little dog sweater on Peanut and tuck him inside his coat against his chest so the chihuahua wouldn't get cold outside.

Everything inside of Ally went gooey, but she quashed the emotion. He'd made his feelings clear, even if it still felt like something was humming beneath the surface every time he looked at her. "It doesn't matter how much I want him," she whispered to Deenie, keeping her voice low. "He has to want me back."

Ben looked up at that moment, catching her eye.

"Yeah…" Deenie grinned. "Somehow I don't think that's going to be a problem."

The
Twelve Dogs
of
Christmas

The
Twelve Dogs
of
Christmas

Lizzie Shane

FOREVER
New York Boston

Forever
Hachette Book Group
1290 Avenue of the Americas, New York, NY 10104
read-forever.com
twitter.com/readforeverpub

First Edition: September 2020

Forever is an imprint of Grand Central Publishing. The Forever name and logo are trademarks of Hachette Book Group, Inc.

The publisher is not responsible for websites (or their content) that are not owned by the publisher.

The Hachette Speakers Bureau provides a wide range of authors for speaking events. To find out more, go to www.hachettespeakersbureau.com or call (866) 376-6591.

ISBNs: 978-1-5387-3587-9 (mass market), 978-1-5387-3588-6 (ebook)

Printed in the United States of America

OPM

10 9 8 7 6 5 4 3 2 1

Chapter One

The residents of Pine Hollow, Vermont, liked to think of it as the Mary Poppins of towns. Practically perfect in every way. Which was cute and all—as long as you weren't one of the town council members responsible for making sure everything *stayed* perfect. After two solid years of listening to every little complaint, Ben West figured he'd now sufficiently paid for any crimes committed in a past life.

And Christmas...Christmas was the worst.

The town went nuts for the holiday every year—and Ben's phone exploded with demands from overly enthusiastic citizens. More lights for the tree lighting. New garland for the library. More padding for the Santa costume since their regular jolly elf impersonator had started running marathons over the summer and lost fifty pounds.

It all had to come out of the town budget—which meant it all went through the town council. And Ben had the dubious distinction of being the swing vote on that council.

He was lucky if he could walk from the house to Astrid's school to work without being stopped half a dozen times with a cheerful, "Oh, Ben! I was hoping I would run into you!" And his phone never seemed to stop vibrating.

Right on cue, a snippet of the *Jaws* theme music *duh-duh*ed from his pocket, alerting him to a new email in his council account. He ignored the sound as he crossed the kitchen, making a beeline for the Keurig. Town business before caffeine was never a good idea. Though maybe this time it wouldn't be anything he needed to deal with. Maybe it would be a Christmas miracle, and someone would be offering a solution rather than heaping another problem onto his plate.

The ominous *Jaws* music came again as he popped in the K-Cup and pushed the button, waiting for the machine to groan to life and dribble salvation into his cup. But nothing happened. He bent closer, studying the face of the machine. It was lit up, just like it was supposed to be. Everything looked fine, but when he pushed the button again—nothing.

The Keurig sat there, silently taunting him, and Ben found himself confronted by the horrible catch-22 of needing caffeine to figure out what was wrong with the machine that was supposed to give him caffeine.

"Morning, Uncle Ben!"

He grunted something vaguely g'morning-ish as his niece bounded into the kitchen.

Astrid, apparently unaware of the imminent caffeine crisis, pulled open a cabinet. "What do you think? Cupcakes, brownies, or gingerbread?"

Ben turned his head just enough to study her as she pulled cereal out of a cupboard. Astrid was that terrifying creation—a morning person—but she didn't usually ask him for sweets over breakfast. "None of the above? Too early for sugar."

"For the bake sale?" Astrid reminded him as she dropped a box of cornflakes on the island. "The Christmas fair? Everyone has to sign up to bring something."

"Right. The fair." Ben turned his attention back to the Keurig. It was plugged in. It had water. What if he turned it off and turned it back on again like rebooting a router? That should work, right? "That's soon?" he asked absently.

"A week from Sunday." Astrid gathered milk and blueberries from the fridge, taking her entire haul to the island. "We have to turn in the forms today, and we can't do cookies because Merritt Miller said she's doing cookies this year and her aunt runs the bakery so hers are going to be, like, the best cookies ever in the history of cookies and anyone else who does them is going to look pathetic." She poured flakes and milk and blueberries into her bowl, pausing with her spoon poised. "Have you *seen* the cookies they sell? They're like, *amazing*. So we have to do cupcakes or brownies or gingerbread or something, and I don't know what to put."

Ben opened his mouth, but no answer came out, his noncaffeinated brain completely empty of inspiration. *Brownies, cupcakes, or gingerbread?* "Uh…"

If someone had told him two years ago that some-day the question of Christmas fair baked goods would be more complicated than the riddle of the Sphinx, he would have laughed them into next week—but a lot of things had changed in the last two years. His obnoxiously perfect overachiever sister and her most-reliable-man-on-the-planet husband were gone. Astrid was his responsibility. And he was now on a Facebook group for parents in Astrid's class, which seemed to double as a master class in passive-aggressive mommy shaming—or uncle shaming, in his case.

Brownies, cupcakes, or gingerbread—whichever he chose, he needed to be prepared to defend that choice with the latest child nutrition studies, or he'd be shredded on the group. Were they gluten-free? Were they prepared on a surface a nut had touched in the last two decades? How many grams of sugar? How many carbs? Were the eggs from organic, cage-free, happy chickens with a quality of life that would rival his own? Had an ancestor of the dairy cow that produced the milk once been given antibiotics?

He wanted to be a responsible guardian. He wanted Astrid to be healthy and happy, which meant worrying about all the things that he was supposed to worry about. But sometimes it seemed like there was no winning except for the oh-so-helpful people who wanted to tell him he was doing something wrong—because he was *always* doing something wrong.

Brownies, cupcakes, or gingerbread?

He needed coffee for this decision.

Every choice had become an important one the second he'd become Astrid's guardian, but this felt like he was being set up to fail. Why were they constantly doing bake sales if half the parents thought sugar and flour were poison? Sometimes he just wanted to wear a T-shirt to drop-off with I SURVIVED HIGH-FRUCTOSE CORN SYRUP on the front in block letters, but he wasn't sure he'd live to tell the tale. This parenting stuff wasn't for the faint of heart.

"We can just do brownies." Astrid spoke to his back as he faced the useless coffee maker. She didn't sound upset, but the *just* dug into his chest.

Katie never would have done *just* anything. She was Supermom, Queen of Bake Sales, but she'd also had a wicked sense of humor and never taken herself too seriously. She was the kind of mom every kid wanted to grow up with. She was the mom Astrid *should* have grown up with, but now his niece was stuck with him and his less-than-stellar baking skills. And he refused to let her down.

"Nah, let's do something fun," he insisted, forcing cheer into his tone, as if his entire neural network wasn't begging for coffee. "How about gingerbread?"

He'd never made gingerbread a day in his life.

Please let gingerbread be easy.

"Really?"

The note of disbelief in Astrid's voice had him doubling down. "Yeah. How hard can it be?"

His niece grimaced. "Maybe we should do the brownies."

"Are you implying I can't do gingerbread?" *I might not be able to do gingerbread.*

"Kinda."

Ben huffed out a laugh at her honesty. "We're doing it. Gingerbread." His phone *duh-duh*ed another *Jaws* warning, and he resisted the urge to fish it out of his pocket, catching sight of the clock on the microwave. *Crap.* "You gonna be ready soon? We're running late." Again.

Astrid was already dressed in her school clothes, but he was going to have to hurry to find a clean-enough work shirt if he was going to get her to school on time. The washer had been on the fritz for the last two weeks, and he was running out of clean options. With the Thanksgiving holiday messing with schedules, the only time the repairman had been able to come out had conflicted with Astrid's parent-teacher conferences, so they were making do with sink laundry until he could reschedule.

Just another of the many things he wasn't quite keeping up with. And now he had to add fixing the Keurig to the list.

How novel it must be to actually have enough hours in the day. He vaguely remembered what that felt like, though the memory was distant.

Astrid slid off her stool, taking her bowl to the sink. "Brownies are cool, too..."

"Have a little faith in your elders."

"I have faith. I just also remember last year."

Ben opened his mouth to refute her—somewhat warranted—concerns, but his cell phone rang, cutting off his defense. The words *Boss Lady* flashed on the screen. *Saved by the bell.* He plucked the phone off the counter, connecting the call. "Hey, Delia. I can't talk long. I've got to get Astrid to school."

"Did you get my emails?" The mayor's voice

reverberated against his eardrums. Delia Winter had one volume: bullhorn. And one mode—impatient. Her question explained the *Jaws* warnings. She'd probably been sending a new email every five seconds—she never could wait to get a reply. But she loved the town, and no one had done more for Pine Hollow than she had. Delia charged on before he had a chance to answer. "I think I have a solution for the budget shortfall."

"Great."

"It's the dog shelter," Delia boomed.

Ben flinched, but thankfully, Astrid didn't seem to have overheard anything from the other side of the island, where she was packing her lunch. His niece had been hinting at wanting a dog for months. Ever since her tenth birthday. And he'd been shutting her down every time. Now it had gotten to the point that even the mere mention of the infamous *D-O-G* word was enough to restart the argument that never seemed to end.

"Just a second, Delia," he said. He mouthed, *"Five minutes,"* at Astrid and rushed out of the kitchen like he was being chased, stubbing his toe on the loose trim on the second stair and swearing under his breath at the reminder of yet another thing that he hadn't gotten around to fixing in the creaky old house.

Delia waited her obligatory one second and forged on. "The funding for the animal shelter was always part of the mayor's discretionary budget. So we just reallocate it. I don't know why I didn't think of it before."

"Won't that hurt the shelter?" he asked, keeping his voice down so it wouldn't carry to Astrid. He'd never gone to the shelter himself, but he had a vague image of a nice older couple on a piece of land at the edge of town.

"We'll fund them until the end of the year to give them time to find homes for the dogs. Rita and Hal are getting up there, and their granddaughter had to come up from the city to help out, but I'm sure she'd like to get back to her own life—and rumor has it Hal and Rita were looking to move out to the Estates but couldn't because of the dogs. Everybody wins."

Ben found a shirt that passed the sniff test and pulled it on. It felt like there was a catch about this perfect solution he wasn't seeing, but he couldn't put his finger on it.

"We have to find the money to fix the rec center roof somewhere, and this is the thing that impacts the town as a whole the least," Delia boomed. "It's not like we can cut schools or the firehouse. And the last time we tried to cut the budget for the Christmas tree lighting, I thought we were going to have a riot. This is the obvious choice."

"Right…" His socks weren't going to match today, but did people really look at socks?

"So I have your vote? We can pass the budget this afternoon, notify the shelter, and recess for the holidays if you're onboard."

He hadn't known what he was getting into when he'd volunteered to take over the rest of his brother-in-law's four-year term on the city council. He'd only been thinking that Paul's and Katie's responsibilities were his responsibilities now and that the consistency would be good for Astrid. But two years of budgets and zoning disputes had shown him the error of his ways. "Recess for the holidays" was the most tantalizing phrase he'd heard in a long time.

He loved Pine Hollow, but one less thing on his list sounded like heaven.

"Sure." He shoved his feet into his shoes and grabbed his laptop bag. "It makes sense." He charged down the stairs, dodging the loose step this time. "I've gotta go, Delia."

"I'll see you later. Thanks, Ben!"

Astrid was waiting at the bottom of the stairs, already wearing her puffy down coat and her backpack—and making him feel like even more of a screw-up as the so-called parental figure.

"You all set?" he asked, even though she obviously was. He grabbed his coat off the hook by the door, checking the time on the grandfather clock in the hall. If they hurried they would make it—and then he could grab a coffee at the Cup before he had to be at work. He pulled open the door, holding it for Astrid to pass through and feeling like he'd dodged a bullet—or an entire firing squad—until he fell into step beside his niece on the front walk and she tipped her head at him innocuously.

"What's going on with the dog shelter?"

The six blocks from Katie and Paul's house to the school cut through the heart of Pine Hollow—and were usually punctuated by Astrid's familiar complaint that there was *no reason* the sixth graders should be allowed to walk themselves to school while the fifth graders who were barely any younger at all should have to be escorted to drop-off like babies. She probably had a future in debate—and a very valid point, at least according to the parenting podcasts Ben had been listening to lately about encouraging independence and autonomy—but that didn't change the school policy.

Today, however, Ben was treated to Astrid's other favorite refrain—All of the Many Reasons Astrid K. Williams Was Responsible Enough to Have a Dog. Luckily, she didn't seem to have overheard that the funding for the shelter was being cut, or she'd probably have added that to her treatise.

Ben's caffeine headache started halfway between the Bluebell Inn and Magda's Bakery. By the time they crossed the last crosswalk onto Pine Hollow Elementary grounds, he was praying for patience and counting the steps to the Cup so he could get an espresso before work.

"What if I could *prove* I'm responsible enough to take care of a dog?" Astrid wheedled, undeterred by his multiple attempts to end the conversation.

Ben considered telling her he would only adopt dogs who were trained to bring him coffee, but he was afraid she'd take it as encouragement. "Astrid, I appreciate the perseverance, but we've talked about this. We don't have a yard."

When he'd moved into Katie and Paul's fixer-upper after the accident, he'd had the best intentions of fulfilling their two-year plan, finishing all their projects and selling the house to move into a bigger place with plenty of land. He just hadn't expected that his fiancée would leave him to do it alone. Or that taking over Paul's town council seat and Katie's position on the PTA board would suck up every spare second of his life. Now, every time Astrid asked him for a dog, he was reminded that she should have been living in a big house with a yard by now.

"I'd walk him," she insisted. "And feed him. You wouldn't have to do anything. Please? We could get a small one. You'd barely notice him."

"Except when it barks. And when I have to pay the vet bills."

"I'd teach it not to bark. And I'd pay for all the shots and stuff. I've been saving my allowance."

Since he paid her allowance, he knew exactly how much she'd been saving, but he had to admire her determination. "We aren't getting a dog," he repeated for the seven millionth time in the last four months.

Never one to give up, she smiled angelically. "Learning to take care of a dog would be beneficial to my education—"

"Being on time to class would be even more beneficial to your education." He slung his arm around her shoulders, giving her a side hug and a nudge toward the school. "Go. Shoo. Have fun. Learn lots."

Astrid rolled her eyes but spotted her best friend, Kimber, and took off running, her backpack thumping rhythmically.

"*Walk*, Astrid!" Elinor, the school librarian overseeing drop-off today, didn't need to raise her voice to be instantly obeyed.

"Sorry, Aunt E!" Astrid rapidly downshifted to power-walk toward Kimber.

Elinor Rodriguez had been Katie's best friend and like a member of their family. "Ben!" She lifted a hand to flag him down before he could escape toward the promise of the Cup. "Don't run off. I need to talk to you for a second."

He resisted the urge to pretend he hadn't heard her. Elinor was probably the smartest person he'd ever met, but he'd always found being the object of her laser-beam focus a little terrifying and her unusual non sequiturs made him feel like he never knew what was coming. He needed caffeine in his system to keep up.

She poked her glasses up her nose as she closed the distance between them.

"What's up?" he asked.

"I need your volunteer schedule for the Christmas fair." She spoke to him, but her attention flicked back the kids filing past her into the school. "Put down the snowball, Jeremiah!"

"I thought the kids were working the booths now that they're responsible fifth graders." He'd apparently entered some caffeine-free dystopia where nothing made sense. He may have been checking his email during the last PTA meeting, but he distinctly remembered hearing the kids were in charge.

"They are, but we have to have adults overseeing operations so they actually give correct change and don't eat all the goodies when no one's looking."

Ben nearly groaned aloud. He should have known. The kids' responsibilities were always the parents' re-sponsibilities. Just one more thing to pile on.

"You just need to sign up for one three-hour block so Astrid can participate in the fair—"

"Three *hours*?"

Plus however much time it took them to make gingerbread and tie it up into cute little packages. Shopping for ingredients and taking Astrid to and from…no one talked about that stuff when they said, "Let's do a Christmas fair for charity. It'll be fun."

"I can fill in for you as a chaperone if you want," Elinor offered, but he jerked his head in an automatic rejection of the offer.

"No, I've got it." He wouldn't let anyone say he was shirking his responsibilities. "Where do I sign up?"

Elinor whipped a tablet out of one voluminous coat pocket and passed it over. "Just fill in any of the empty slots."

Ben skimmed through the available hours, trying to find something he could make work on a Sunday in December. The town went nuts for the holidays, and there were always a million things to do—and he felt like he needed to do them all for Astrid.

He'd managed to get the Christmas decorations up over Thanksgiving weekend—because Katie *always* decorated early, and he refused to let Astrid down—but he still had all the Christmas shopping to do. And wrapping. And stocking stuffing. Plus now gingerbread and the freaking washer and the Keurig, and at some point he was going to have to clear out the guest room before his parents arrived for Christmas in three weeks and noticed he still hadn't finished any of the half-finished projects around the house.

He needed a clone.

"Just curious. Are you trying to scare the children?"

"What?" He looked up from the tablet, belatedly realizing he was glowering when Elinor mimicked his expression. "Cute."

"As your friend, I feel I should warn you. You're getting a reputation around town." She wrinkled her nose, her glasses slipping downward. "The name *Ebenezer* may have been mentioned."

"I'm not a Scrooge," he snapped, a little more defensively than he'd planned. "I'm just *stressed*. There's a lot to do." And there was no coffee.

"Stress is bad for your brain," Elinor commented conversationally. "I was just reading this study about how it puts you into a reactive mode and cuts you off from the creative and problem-solving portions of your brain. Did you know saturating your brain in stress hormones for long periods of time can rework your brain chemistry and cause depression? Isn't that fascinating?"

Great. Now he had that to look forward to. "Yes, fascinating. Very helpful. Thank you."

Elinor shrugged. "I'm just saying. You need to find a way to destress."

"I'll get right on that. After Christmas." He tapped his name into one of the slots at random and handed the tablet back to her. He'd just have to make it work. Like he always did.

The bell had already rung, and the kids were all inside the school. Elinor accepted the tablet. "Kaye Berry's always thought you were hot, and she's divorced now—"

"No," he interrupted before she could get any ideas. "I'm not dating one of the moms from Astrid's class. I need to get a handle on what I've already committed to before I commit to anything—or anyone—else."

He couldn't deal with one more thing. No dogs. No dating. No crazy complications to a Christmas season he just needed to get through. Astrid was his top priority, and until he figured out how to give her the life she should have had—complete with a big yard and a dog—he couldn't think about anything else. He owed that to Katie and Paul. Now he just had to figure out how to do it.

Chapter Two

"Come on, Partridge. Look over here. Come on, baby." Ally Gilmore, professional fashion photographer, crouched in front of the world's drooliest bulldog with her camera in one hand and a squeaky toy in the other.

She'd always been willing to contort herself into whatever position was necessary to get the shot, but her former subjects tended more toward pouty-lipped models with angular bodies and less toward big-eyed pooches with rolls of white fur.

Still, the concept was the same. Sell the product. Get the best angle to make it look the most appealing. And in this case the product *was* the drooliest bulldog in the world—and the longest-running resident of the Furry Friends Animal Rescue. The bulldog had come to the shelter three years ago as a stray, and poor Partridge still hadn't managed to find a forever home, despite all her grandparents' efforts to showcase his unique charms.

Yes, he had a distinct underbite, his eyes were different

sizes, and he drooled when he got excited...or when he was hungry...or when he was sleeping...or really any time at all, but he still deserved love just as much as all the rest of the dogs at Furry Friends. And Ally was determined to capture the perfect photo for the website to make someone fall in love with him.

Provided she could get him to stop trying to lick the camera.

"Come on, honey. Work with me here. You'll thank me later."

Her Saint Bernard, Colby—the laziest animal on the planet, who would probably sleep for twenty-two hours straight if that didn't mean missing mealtimes—suddenly lifted his head, looking toward the front of the kennels a fraction of a second before a cascade of barks rippled through the building, echoing off the vaulted ceiling.

"Gram?" Ally raised her voice over the dogs.

It was still early, much too early for pet seekers—though there hadn't been many since Ally had arrived to help out three weeks ago. Her grandparents said it was just the season, everyone busy getting ready for Thanksgiving, but Ally had a feeling the outdated website might have also played a part. Which was why she'd crawled out of bed while it was still dark on the first of December, determined to do something about it.

"Ally girl?" Gram's voice warbled over the barking.

"Back here, Gram!" Ally called back, yanking her camera away at the last minute to avoid another lick attempt by Partridge.

"What are you doing?" Gram asked as she rounded the corner from the front of the barn, carrying a box that looked entirely too heavy for a woman who'd torn the ligaments in her shoulder less than two months ago.

"I'm getting photos for the website." Ally rushed out of Partridge's pen, quickly setting down her camera so she could take the giant box of Milk-Bones from her grandmother's arms. "What are *you* doing? Where's your sling?"

"Oh, I don't need that. It was just for the first couple of weeks." She crouched down, stroking Colby's ears in greeting before moving to say hello to Partridge.

Rita Gilmore was barely five feet tall—which made her only two inches shorter than Ally, but who was counting? Her wild white curls were mashed down beneath a bright red knit cap today, but there was always something unfettered about her—like she had been born wild and wasn't about to be tamed. Which was great, as long as you weren't causing yourself potentially permanent injury with your stubbornness.

"The doctors said the risk of reinjury—"

Her grandmother flapped a hand at her. "Doctors have to say things like that so they won't get sued if I hurt it again and decide to blame them. I'm fine. Don't fuss."

Ally clung to her patience with both hands. Ever since she'd arrived in Pine Hollow that had been the refrain. *I'm fine. Don't fuss. Don't help. Don't do or say anything to imply that I might be too old to get along on my own.*

Except she was. Gram had dislocated her shoulder and shredded her ligaments doing nothing more taxing than walking one of the dogs at the shelter. Admittedly, it was Maximus, the Irish wolfhound mix the size of a small pony, who had no idea of his own strength, but still. Gram couldn't just keep on pretending a couple in their eighties could handle the physical labor of running a dog shelter by themselves. Ally had reason to worry about them.

Especially because they hadn't told her about the injury for weeks. Not wanting to worry her. Not wanting her to interrupt her life in New York to help them. Her grandfather had been running himself ragged trying to keep her grandmother from taking off her sling and jumping back into work the second she got home from surgery. When Ally had come to Pine Hollow for a weekend visit and seen that, she'd done the only thing she could think of.

She'd dropped everything and come for an extended visit.

Her lease was up, her planned out-of-town shoot had just been canceled, and she'd already been feeling unsettled, trying to figure out whether she wanted to stay in New York. Gram's injury had felt like a giant flashing sign from the universe pointing her toward Pine Hollow. The perfect chance to spend the holidays with her only remaining family, soak up the too-adorable-to-be-real small-town Christmas charm, and figure out what she wanted to do next, all while helping out around the shelter.

Except her grandparents seemed morally opposed to her pitching in.

Gram frowned at the camera resting on the bench beside Partridge's pen. "You don't have to do that, dear."

"I want to help." Ally set the Milk-Bones at the entrance to the main storeroom and turned back to her grandmother. "I know you don't want to change the website because somebody made it for you as a favor ten years ago, but trust me, this is how a lot of people look for pets now. They want to see pictures and cute descriptions."

"People don't fall in love with pictures. Do they, Partridge? No, they don't."

"Pretty much my entire job is making people fall in love with things by taking pictures of them," Ally argued, picking up her camera. "But even if you're right and people won't adopt because of a picture—that picture might at least get them in the door. Or maybe some cute videos—we could start a Twitter account or Instagram. It could let people know what kind of dogs we have here. Maybe there's someone who's searching for a bulldog or a wolfhound on Petfinder right now. We have to get our dogs on there, which means bringing the website into this decade."

"All that webby nonsense is too complicated for your grandpa and me. I know you want to help, but the way we do things has always worked perfectly well, and it'll find these pups their forever homes in due time."

"But if having an updated website could help them find homes faster, what's the harm?"

"It's just too much for us to manage. And you should be enjoying your holiday." Gram linked her good arm with Ally's, tugging her back toward the front of the shelter. Colby heaved to his feet with a sigh, padding at their heels. "Weren't you talking about walking into town and getting some pictures of the town square before the latest snow gets all trampled?"

"I was," Ally admitted, "but I can do this, too. I'm happy to help, and not just with the website. I want to be useful."

"And you are, darling." Gram patted her arm. "In fact, I was just coming out here to ask if you can help us this afternoon by keeping an eye on things around the shelter."

Ally had a feeling Gram had just invented the request for help to placate her, but she wasn't going to argue with a chance to sneak a few more photos on the website while she was in charge. "Of course I will. Are you going somewhere?"

"Your grandfather wants to join a poker tournament they're having out at the Estates. We won't be late. Everything out there runs on early-bird hours."

The Summerland Estates retirement community on the edge of town looked, at first glance, more like a posh country club than a home for the elderly. But in addition to the golf course and swimming pools, they also had nursing and assisted-living amenities for residents who needed them—or would in a few years.

Her grandmother had always loudly proclaimed that she wouldn't be caught dead in a nursing home and planned to stay in her house until they carried her out of it, but so many of her grandfather's poker buddies had moved up there in recent years that he now spent almost as much time at the Estates as he did at home. It was a beautiful place, but Ally was relieved her grandparents didn't seem inclined to move out there. She already felt untethered enough, and their place was the closest thing to home she had.

Ally grabbed her coat from a peg by the front door and pulled it on. She held the door for Gram and Colby, and together they crunched across the snow-covered gravel driveway toward the house.

The big white farmhouse had been thoroughly doused in Christmas cheer, with twinkle lights on the covered porch, garland on the banisters, and a wreath on the door—though Gram kept insisting they needed to decorate the barn, too. She'd thrown herself into Christmas the second Thanksgiving was over, and Ally and her grandfather could only do their best to keep up—and keep her from overusing her shoulder. Gram had always loved the season, but she seemed even more fanatic this year. Or maybe it just seemed that way because Ally was here to see it firsthand.

Not that she was complaining. She could use an infusion of Christmas magic. It had been too long since she'd had that holiday feeling. The warmth and peace. She loved Christmas in the city, the lights and excitement, but she always felt more centered somehow when she made the trek up to Pine Hollow to spend Christmas with her grandparents like she had when she was little. She'd thought this place was magical back then, and that feeling had never quite gone away.

"You go get your photos," Gram encouraged. "Get out and enjoy the town a little bit. We've been monopolizing you here."

Ally squeezed her grandmother's arm where it linked with hers. "I like being monopolized by you."

When she arrived in Vermont, she'd just wanted to soak up the time with her grandparents and look after the dogs. The last few years she'd been working free-lance and traveling whenever the job demanded—which meant a lot of time on her own. It got lonely. She'd missed having someone to share the day-to-day with.

But Gram was right. If Ally wanted the full Pine Hollow Christmas experience, she couldn't get that hanging around the shelter all the time. It would do her good to get out into the town.

Fifteen minutes later she headed down the long driveway with a scarf wrapped around her neck and her camera in her hands.

Pine Hollow was the foundation for every fantasy of small-town life she'd ever had. Every block looked like another Christmas card. If she headed one direction she'd find covered bridges and the winding road that led out to the ski resort. In the other direction lay the adorable town square, complete with a gazebo at one corner, all of it covered in snow and the peaceful hush of winter.

Lifting her camera to shoot as she walked, Ally wandered toward the square, taking everything in through the filter of her lens. The historic town hall. The cute little inn. There were a few pedestrians, townspeople going about their daily lives, but the December morning still felt marvelously still, the air crisp and clean and cold in her lungs.

The lyrics of Christmas songs ran through her head, and she found herself humming as she wandered toward the heart of town. As she grew closer to the square, she heard voices shouting instructions before she even turned the corner and spotted the bustle of activity.

A group of people was directing the delivery of a giant pine tree for the tree lighting next week. Ally moved along the street opposite to get a better angle, framing the shot—and right on cue an actual horse-drawn sleigh rounded the corner, gliding toward the square. Did a moment get any more classically Christmas?

Ally grinned and backpedaled to get the shot before the sleigh moved out of position. She hadn't brought her wide angle, but with just a few more steps...

Jingle bells jangled over her head. Ally focused entirely on the viewfinder as she scrambled back—

And slammed into something hard.

"Son of a—" The brick wall at her back broke off mid-curse, and Ally whirled, embarrassment rising as she lowered her camera.

"I'm sorry! I wasn't..." The words trailed off as she looked up.

And up.

Past the broad shoulders and the dark, scruffy beard. All the way up to the startlingly pale blue eyes. Winter blue. Her heart leapt into her throat, stoppering the words there, and her hands tightened reflexively on the camera—until she realized Tall, Dark, and Scruffy was glaring at her.

And dripping.

He held a crushed to-go cup away from his body, a giant coffee stain spreading across his shirt where his coat hung open.

"Oh." Ally groaned. "Your shirt..."

Chapter Three

Ben could not catch a break today.

The line at the Cup had been massive, so he'd made the snap decision to get his caffeine fix at Magda's Bakery instead. His head had already been throbbing, his patience hanging by a thread—so of course Gayle Danvers, the head of the town's Christmas Pageant Committee, had chosen the moment he stepped into the bakery to corner him and deliver a fifteen-minute treatise on why the theater that hosted the pageant absolutely *needed* new curtains, and couldn't he find the money in the budget for them somewhere?

He'd said no. Because he was always the one who had to say no. Someone had to be realistic. Someone had to consider the costs.

But Gayle hadn't wanted to take no for an answer. The entire town seemed to think if they badgered him enough he would have to give in—so he got to be the bad guy over and over again. His life had become an exercise in disappointing people.

But that was no excuse for Gayle to accuse him of trying to ruin Christmas when he was just trying to get *one* cup of coffee so his head would stop exploding.

When Magda had handed him his cup, he'd practically run out the door.

So yes, maybe he had been moving a little too quickly, trying to escape before anyone else latched on to him and asked for money—but the camera-wielding tourist hadn't been looking where she was going. She'd backed into him before he could dodge out of the way or save his coffee.

He hadn't gotten a single sip before the contents of his cup were splashing all over his chest. He managed to get the fabric of his shirt away from his skin before second-degree burns could set in, but now the winter air was cooling the sopping fabric and turning his last semi-clean shirt into a clammy mess.

All because some tourist had been too busy gawking to pay attention to the world around her.

She was tiny, though the knot of curly black hair piled on top of her head gave her an extra couple of inches, and she'd still rammed into him with the force of a freaking linebacker. She held a massive camera in her other hand—classic tourist. Treating Pine Hollow like it was Christmas Land at an amusement park. Just here for her entertainment.

"I'm so sorry," the woman said again. She had one of those sweet, round faces that screamed "nice girl" and was currently drawn into an expression of exaggerated contrition. "I wasn't looking where I was going—"

"I noticed," Ben growled, plucking clinging fabric away from his skin.

"I was trying to get a picture of the tree and then the sleigh came around the corner." She waved behind her toward the square. "Sorry. I can pay for your dry cleaning."

Ben made it a point not to own anything that was dry clean only, but her words only reminded him that he was currently without a functional washing machine, because Murphy's Law was actively messing with him. "It's fine."

It was not fine.

"At least let me get you another coffee—"

"I don't have time to get another coffee," he snapped, the words sharpened by the caffeine headache still pounding merrily away at his temples. "I'm already late to work, and now I have to go home and change because some tourist thinks my town is an adorable little Christmas prop put here for her amusement. People live here, you know. We aren't just a photo op."

Her eyes widened. "I never said—"

"Maybe next time you can watch where you're going instead of expecting the entire world to revolve around you and your camera."

The nice-girl expression vanished, fire sparking in her dark brown eyes. "I'm trying to apologize. It was an accident. I didn't run into you on purpose."

"Well, that's comforting. If you'd been throwing coffee on people *on purpose* we'd really have an issue." He could hear himself being a jerk, and the words just kept spilling out, propelled by the frustration that had been building all morning—not to mention the little drummer boy currently doing a number on his brain.

"I'm *sorry*. What is your problem?" she demanded, drawing herself up to her full height as the bakery door opened again with a jingle of bells.

The broken washing machine was his problem. The defunct Keurig. The home improvement projects that never got done. The never-ending demands from Paul's town council seat and Katie's PTA position. The guilt that he couldn't give Astrid the yard and the dog that she wanted. The feeling that he was letting everyone down and falling farther and farther behind.

It was all his problem.

And now he was taking his frustrations out on random strangers in the town square. *Way to be a role model, West.* His old friend Guilt rose up again.

"Just watch where you're going," he growled. "This isn't Christmas Land." He moved past her—and locked eyes with Gayle Danvers, who stood outside the bakery door, watching him.

Exactly what he needed.

Everyone in town was going to hear about this. Ben sniping at a tourist. The perfect start to the holiday season.

His face heated, and he jerked a terse nod at his audience. "Mrs. Danvers," he grunted, stalking back toward Katie and Paul's house to find something dry to wear. Officially sucking at life.

"Don't mind him."

Ally yanked her gaze away from the retreating back

of Tall, Dark, and Cranky to face the elderly woman who had exited the bakery.

"That's our resident Scrooge," she explained. "Every town needs one, right?"

Ally smiled uncertainly. "I guess."

She hadn't exactly been blameless. She hadn't been paying attention, focused completely on the world in front of her lens, and she'd backed right into him. He'd been a jerk to refuse her apology and treat her like she'd done it on purpose, but she had doused him in coffee—however accidentally.

"Really, don't worry about it," the woman insisted, coming forward to pat her arm. "You're Rita and Hal's granddaughter, aren't you?" She nodded at the camera in Ally's hands. "The photographer?"

"Uh, yeah. Yes, that's me."

The woman beamed. "You probably don't remember me. I knew you when you were this big." She held her hand up at her waist. "When you used to come up here with your parents. Gayle Danvers? I live just down the street from your grandparents."

"Right. Of course. Mrs. Danvers. It's good to see you."

"I just wanted to say you're doing a wonderful thing. Putting your life on hold to help your grandparents. How many people would make that kind of sacrifice?"

"Oh, well, it wasn't such a sacrifice—"

"It *was*," Mrs. Danvers insisted, making Ally squirm internally. "And don't let anyone tell you otherwise. You're a good girl, Ally Gilmore." She gave Ally's arm a final pat. "Don't you give old Ebenezer West another thought."

Ally smiled awkwardly, discomfort swirling through

her as Mrs. Danvers headed off. She hadn't come to Pine Hollow because she was some kind of saint. She'd needed this.

In the town square, the tree was upright now, towering over the gazebo. Her camera was still in one hand, but the idea of wandering through town taking pictures had lost all its appeal. She grabbed one last shot of the square and the sleigh—just to spite the Scrooge wannabe—and then tucked her camera inside her coat, heading back toward her grandparents' house.

A cold wind had kicked up, and she ducked her head against it, trying to put the moment with Pine Hollow's answer to Ebenezer out of her mind. She'd felt so good before she slammed into him. And yes, maybe she had been seeing a fantasy version of the town—that soft-focus vision of life that only existed in Christmas movies—but was that really a crime? She should have paid more attention, but was that any excuse for him to be so rude?

She'd actually thought he was attractive, in the fraction of a second before his personality changed her mind. Six feet tall with dark hair, unfairly broad shoulders and those winter-blue eyes. With the scruffy beard, he might look more like a sexy lumberjack than a white-haired miser, but a Scrooge was a Scrooge, and he didn't deserve one inch of real estate in her brain.

So of course she was still thinking of him that afternoon when her grandparents headed out to the Estates and she closed herself in the office to work on the website. She tried to focus, but she couldn't stop reliving the moment she'd crashed into him.

Colby sprawled on one of the ragged dog beds that littered the small office, snoring softly. Most of the dogs were napping, the only sound being the Trans-Siberian Orchestra crackling from the old radio. She didn't know how long she worked, uploading photos and updating descriptions. It could have been minutes or hours later when Colby lifted his head, turning toward the open door to the office and releasing a soft, huffing *"Woof."*

Ally angled her head to see through the open office door as the exterior shelter door creaked open and a tentative voice called, "Um...hello?"

A few scattered barks responded as the dogs woke up to greet the new arrival.

A *customer*.

Ally instantly perked up. "Be right with you!" she called, shoving away from the desk. Colby reluctantly heaved himself to his feet to pad at her side. "I think we've got a live one, Colb."

She pushed the office door all the way open, smiling welcomingly—and forced her smile to remain pinned in place when she saw who was standing inside the exterior door.

Two little girls stood side by side, gripping their backpack straps and glancing around uncertainly. Ally wasn't great at guessing ages, not having been around children much, but she'd place these two in a vaguely upper elementary school age bracket. Old enough to be running around town on their own, but young enough that they hadn't yet hit the obnoxious teen years.

And not nearly old enough to adopt a dog without their parents in tow.

Chapter Four

H i there," Ally greeted the pair, keeping an eye on the door in case the parents were on their way inside, as the radio shifted into a bluesy rendition of "White Christmas." "Can I help you?"

The two stood close together, as if drawing support from each other. One was taller and slim with tight reddish curls, while the other was tiny with glasses and black braids on either side of her face.

Colby wandered forward at his maximum speed— roughly half that of a tortoise—and both girls instantly locked eyes on him, though they seemed more entranced than fearful of the big guy.

"He's friendly," Ally assured them. "But this one's not available for adoption. His name's Colby."

"Hi, Colby," the girls cooed at him in unison, extending gloved hands. Colby gave them a half-hearted sniff and, having maxed out his cardio for the day with the ten-foot walk, released a dramatic sigh, sinking onto the floor in a Saint Bernard–shaped heap.

"Don't be offended by the lack of welcome. The only thing that ranks above sleep for Colby is food. Are, uh, are your parents with you?"

The girls tore their eyes off Colby and exchanged a look. An unspoken agreement passed between them and they drew themselves up, lifting their chins as if they were girding for battle. "I'm Astrid," the taller of the two announced. "And this is Kimber."

Ally nodded. "Ally. Nice to meet you."

The little one with the braids—Kimber—took a deep breath and announced, "We're looking for a job."

Ally blinked, barely stopping her lips from twitching. Kimber's voice was firm and direct. This was serious business. But she also looked to be about eight. "I think there might be some child labor laws against that."

"Not a real job," the girl clarified.

"We want to volunteer," the redhead—Astrid—put in, less forceful, but no less earnest. Her eyes were pleading, begging Ally to listen. "Help out. Walk the dogs or feed them—"

"Or give them baths or teach them tricks—"

"Whatever you need us to do," the redhead finished. "Anything."

A lightbulb went on, and Ally allowed herself a smile. "Let me guess. Your parents won't let you get a dog until you can prove you're responsible enough to take care of one, so you're out here to prove it?"

Kimber's eyes rounded behind her glasses. "How did you know?"

Ally grinned. "I've been there. When I was your age,

I wanted a dog so badly I could barely breathe. It was all I could think about."

Astrid nodded eagerly, taking a small step forward. "That's exactly how we feel. Please. We'll work so hard."

It was tempting to say yes—in part because they reminded her so much of herself, but also she'd kind of like the company. But that didn't mean she could just put these girls to work. "Do your parents know you're here?"

"Of course." Astrid's gaze slid to the side, evading hers.

So the parents have no idea where they are. Great.

What was she supposed to do in this situation? Rat the girls out to their parents because they didn't technically have permission to be here? Was there really any harm in letting them walk a dog or two? She could start with Fred and Ginger. The elderly dachshund mixes were angels on a leash and wouldn't give them any trouble. If that went well, they could throw a ball for Harry in the back paddock—the Australian shepherd didn't have an aggressive bone in her body, but she needed to get her zoomies out on a regular basis.

It sounded harmless enough, but if either of the girls so much as got a skinned knee and their parents didn't know they were here..."I'm sorry—" Ally started.

Gravel crunched beneath tires in the front drive, sending a cascade of barks bouncing off the rafters.

"We're really good with dogs," Astrid pleaded, until a shout from the driveway outside cut her off—and saved Ally from having to break the girls' hearts.

"Hallooo!"

Even Colby summoned the energy to lift his head at that familiar voice and relief whispered through Ally. Gram would know if it was kosher to accept kids as volunteers.

"That's my grandmother," Ally explained. "We'll see what she thinks." She moved past the girls to the door, pushing it open to find Gram opening the tailgate of her ancient Subaru. "Hey, Gram."

"Hey, sweetie," her grandmother called back, without looking away from whatever she was messing with in the back of the hatchback.

A gust of wind blew across the driveway, and Ally shivered in her sweater. She'd forgotten to grab her coat from the shelter office, and she wrapped her arms around herself to hold the warmth in. Astrid and Kimber stood just outside the barn door, both still in their puffy winter coats, hovering nearby as if watching for an opportunity to press their case.

Ally headed toward the back of the Subaru, looking around for her grandmother's chauffeur. "Where'd Gramps go?"

"Hm?" Her grandmother barely glanced up. "Oh, you know your grandfather. He's still cleaning up at that poker tournament."

Ally frowned at the old Subaru parked crookedly across the driveway. "Did you drive yourself back?"

"I got a call from Selina over in Franklin," her grandmother replied, as if that answered the question. She crooned into the back and Ally heard a definite canine whimper. "This precious girl needed us. She'd been abandoned. Running around loose after her family moved away and just left her behind. Can you imagine?"

"Gram." Ally groaned, ignoring the dog for the moment. "Tell me you didn't go all the way to Franklin and back by yourself. You know you're not supposed to be driving." The old Subaru was a stick shift, and Gram was supposed to be resting her right arm. "You should have called me," Ally insisted. Though she shouldn't be surprised her grandmother had driven fifty miles the second someone told her there was a dog in need. Gram had the biggest heart of anyone Ally had ever met—and a definite tendency to leap before she looked.

"It was a little drive, and I'm fine. See?" Gram waved her right arm vigorously, her gaze sliding past Ally. "Hello, Astrid. Hello, Kimber."

"Hello, Mrs. Gilmore," they chorused.

They knew each other. Of course they did. Everyone knew each other. Ally was the odd one out around here. And the only voice of reason in this insanity.

"You could *lose the use of your arm* if you reinjure it," Ally reminded Gram, though the words didn't make a dent in her grandmother's fixation on the carrier crate in the back.

"Then it's lucky I didn't," Gram said blithely. "Besides, this was an emergency. Look at that face." It was an adorable face. Part spaniel, by the look of it, with long silky ears and huge help-me eyes. "I've been thinking we can call her Dolce. Doesn't she look designer?"

Ally refused to get distracted. "Does Gramps know you took off with the car?"

"You know how he is when he's playing. I'll be back there before he knows I'm gone."

Oh no. "You are not driving yourself back out there. I'll pick Gramps up. And next time you have to *call me*. This is exactly the stuff I'm here to help with."

"Fine." She rolled her eyes. "I'll call you next time. But isn't she sweet?"

Ally sighed. "Very sweet," she admitted, conceding defeat for the moment—and wondering what her grandfather would think when he looked up from his game to find Gram gone. He'd always been the sensible one in their relationship—and the only one who could get Rita Gilmore to do anything she didn't want to do.

"We'll need to have Jeb look her over to make sure she's healthy and up-to-date on her shots, and I'm not sure she's been spayed yet, but after that she'll be ready to go to a good home. Won't you, sweet girl?"

"We don't have a run for her." These last few weeks they'd been taking in more dogs than were going out. In fact, none of the twelve dogs had been adopted since Ally arrived.

"We'll keep her in the office for now," Gram said with a casual hand flap. "Though I don't think she'll be with us long. I have a feeling. Someone's going to snap her right up." She sent her beaming smile past Ally. "Are you looking for a dog, girls?"

The girls exchanged a look. "We're just volunteering for now," Astrid said.

"What a lovely idea! Aren't you sweet? Do you want to help me introduce little Dolce to the office?"

Handing a strange dog who hadn't even been checked

for rabies yet over to a pair of children sounded like a recipe for a lawsuit. Ally stepped forward quickly before her grandmother could reach for the carrier crate. She didn't even want to think about her grandmother trying to carry the bulky thing. "I'll take care of Dolce. Why don't you show the girls where the leashes are so they can take Fred and Ginger for a walk?"

"Good idea. You'll love them," Gram gushed, putting one arm around each girl's shoulders and guiding them toward the kennels, leaving Ally alone with the timid little spaniel.

The dog watched her cautiously, and Ally bent down to make herself less intimidating.

"Hello, sweet girl." She reached out her hand, letting the pup sniff her through the cage. "It's okay. You're okay now." In her pocket, her phone chimed with an email alert, and the spaniel scrambled to the back of the crate at the sound, hiding her face.

"That's okay," Ally murmured soothingly, taking a step back to pull out her phone. "You take your time. Maybe this is someone putting in an application to adopt a sweet girl just like you."

She'd only gotten the application form to go live on the website a few hours ago, so that might be overly optimistic, but a girl could hope. Maybe this was the first of many.

But when she opened the email, it wasn't an application.

Regret to inform... budget shortfall... discontinuing funding... January first... She skimmed the words, trying to make sense of them, but they refused to compute.

The town couldn't actually be cutting the shelter funding. The shelter had been here for decades. Almost as long as she could remember.

"Ally girl?" Her grandmother's voice penetrated the fog she'd fallen into as she stared at the email, as if she could change the meaning if she just read it enough times. "Are you all right? You've gone white as a sheet."

Ally looked up from the phone, the words spilling out of her mouth and making it real.

"They're shutting us down."

Chapter Five

"Who does that? Who cuts the funding for an animal shelter right before Christmas?"

Ally stalked back and forth in the tight confines of the shelter office while her grandmother sat cross-legged on the floor, trying to lure Dolce out of the crate beside her with a cheddar snack. They'd carried the new dog inside, and in the process Ally's shock had melted away, leaving frustration and indignation in its wake.

"I'm sure it's just a mistake," her grandmother soothed, keeping her voice soft for Dolce's sake. "The town would never cut our funding."

"It says they expect us to find homes for all the dogs and cease operations by the first of the year."

The shelter got some money from donations and adoption fees, but the town funding kept them afloat. Ally hadn't realized how expensive the little shelter was until she'd gotten a look at the books. Food, vet bills, dog beds, and chew toys she'd expected, but she hadn't considered propane to heat the barn and liability insurance and maintenance costs. Her grandparents had opened the shelter after they retired and made it look easy for twenty years—and they weren't exactly business savvy—but three weeks after she showed up the whole house of cards was collapsing.

"I'm sure that's not what they meant," her grandmother insisted. "It's all a misunderstanding. Who sent the email?"

Ally scrolled to the bottom of the email, the same one she'd been reading over and over again for the last fifteen minutes. *Sincerely, Benjamin West, Pine Hollow Town Council.* "Benjamin West."

A flicker of a frown crossed Gram's brow. "Hm."

"What does that mean? Hm? Who is he?"

"He took over Paul Williams's spot on the council two years ago and he...well..."

Ally groaned. "Don't tell me. He would actually do this. Shut down a charitable organization right before Christmas."

"Of course not. Though he can be a little prickly, I suppose, but some people are just a little more abrupt than others. There were all those rumors with his fiancée, but he's a *wonderful* uncle and I'm sure he isn't *trying* to run the shelter out of business—"

That was all the confirmation Ally needed. Her grandmother would bend over backward to say nice things about everyone she met, but Ally could read between the lines. This *prickly* councilman was probably rotten to his core. Evicting poor helpless dogs right before Christmas.

She shoved her cell phone into her pocket. "I'm going down there."

Her grandmother looked up, frowning. "Down where?"

"Town hall." She yanked her coat off the hook, flinging her scarf around her neck. "I'm dropping the car at the Estates for Gramps and then I'm fighting this."

Her grandparents would dip into their retirement savings without a second thought to keep the shelter afloat, but they needed that money to support themselves. And she wasn't going to let any power-mad bureaucrat take the shelter away from them.

"I can pick up your grandfather—"

"*Gram.*"

"All right, all right, fine. I'll stay here and keep an eye on Dolce and Astrid and Kimber." She tipped her head to the side speculatively. "Though maybe you should take Astrid with you. Ben West's her uncle, and she might be able to persuade him where you can't."

Ally was pretty sure Astrid hadn't told her parents she was volunteering here, and this Benjamin West sounded like the kind of guy who would absolutely rat her out.

Ally shook her head. "I don't need a kid to fight my battles. I'm going to give this Benjamin West a piece of my mind. This shelter is staying open. That prickly..." She couldn't think of a word insulting enough that she could say in front of her grandmother. "*Whatever* won't know what hit him."

"It just *stopped.*"

Ben silently counted to ten in an attempt to cling to his patience as Linda Hilson flapped her hands helplessly over the blank computer monitor. He'd been the one-man IT department for the town for the last six years now, and he never ceased to be amazed at the different ways people could screw up perfectly good electronics.

"Go grab yourself a cup of coffee and I'll see what I can do," he suggested.

"Thank you," Linda gushed, before leaving him in peace so he could diagnose the problem.

Ben crouched on the floor, checking all the cables and connections. The desk had been buried under a mountain of Christmas cheer, and he found the power strip beneath a swath of garland…with the power switched off.

He flicked the switch, heard the familiar hum of electronics whirring to life, and climbed out from beneath the desk, borrowing Linda's chair as the machine powered up so he could confirm that was the only issue—the wiring in the historic town hall building was notoriously finicky and could wreak havoc on electronics.

If only all of life's problems were as simple as flipping a switch.

While he waited, he pulled up the to-do list on his phone, adding *research gingerbread* and *figure out which time slot I blindly volunteered for at the freaking Christmas fair* to the never-ending list. Along with *fix Keurig.*

Two years ago, he probably would have just ordered a new machine and not thought twice, but two years ago every dollar he spent on himself wasn't a dollar he could be saving for Astrid's college fund. Katie and Paul had tucked some money away for Astrid's future, but the good schools were only getting more expensive, and Ben wasn't bringing home Silicon Valley paychecks anymore. Working for the town had sounded *relaxing* compared to the eighty-hour weeks he'd been pulling in Palo Alto—but at the time he'd never expected to become a single parent or a town councilman. Relaxing felt like a distant memory.

He tucked away his phone, glancing around the town hall. Garland and twinkle lights draped every surface, and there was even a bough of mistletoe hanging over the door—which seemed like an odd choice in a work environment, but Ben wasn't about to suggest taking it down and earn himself another Grinch strike.

New plan: Keep his head down and avoid pissing anyone else off between now and Christmas Day.

As the computer booted, he stared at the bough of Sexual-Harrassment-Lawsuit-Waiting-to-Happen—so he was perfectly positioned to see the tourist from this morning appear beneath the mistletoe, storming into the building.

And she was definitely storming.

Her purple wool coat flew open as she moved, and a white scarf flapped in the gust of wind as the door slammed shut behind her. Her expression only darkened when her gaze landed on him.

"You!"

Ben frowned. "Me?"

"You're him, aren't you?" The words cracked like a whip. "Of course you are. Benjamin West. As in the Wicked Witch of."

He straightened from Linda's chair. "No relation, actually."

"I should have known it would be you," she snapped—which didn't help him figure out what she was doing here. "Did you do this because I spilled coffee on you? Are you really that petty?"

"Look, I'm sorry about this morning. My coffeemaker was broken, and I'd had a lousy start to the day. It was a whole thing, but I shouldn't have taken it out on you."

"Apology not accepted. Lots of people have bad days. My day hasn't exactly been peachy. And you know why? Because some jerk yelled at me this morning when I was trying to apologize to him, and now he's shutting down my shelter. Who does that? Oh, that's right, Ebenezer West. The Scrooge of Pine Hollow. Determined to destroy Christmas for all of us."

Frustration flashed through him. "What is it with everyone thinking I'm anti-Christmas all of a sudden?"

"Maybe if you don't want to be known that way, you shouldn't go around shutting down animal shelters three weeks before the holiday. My grandparents put their *lives* into that shelter. They've been running it for over twenty years, and now, what? You're just going to cut their funding because you had a *bad day*?"

The pieces clicked into place—though one still didn't quite fit. "*You're* Rita and Hal's granddaughter?"

"You were expecting someone else?"

"I was expecting a city girl," he admitted, before he thought through the words. He'd heard Hal and Rita's granddaughter was some New York fashionista. He'd pictured a six-foot model-gorgeous woman with flat-ironed hair and fake eyelashes. And heels. Definitely heels. But this pint-sized tornado had clomped in here in snow boots without a lick of makeup to cover her freckles. They were kind of cute, those freckles. If you could ignore the glare coming over them.

"Yeah, well, I am a city girl. And city girls don't take shit from anyone. So explain to me why my funding is being cut for no good reason three weeks before Christmas."

Ben felt his eyebrows climbing at her assessment of the situation. No wonder she thought he was the second coming of Scrooge. "How long have you been in Pine Hollow, Ms. Gilmore?"

She tipped back her chin pugnaciously. She was kind of adorable when she was mad, but he had too many self-preservation instincts to tell her that. "A few weeks, but that shelter has been here for decades. My grandparents are *pillars* of the community."

"So you were here two weeks ago when we had that big snow? And I'm sure you heard about how all that wet, heavy snow caved in the roof on the community center? The building that houses dozens of town events every month and is currently unsafe to enter?"

"I don't see what that has to do with the shelter."

"It's a town building. Which means the town has to pay for the repairs. And that money has to come from somewhere," he explained. "No one wanted to make the call to cut your funding, but it was one area we *could* cut. We couldn't take the money away from schools or first responders without impacting the entire community. There just isn't any extra to go around."

She pressed her lips together, still glaring at him,

though some of the heat had gone out of it. "Couldn't you have..." She trailed off with a frustrated noise.

"The council didn't do this to spite you. Or anyone else. If it's any consolation, that money is going to do the community a lot of good."

"The shelter does the community good, too," she insisted, but there was the awareness of impending defeat in her eyes. "What are we supposed to do with the animals?"

"Find them homes?" he suggested. "Isn't that what you do?"

"It's not as easy as just waving a magic wand and the perfect home for every dog instantly appears. There's always more supply than demand, and we haven't had a single adoption since I got here. And now we have to find homes for all of them in less than a month? It's like I'm cursed." She looked up at him, a rosy flush rising to her cheeks. "I can't believe I just told you that."

"It's okay. I'm really not Ebenezer Scrooge, you know." Her dejection dug into his chest, but he pushed down the urge to help the damsel in distress. *You don't have time for one more thing, moron.*

"I didn't mean to call you—Okay, yes, I did, but I was just thinking about the dogs and my grandparents and only having four weeks and it being Christmas and a new dog just arrived today and I have no idea what to do with her and... You know, it really doesn't help that you had a good reason to cut the funding. We need it."

"The town budget doesn't have any wiggle room. I wish it did." Especially since his vote had been the tie-breaker, sealing the shelter's fate. "Look, the town can't extend the funding past the first of the year, but maybe we can help you find homes for some of the dogs. I can put the word out—I handle the town's newsletter. And if I hear of anyone looking for a dog"—other than Astrid— "I'll send them your way."

"Great," she mumbled. "Thanks. Sorry for calling you Scrooge."

He grimaced. Right now he felt like one. "Merry Christmas."

Her smile was humorless. "Bah humbug."

Chapter Six

Ally stalked back toward the shelter, her head tucked down against the wind, as she tried to think of some way to fix this. She should have known the jerk who cut their funding was the same bearded guy from this morning. And it didn't help that he had a good reason for doing it. It just made her feel that much more helpless to undo it.

Yes, she understood that the money had to come from somewhere, but they'd found it in the past, hadn't they?

She couldn't escape the feeling that she'd caused this mess for her grandparents somehow. She'd always believed in signs. In messages from the universe. Or maybe she just wanted to believe in them because she wanted to believe her parents were still out there, silent voices guiding her.

She'd come to Pine Hollow in part because it had felt like the universe was pointing her away from New York. Everything had lined up so perfectly—the end of her lease, a gap in her freelance work, her grandparents needing her. But now it was like Pine Hollow was kicking her out—and punishing her grandparents for taking her in at all.

A car rolled to a stop beside her, and Ally glanced over to see her grandparents' Subaru. For a fraction of a second she thought Gram had gotten behind the wheel again—but then the passenger's side window rolled down and her grandfather leaned across the gearshift. "You need a ride?"

"Hey." Anger still hummed through her, but some of it unknotted as she reached for the door handle.

Her grandfather had a dry, raspy voice and an impenetrable calm. He'd always been the voice of reason and logic in their family—but he was also the one who would do things just to wind his wife up and then wink at Ally when he got a rise out of her. Ally had always thought she took after him—a planner, pragmatic rather than emotional. But throw one little obstacle in her path and she immediately became her grandmother, storming town hall and calling civil servants Ebenezer.

Copper—the mini mutt with a wizened little old man face that her grandfather insisted was Gram's dog but was never more than two feet away from Gramps—stood on her grandfather's lap with his paws on the driver's side window. When Ally climbed into the warmth of the car, holding her frozen fingers up to the vents, Copper scampered across the stick shift to sniff at her before resuming his post, keeping watch for traffic threats.

"Did you win?" she asked.

Her grandfather's shrug was nonchalant. "A few dollars. Figured I'd let 'em keep the rest until next time. Your gram called me."

Ally hadn't wanted to interrupt her grandfather's card game when she dropped off the car, so she hadn't gone inside. She'd also been impatient to get to the town hall—and hopeful she'd have the whole funding thing worked out before her grandfather even heard about it. "Did she tell you she drove to Franklin and back for a dog?"

"Sounds like something she'd do," he said mildly. "But that wasn't why she called."

"She isn't supposed to be driving."

"Mm-hmm." That was her grandfather. He almost never directly contradicted her. He just agreed with her in a way that made her feel foolish.

Ally squirmed in the passenger seat, his calm unnerving her, the silence working on her like a master interrogator. "She told you about the email. About the funding."

"She mentioned it." He flicked his turning signal.

The hatchback glided slowly along the streets of Pine Hollow. With the one-way streets, school zones, and overabundance of stop signs, she probably could have walked home faster—especially since her grandfather always drove ten miles per hour below the speed limit. Most days it made Ally a little crazy, but today was worse than most. His lack of panic, the methodical, unhurried pace of it all was making her want to shake him and scream *Don't you see we have a problem here?* But she forced her voice to remain calm. "Apparently they need the money for the roof of the community center."

He nodded, not taking his eyes off the road. "Heard it caved in. That big snow we had."

"So we have four weeks to find another source of funding or find homes for all the dogs."

Her grandfather grunted, not responding right away, but then he never did. Hal Gilmore was notorious for thinking before he spoke, even when she might wish he would hurry up and say something.

"It's not ideal," he admitted finally. "But that funding from the town was always a casual agreement, not a guarantee."

Frustration flashed through her. "Why aren't you upset?"

"Would it help?"

Maybe not, but the fact that her grandparents never seemed to worry about anything only made her feel like she needed to worry more.

"We could try for some grants," Gramps suggested. "In my experience you get approved for one for every fifteen requests you fill out, but that doesn't mean you don't fill 'em out. Seems I heard something about some online funding thingy—"

"GoFundMe. It's charity crowdsourcing."

"There you go."

She watched him, trying to absorb his calm. "You aren't worried at all?"

Gramps shrugged, scratching Copper's head. "Your generation is always in such a hurry—demanding solutions as soon as problems pop up. Maybe it's the city in you or the internet streaming stuff at you the second you ask for it. I don't know. I just know that when you take a breath and let things unfold, sometimes the problems work themselves out."

Ally resisted the urge to grind her teeth. Her grandmother rushed into things with no thought to the consequences, and her grandfather just waited for the universe to solve everything. How had they survived in the world for eighty-plus years?

"You don't need to be worrying about this. The funding—it'll come or it won't, and we'll deal with it. All you need to worry about is enjoying being home for the holidays."

Her grandmother had said the same thing. Enjoy being home. Except it didn't feel like home. Nowhere did.

Pine Hollow wasn't where she'd grown up, but she didn't have any family left in New Jersey, and she'd long since drifted away from her childhood friends. She'd changed when her parents died, in ways none of them had quite understood. There wasn't anything there for her anymore. She didn't really belong anywhere, but coming to Pine Hollow was a chance to spend time with people who really mattered and figure out her next step. Start fresh.

She'd grown tired of how temporary everything in her life felt—the freelance work, always scrambling. She'd applied for a couple of more stable jobs in the city, but if those didn't come through, she didn't know where her future would be. And yes, maybe on some level she'd fantasized that everything would magically fall into place and she would find a home in Pine Hollow, looking after the shelter and her grandparents. But now...

Gramps pulled into the driveway for the shelter and the farmhouse next to it, where her grandparents had lived for fifty years. They'd built a life here, built this shelter out of an old barn and desire to help. This was their legacy, and Ally wasn't going to let anything threaten that.

"We'll get funding," she assured her grandfather, though she had no idea where that money was going to come from. "We'll make it work."

"Mm-hmm." He set the parking brake but didn't shut off the engine, warm air continuing to blast through the vents.

"And we'll find homes for the dogs. Even if—*when* we get the funding to stay open, the dogs still need families."

"And they'll get 'em. You'll see. Dogs have a way of finding their people." He scratched Copper's chin. "It's love—you can't force love. Just wait. When you see an animal wiggle their way into someone's heart, there's nothing like it."

Love was nice and all, but Ally wasn't going to wait around for lightning to strike. They had a deadline now. For the funding and for the dogs.

Four weeks.

She needed to make that website shine.

"Did you leave your game to come find me?" she asked.

Gramps glanced over at her, his bushy eyebrows arched. "I figured you could use an ear."

Ally unbuckled her seat belt and leaned across the gearshift to hug him. "You're the best, you know that?"

Copper, excited by the movement, scrambled between them to lick her chin.

Gramps coughed gruffly. "I didn't do much of anything."

"You came," she said softly. And that was worth a lot. It had been too long since she'd had someone to share the victories with or talk her down when things went wrong.

She wouldn't fail her grandparents. She was going to find all the dogs homes and save the shelter. And no Councilman Scrooge was going to stop her.

Chapter Seven

Guilt, it turned out, was a powerful motivator.

There was no other explanation for why Ben was crunching up the long gravel driveway toward the Furry Friends Animal Rescue on his lunch hour. He didn't have time for this, but he hadn't been able to stop thinking about the shelter. Or the woman who ran it.

He hadn't gotten her first name yesterday. Rita and Hal's granddaughter. She hadn't exactly been focused on pleasantries when they met. But he couldn't get the memory of her dejection out of his head.

It didn't help that the Keurig was still out of commission, so he'd had to swing by the Cup for coffee this morning. He'd thought avoiding the bakery would dodge the guilt over the way he'd snapped at her yesterday morning, but he'd failed to take into account how gossip spread in Pine Hollow. At least four people had approached him with helpful comments like "So I hear you're closing the shelter," and "Is it true you attacked Hal and Rita's granddaughter in the square yesterday?" Just another stop on his lifelong guilt trip.

Astrid had nagged him for a dog nonstop during dinner last night. She'd even suggested volunteering at the shelter as a way to prove how capable and responsible she was—which only made him feel that much worse because he'd been the deciding vote to close it. He didn't dare tell Astrid the shelter was closing, or she'd probably try to get him to adopt every dog in the place.

He couldn't do that. But he could help find them homes before the shelter had to close its doors.

He'd gone on their website this morning to find a couple of dogs to feature in the newsletter and had gotten more than he bargained for. The homepage was covered in dog photos, each one cuter than the last. It was visual emotional blackmail—but he couldn't feature all of them in the newsletter. He needed to focus on one or two. So he'd come out here to talk to the shelter lady about which ones needed the most help.

He could have sent an email. He probably should have sent an email. But he still felt like he owed her. Like her entire situation was his fault rather than the unfortunate side effect of a roof caving in.

"Hello?" Ben called, setting off a chorus of barks from the barn.

The big barn with the Furry Friends sign sat to one side of the driveway, and a farmhouse with a wraparound porch squatted on the other. There wasn't any human movement from either of them, so he took a chance and headed toward the barn. "Ms. Gilmore?"

She probably couldn't hear him over the barking. He

didn't know exactly how many dogs the shelter housed, but it sounded like dozens. The niggling guilt spiked even more with the realization that he hadn't even looked at what the shelter did before voting to cut their funding. He'd never been a dog person. All he'd been thinking of was being done with town council business for the rest of the year.

He tried the door to the barn, and a bell jangled over his head as it opened, setting off another chorus of barks and a frantic scrabble of paws on the worn hardwood floor. He let the door slam shut behind him—a fraction of a second before half a dozen dogs raced around the corner, rushing toward him in a pack.

He'd expected cages. He hadn't expected the dogs to be running around loose and unsupervised.

Ben did the manly thing. He screamed.

Ally's head jerked up at the strangled yelp on the other side of the office door.

When her grandparents had left to take Dolce to her vet appointment, she'd closed herself in the office to fill out grant applications, squinting at the computer until her eyes burned. She'd googled last night until the wee hours, looking for grants and tips on how to keep a shelter afloat.

She'd set up a GoFundMe page, but there were so many important causes vying for attention that she didn't have a lot of faith that the fund drive alone was going to save them. So she'd tackled the grants, so focused on her task that she barely registered the increased barking on the other side of the door until that yelp. Even Colby lifted his head, stirring himself to investigate.

"Gram?" Ally glanced at the clock, but it was still too early for her grandparents to be back with Dolce, unless they'd teleported to Burlington.

The barking was frantic now, the kind of frenzied enthusiasm that usually happened during mealtimes or when they had a visitor. Ally rushed for the door and yanked it open—and her jaw dropped at the sight that greeted her.

Ebenezer West stood with his back pressed against the exterior door, half the dogs in the shelter crowding around him in a squirming, barking mass.

"What did you do?" she cried. All the pen doors she could see hung open.

Ben's gaze snapped toward her—and for the first time she registered the panic on his face. "Get them off!"

The dogs rushed toward Ally en masse, and she snapped the office door shut before they could make it past her. "Why did you let them out?" she demanded, hurrying forward to take stock of the damage.

"I didn't!" Ben protested.

"Well, someone did!"

The section of the barn that housed the dog runs was L-shaped, with the rest of the space taken up by two storage rooms and the tiny front office. Ally rushed to the corner so she could see down the long stretch of pens with Colby right at her heels.

Partridge waddled into view—and Ally came to the L-bend in the corridor.

The inmates were running the asylum.

Half a dozen more pens were open. Jelly, a boisterous

yellow Lab–pit bull mix, bounded nearby, while black-and-tan mutt Biscuit trotted around the corner, dragging a dog bed as big as he was with him as an offering. JoJo, a papillon with more moxie than sense, yapped at the paws of Maximus, who peered down at the baffling little furball.

Their newest arrival, an energetic Aussie somewhat strangely called Harry, given she was female, darted down the hall to one of the few pens that was still closed. She bounced up on her hind legs, her front paws landing against the latch. She pawed at it, and as Ally watched the latch flipped up.

Little Harry was staging a jailbreak.

"Are they supposed to be able to do that?" a deep voice asked beside her. Ben stood at her side, looking decidedly out of his depth.

The newly freed golden retriever bounded past them, eager to join the fun. Harry and Jelly gave chase—right through Ben's legs. That high-pitched yelp came again as he tried to dance out of the way, ricocheting off one of the pens and tumbling to the ground, and Ally couldn't help it.

She started to laugh.

It took nearly an hour and a lot of patience to get all the dogs back into their pens.

Ally quickly realized they needed to catch Harry first, or she'd just keep freeing more of the others, but an Australian shepherd who thought chase was a super-fun game was incredibly difficult to catch. Especially when her other favorite game appeared to be herding the other dogs up and down the corridor of the shelter.

Ben was visibly uncomfortable with the dogs, and she expected him to run for the hills in under sixty seconds, but he surprised her by sticking around—and even using his body to herd Harry, though he seemed convinced the friendly little Aussie was going to leap on him at any moment.

When they had Harry securely padlocked back in her run, the task of rounding up the other dogs was much easier—especially with both of them armed with treats. She chucked a bag of liver snacks at Ben, forcing him to catch it reflexively against his chest.

"You go for the little ones," she instructed, making a beeline for Jelly, who crouched with his front end low and his rear high in the air. When she'd wrangled Biscuit, Jelly, and Captain America back into their runs, Fred and Ginger retreated to their pen on their own, curling up together, so all she had to do was shut the gate. She shut Colby in the office and manhandled the giant doofus Maximus back into his run, scanning to see who else was still roaming.

"Come on, Drooly Dog. Come on..."

Ally turned to find Ben coaxing Partridge toward his pen, wagging a liver snack at the bulldog, who gazed at the treat adoringly.

"His name is Partridge, actually," she corrected, coming up behind him.

Ben looked over his shoulder at her, still looking shell-shocked, the treat bag clutched in one large hand.

"You haven't been around dogs much, have you?"

"Does it show?"

She couldn't help her smile as he slipped out of Partridge's pen and she latched the gate. "A little. You okay? That sound you made right before I came out was...interesting."

His cheeks flushed above his beard. "You heard that, huh?"

"Yeah." She was exhausted. Thankfully, so were the dogs, all sprawled in their beds after their adventure. Ben faced her in the suddenly peaceful shelter corridor, and she studied him, trying to figure out why he was still here—or why he was here at all. It didn't fit with the idea she'd built of him. "What are you doing here? Don't tell me you're looking to adopt."

"No. Absolutely not."

Her eyebrows lifted. "Okay..."

He practically squirmed where he stood, the big strong man visibly uncomfortable. "I told you I'd help."

She blinked. "I didn't think you actually meant that."

He drew himself up, swelling before her eyes. "I'm not in the habit of making promises I don't intend to keep."

Great. Now she'd offended him. "Look, I'm not trying to insult you. We didn't exactly get off to the best start. I figured you'd say anything to get me to leave."

He grimaced. "Can we start over? Contrary to popular opinion, I'm not the Grinch." He thrust his hand at her. "Ben West."

"Ally Gilmore." She took his hand, briefly noting the sheer size of it, how completely it enveloped hers, before she flushed and dropped it.

Two hours ago she would have declared he was the

enemy, but it was hard to hate someone after she'd seen him leap away from a nine-pound papillon like it was a feral wolf but still help out until every single dog was back in its designated pen.

He might not actually be the bad guy—but she didn't want to get her hopes up about his offer of help. She somehow doubted he was offering funding.

"So you're here to volunteer? I can always use help walking the dogs, practicing basic training—even playing with them is good. We want them to be able to move out of the shelter and into forever homes as seamlessly as possible, which means giving them as much socialization as we can—"

"Actually I'm here about the newsletter."

"Right." Definitely not as good as funding.

"You have too many dogs to feature them all—it would just overwhelm people," he explained, looking plenty overwhelmed himself. "So I thought we'd pick a few and spread them out in emails over the next couple of weeks so people can focus on each one instead of being bombarded by the magnitude of the problem." He glanced at the pens around them as if they contained fire-breathing dragons rather than snoring mutts. "How many are there?"

"A dozen. Plus the one my grandparents took to the vet today, but until we know she's healthy we can't advertise her." She cocked her head. "How many did you expect?"

"I don't know. Three or four? We're a small town. How many stray dogs could there be?"

"Twelve apparently. Or thirteen, if we count Dolce."

"Twelve..." He rubbed his eyebrow, glancing toward

Partridge's pen, where the bulldog was still watching him devotedly—living in hope of another treat. "We could call it the Twelve Dogs of Christmas."

A startled laugh popped out of Ally's mouth. "That's actually kind of cute."

Ben frowned at the dog, who was still staring fixedly at him. "Why is he called Partridge?"

"He first came to the shelter at Christmas, and my gram had that song stuck in her head."

Ben frowned. "He's been here a year?"

"Three years, actually. That's not as uncommon as you might think. Some dogs get rescued right away— in the door and out the same day—but a lot of the others..." She shook her head. "Some dogs are harder to place. Too old, too excited when they meet someone new, too shy when they meet someone new. Every dog has a good dog inside them, but they don't always put their best foot forward when they're competing for love in a place like this. A bunch of the ones that end up here have already been bounced from shelter to shelter, looking for the right person to love them. My grandfather seems to think it's all about finding the right fit, but it's hard to know what people are looking for when you don't know the people, you know?"

"I could help with that," he offered. "I've lived here most of my life. If there's one thing I know, it's this town."

She looked at him, skeptic of the town Scrooge offering more help. "Really?"

"Sure. I need to get back to work now, but I could come by over my lunch hour tomorrow. You could show me which dogs you've had the hardest time getting adopted, and I'll try to think of the person who would fit them the best. We can even take some new photos for the Twelve Dogs of Christmas feature. Add a cute Santa hat or some tinsel or something."

"It's a better strategy than anything I've got." And way more than she had expected from him. "Are you sure you don't mind?"

"Of course not."

Ben walked quickly back toward town hall, kicking himself for volunteering time he didn't have. He'd intended to talk to her about the newsletter, nothing more, but something about her skepticism had made him want to prove her wrong. To show that he *wasn't* the Scrooge everyone seemed to think he was.

Not to mention the fact that he could really use a win right now. He might not be able to give Astrid the big house with the yard, or make everyone in town happy with an unlimited budget for town events, or even get his washing machine fixed in a reasonable amount of time, but he could find homes for these dogs.

He'd dedicate one more lunch hour to the cause of helping the shelter, and that would be it. One easy victory and redemption in the eyes of the town.

He knew this town. He knew these people. How hard could it be?

Chapter Eight

Ally was still thinking about Ben's offer an hour later when her grandparents returned from Burlington. The Twelve Dogs of Christmas. It was a cute idea. Cute enough that she wished she'd thought of it herself. She couldn't seem to focus on the grant application in front of her, so as soon as she heard the crunch of gravel under tires, she flipped the laptop closed and headed outside.

Gram still wasn't wearing her sling as she climbed out of the car, but at least she didn't make a move to lift the pet carrier.

"What's the verdict?" Ally asked as Gramps opened the driver's side door and Copper tumbled out in an excited rush. She opened the tailgate and reached for Dolce's carrier. "Is she healthy?"

"Very healthy," Gram gushed.

"And pregnant," Gramps added.

Ally froze. "Oh no."

"Don't worry. The puppies will get snapped up fast,"

Gram assured her—but Ally's thoughts were already spiraling.

The vet bills. The *time*. Dolce couldn't be spayed until the puppies were weaned, which would be *weeks*. Well after the first-of-the-year shutdown deadline. Then the puppies would all need shots. And to be spayed and neutered... "When's she due?"

"A couple of weeks. Give or take. She seems most comfortable in the crate, so we'll set it up in the office so she feels nice and safe—" Gram opened the shelter door, frowning when there wasn't a riot of barking to greet her. "They're all so quiet. Did you drug them?"

Ally snorted. "They're tired. We had an adventure while you were gone. You know Harry? Turns out she knows how to open doors. She let everyone out and had them running up and down the aisle."

"No!" Gram gasped, her eyes alight. "I wished I'd been here to see it."

"Explains why they call her Houdini," Gramps grunted, nudging Colby out of the way so Ally could set Dolce's carrier in the corner.

Ally's head snapped up. "Houdini?" she demanded.

"Mm," Gram mused. "It was such an odd name for her, and she never responded to it, so we just started calling her Harry—short for Harriet—but now it makes sense. An escape artist. Isn't she clever?"

"You aren't the one who had to chase them all back into their runs." Though it was probably a good thing Gram hadn't been there. She would have reinjured her shoulder for sure. "I was lucky Ben was here or it would have taken all afternoon."

"Ben?"

"Ben West came by. He had some ideas for helping us find homes for the dogs. Some feature in the town's email newsletter."

"See? I knew they didn't mean to take our funding."

"They still revoked our funding, Gram. I think he just felt…I don't know. Responsible." Which made it a lot harder to keep thinking of him as the villain. "Do we have any Christmas stuff that would fit the dogs? Santa hats or scarves or anything?"

Her grandmother's eyes flared with excitement. "Do we have Christmas stuff? I am almost insulted you had to ask."

Her grandmother's Christmas stores were impressive, to say the least. Ally didn't find a Santa hat, but she did collect some cute options, piling them in the office the next day so she'd be ready when Ben arrived—though part of her still doubted he was coming. He had no reason to help them.

She could do this without him. She might not know which townspeople were right for which dogs, but it wasn't like she didn't know how to take pictures—

A cascade of barks alerted her to his arrival. Ally straightened, moving to the open doorway of the office as the outer door opened.

"Hey." Ben nodded, stripping off his gloves.

"Hey." Awkwardness hummed in the air between them. "Are you hungry? My gram made some sandwiches, since I mentioned you might be coming during your lunch hour. My grandparents had lunch plans, but she wanted to make sure I was being a good host."

"You don't have to feed me. I pretty much invited myself—"

"To help us. This whole Twelve Dogs thing is for the shelter. The least we can do is feed you. And Gram makes a mean ham and cheese. Seriously, you don't want to miss it."

A smile quirked up one side of his beard. "In that case..."

Ally stepped back into the office, where the picnic basket her grandmother had shoved at her sat on the desk. Gram had even wrapped the handle in a bright red ribbon. "Gram's all about presentation," Ally muttered as she unpacked the lunch.

Ben sat on the couch while Ally took the chair behind the desk. Colby padded over to lay his head on her lap, sighing dramatically when she failed to immediately slip him some of her ham and cheese.

Ben jerked his chin in Colby's direction. "That one doesn't have a pen?"

"This one's mine." She ruffled his silky ears. "Colby. He's very friendly."

"He's very *large*."

Ally grinned. "That too. Did you have a bad experience with a dog...?"

"No, I just..." He shrugged. "We never had one growing up. Did you always have dogs?"

"Nah. Not when I was a kid. I wanted one so badly. I love Gram and Gramps, but I think the main reason

I always wanted to come up here to visit when I was little was so I could play with their dogs. They only had a couple then—that was before they retired and started the shelter."

"Your grandmother, she was the art teacher, right?"

"At the high school. Yeah." Ally reached into the basket, pulling out a pear and offering it to him. He declined with a shake of his head. "You never took art?" She'd officially reverted to small talk.

"No, I was more of a math and science kid." He lifted his sandwich. "This is really good."

"Right? I can't get her to tell me what the secret ingredient is. Dijon, maybe?" Great. Now she was talking about mustard. Because that wasn't awkward at all.

"Don't ask me. I'm useless in the kitchen."

She didn't know why she felt so uncomfortable around him. Maybe because she'd judged him too quickly.

Dolce gave a soft yip from inside her crate and Ben jumped, braced for the threat. "There's something in there."

"That's Dolce, our newcomer. She's still a little nervous. I'm sure being driven to Burlington and back to see the vet didn't help."

"Right, this was the one who couldn't go on the website until she was healthy." Ben bent down, cautiously peering inside. "Is she okay?"

"Yeah. The crate's just her safe place. She's perfectly healthy. Pregnant. But very healthy."

He glanced up and cringed. "Mazel tov?"

She laughed, the sound equally pained and amused. "Yeah. Not ideal." She stood, feeding the last of her sandwich to Colby and dusting off her hands. "You ready to meet the dogs? Don't worry. They're much easier to handle one at a time. And they already like you."

His eyebrows popped up in high skeptical arches. "They do?"

"Absolutely. Give them a treat and they'll love you forever." She plucked a bag of treats off the desk and tossed it to him. Ben caught it against his chest, still looking dubious.

Ally led the way into the heart of the kennels, greeting the dogs by name and giving Ben a little information about each one as they walked down the aisle.

"I'm sure you remember Harry, short for Harriet. Or Houdini, apparently." She indicated the sweet Australian shepherd who was currently racing through the dog door into the outer portion of her run, then back inside, leaping over her raised dog dish and literally bouncing off the wall before taking another lap. "She's already been adopted and returned to different shelters twice. We just got her about a week ago and yesterday . . . Well. You saw." Ally indicated the elaborate lock system on Harry's run. "We think we have her contained now. She might be the smartest dog in here, and she's as sweet as the day is long, but she needs someone who doesn't mind a challenge. And a lot of energy."

Ally moved onto the next run, avoiding looking directly at Ben as eight tiny feet pattered to meet them. "Fred and Ginger—totally sweet and completely codependent. If we try to separate them, they both stop eating. They're both older, and they came to us when their owner passed away suddenly. Ginger has a bad back, so she can't handle stairs, and she needs a ramp to get up on the couch. And Fred's epileptic. It's managed with medication, but the meds aren't cheap, and with so many other dogs to choose from, most people pick a pet that isn't so complicated."

In the run beside Fred and Ginger, a giant shaggy head pressed against the door. "Maximus—half Irish wolfhound, half Great Dane—we think—and only half trained. But all heart. He was never taught good manners when he was young, and he's so big he's hard to manage. We've been working with him, but he doesn't know his own strength and needs someone who can handle a pony who thinks he's a lap dog."

Another cage, another story. Peanut, the chihuahua who couldn't hear. Trapper the one-eyed Jack Russell. And poor Daisy, who peed in submissive reflex every time a stranger tried to touch her.

None of them belonged here, but there was a reason each one was here. Which was why she'd been so disheartened by the idea of finding homes for all of them in the next four weeks. Shelters in other areas were just as overcrowded as they were, especially at the holidays, so it wasn't like she could transfer them all.

They reached the end of the aisle, and she stopped in front of the final run. "And last, but not least, Partridge."

The bulldog waddled to the front of his enclosure, panting and trailing strings of drool out of each side of his mouth.

"What's wrong with him?"

"Nothing's *wrong* with him." Ally unlatched the

gate and crouched down to ruffle his skin rolls. "He just hasn't found his people yet. Isn't that right, Your Drooliness?"

Partridge gazed up at her adoringly, listing to one side as he leaned into her scratches.

"I was thinking we could start with him, since he fits the whole Twelve Dogs of Christmas theme," Ben suggested from where he stood well back of the open run.

Ally glanced up over her shoulder. "You know someone who would be perfect for him?"

"Not off the top of my head. But I'm sure if we highlight him, let the community know the shelter is closing, and enlist their help to get the word out, we'll find the right person."

He was standing about as far back from Partridge's pen as he could get without leaving the shelter entirely. It was sort of adorable, the gruff man with the scruffy beard holding himself so stiffly aloof. Determined not to let the dogs into his heart.

Partridge snorted and snuffled at her hand, and Ally turned her attention back to rubbing his ears. "What do you need to feature him?"

Ben took a single step closer. "Any information that might make people want to adopt him. And some Christmassy picture."

"Right." She straightened, glancing down at the least photogenic dog on the planet. "I have some costume options in the office. I'll be right back."

Chapter Nine

Ben watched Ally half-jogging away from him down the aisle, and a warm lump settled against his ankle. He startled, glancing down to see Partridge leaning against him.

She'd left him alone with the dog. The cage door was open, and there wasn't a leash in sight. Luckily, Partridge didn't seem terribly eager to make a run for it. He sat half on top of Ben's shoe, gazing up at him fixedly and occasionally licking his—very moist—chops.

"Hi." Ben tried to edge his foot out from under the dog, but Partridge only shuffled closer, replanting himself and brushing close enough to leave a clinging streak of drool on Ben's jeans. "Thanks," he said dryly, and Partridge snorted, staring up at him like it was a contest.

Ben glanced toward the front of the shelter, but Ally was nowhere in sight. He didn't think he'd ever been alone with a dog before now. Especially one who seemed to be trying to will him into doing something with his puppy psychic powers.

"Can I help you?" he asked the dog.

Partridge grunted and leaned more of his bulk against Ben's leg with a weary sigh, as if exhausted by his obtuseness.

"Sorry. I'm not much of a dog person," he admitted, bending down to pat the bulldog awkwardly on the top of the head. Partridge instantly perked up, lunging upward clumsily, and Ben flinched back, anticipating a bite—or at least a really wet lick—but all he felt was a soft, warm snuffling against his fingertips. He scratched Partridge tentatively behind his ear and the dog sighed, gazing adoringly—

At the bag in his other hand.

The treats. The dog had been trying to get the dumb human to give him a snack. And here Ben was, bending over and holding the bag inches away from the poor guy's face. "Is this what you want?" he asked, reaching into the bag and plucking out a dried brown square that smelled strongly of liver.

Partridge went statue-still, focused intently on the treat. His only movement was a wet slurp of his tongue.

Ben dropped the treat toward the dog's mouth—unsure he would keep his fingers if he got them close enough to actually hand over the snack. It bounced off Partridge's nose and the bulldog lunged after it, snarfing it off the scarred hardwood floor in the blink of an eye. And then instantly returning to his position at Ben's ankle, resuming the feed-me lean.

"Sorry, buddy. I don't know if you're allowed to have more than one." He sealed the bag, tucking it into his pocket—but Partridge continued his attempt to

Jedi-mind-trick him into food. Ben leaned down, watching the dog carefully to make sure he wasn't about to lose a finger, and gave him another cautious pat on the head. The dog leaned into the caress, groaning softly, his eyes going half closed.

When Ben straightened, Partridge whined softly, leaning into his leg—and dribbling more drool onto his shoe.

"What? What do you want now?"

"You've got treats."

Ben jumped. He hadn't heard Ally come back, so focused on Partridge and his impressive saliva production. She was still six feet away, walking up the aisle with her arms full of Christmas décor and a fancy camera. The giant, droopy Saint Bernard padded at her heels.

"I already gave him one," Ben admitted.

"In his mind, one is never enough. Partridge is very food motivated." She stopped a couple of feet away, but the huge Saint Bernard kept moving past her toward him.

"Whoa." Ben stumbled back, shying away—and Partridge tipped over with the loss of his shin as support, somehow making the move look slow motion as he listed into a sprawl on the scratched hardwood.

"Don't mind Colby," Ally said. "He just wants to say hello to Partridge. Go on, lie down, Colb."

The Saint Bernard didn't have to be told twice. He'd paused to sniff Partridge, but at the command he turned in a circle and flopped down with a sigh, as if utterly exhausted by life. Ben watched him for a moment to make sure he was down for the count, and when he looked up again, Ally was studying him.

"You really aren't comfortable around dogs, are you?"

"Not uncomfortable. Just...cautious."

Her smile revealed a small dimple in her left cheek. "Well, don't worry. Partridge is easy. He's all heart and stomach."

"And drool."

"That too." The words came out half-laughing. She held up the Christmas things she'd brought. "What do you think? Can we make him look festive? I thought we'd shoot him in his dog bed so it looks sort of cozy. The lighting will be better there, too. Or we could take him up to the house. Put him in front of the Christmas tree..."

"No, this is good." Ben took some of the ribbon from her hands, noticing the camera again. It was the same one she'd been carrying the other day, but this time it had attachments—like something from a professional photo shoot. "That's quite a camera."

Ally glanced down at it as she set the Christmas things she'd brought in a pile. "If we want to do this, we might as well do it right, don't you think?" She pulled a dog biscuit from her pocket and lured Partridge back into his run and over to his dog bed. The dog flopped down with a huff and she crouched, sticking a giant bow right on top of his head. "I could use the practice with live models anyway. I've mostly been doing scenery shots since I came up here—and the occasional shot of locals putting up a tree in the town square. Sorry about that, by the way. I really will pay for your dry cleaning."

"Don't worry about it. I'm sorry I overreacted. I blame caffeine deprivation." He glanced around, eager to change the topic. "You're a photographer?"

She moved back far enough to give herself room to lift the camera, but didn't come out of her crouch, the shutter clicking. "Hm? Oh, yeah. I freelance for a few magazines in New York."

"I heard you were some big deal in fashion."

That pulled her attention away from the viewfinder. She glanced up at him, arching a brow. "You heard?"

"Small town. Gossip is our fuel."

The bow started to slide sideways off Partridge's head, and Ally's attention returned to her subject. "So what have you heard about me?" she asked without looking away from the lens.

"Not much. Just that you're Hal and Rita's big-city granddaughter with some high fashion career."

"It wasn't all that high fashion. I've never shot for *Vogue*, if that's what you were envisioning."

"But you made a living at it."

"Yeah. I made it work." Partridge sneezed, the bow sliding off his head and onto his paws. He immediately tried to eat it, and Ally snapped one more picture before rescuing it from his juicy clutches. She tossed the bow back onto the pile and picked up a long, red velvet ribbon. "I didn't find a Santa hat. Do you think we can get this tied around his collar in a way that doesn't look ridiculous?"

"Here, let me." He took the ribbon and knelt next to Partridge—who immediately perked up and snuffled at the pocket where Ben had stashed the treats. "Be good and you can have another one," he promised the dog, looping the velvet around his neck and tying a tidy little bow.

"You're good at that," she commented when he stepped back.

"Present wrapping is pretty much my only useful holiday skill." For a moment, the only sound was the click of the camera. "Do you miss it? New York?"

She was silent for a moment, even the camera's shutter going still. "I miss feeling like I knew what I was doing," she said finally, the steady click of the camera starting up again.

"I get that." He hadn't felt like he had a clue ever since he became Astrid's guardian. All of the certainty he used to have in his life had gone up in smoke in a single second. "That confidence makes a difference."

"Exactly. I'd gotten to the point where I knew I was good, you know? I liked that. Even if it was just at work."

Ben watched Partridge try to figure out how to chew on the ribbon on his collar, silently agreeing with everything she said. It meant a lot—that feeling that he knew what he was doing at work. If there was a problem with a computer or a database needed to be debugged, he could fix it. There were some days when it felt like work was the only place he had control in his life. "So what are you doing here?"

Another minute pause of the shutter, though she didn't look away from the lens. "My grandparents needed me—it seemed like a sign. The universe telling me to stick around here and help out."

"I've never been much for listening to the universe."

She looked at him over the camera. "Somehow it doesn't surprise me that you don't believe in signs. But don't you ever get that sense that life seems to be shoving you in a certain direction?"

"I guess." He never would have picked the single-dad life if he'd been picking futures out of a catalog, but life had shoved him into it. He wouldn't want Astrid with anyone else, and he wouldn't trade his relationship with her for anything, but when Katie and Paul died, in a way it felt like a lot of his choices had died with them. Now he was just ricocheting from day to day, trying to manage the choices that life had already made for him.

Partridge decided he was done playing model and stood up from the bed, waddling over to Ally and trying to climb on her. She ruffled his ears before standing up to save her camera from his drool. She studied the camera's digital display, toggling quickly through photos until she paused on one.

She grinned, angling the camera toward him. "What do you think? Do we have a winner?"

It was one of the photos with the bow on top of his head. It tilted slightly to one side, making Partridge's lopsided face somehow look even more adorable.

"That's really good." Realizing he sounded insultingly surprised, considering she was a professional, he tried to cover. "I just mean that's sure to get him adopted. He looks very adoptable. Perfect for the feature. In the newsletter."

Ally grinned, thankfully amused by his stumbling. "All right. I'll send this one to you this afternoon. And

I'll look through to see if there are any others we don't want to miss."

"Right. I should probably get back to work." He glanced at his two-year-old smart watch—and cursed under his breath. "I should definitely get back to work."

"Ben...I really appreciate you doing this. The Twelve Dogs of Christmas."

He looked away, uncomfortable with the gratitude. "It's nothing."

"It's not nothing." She gathered up her things and slipped out of the run. Ben tossed Partridge the treat he'd promised him and followed her out.

Colby had been snoring softly in the aisle, but he lifted his head as Ally closed the gate, though he didn't get up to follow when she and Ben headed toward the entrance.

"Is there anything I can do to repay the favor? Anything you need photographed?"

"Do you know anything about making gingerbread?" He didn't know why he'd asked that. It was his responsibility to make the gingerbread, and he didn't foist his responsibilities off on anyone else. He managed. No matter what it took.

"Actually..." For a second his hopes lifted, and then she grimaced. "Not a thing."

He matched her grimace. "Yeah. Me either."

"But I bet my gram does," Ally said suddenly. "She loves baking, and I'm sure she'd love to help."

"No. No, it's okay. I've got it figured out." Google would teach him whatever he needed to know.

They'd reached the front of the barn, and Ally pushed

open the door, cradling her camera in her other arm. "If you change your mind, the offer stands."

"You don't need to do anything. Just concentrate on finding homes for the dogs." Because if they found homes for the dogs, he didn't need to feel quite so guilty about cutting her funding in the first place.

"Will do. Thanks, Ben."

"Ally." He nodded to her, fastening his coat.

He was a quarter mile down the road before he realized he still had a bag of liver treats in his pocket.

Chapter Ten

Ally stepped into the historic town hall building on Friday morning with her hands full of peace-offering coffee and her stomach full of butterflies. She and Ben had reached an unexpected truce, but she still felt bad that she'd jumped to conclusions about him...and spilled coffee all over him. If his coffee machine was broken, this seemed like the perfect gesture to clean the slate and thank him for helping the shelter.

But when she looked to the desk where he'd been sitting the other day there was a middle-aged woman in his place.

"Hi." Ally kept her determined smile pinned in place as she approached the desk. "I'm looking for Ben West?"

The woman's face lit, speculation flickering in her eyes. "Third floor. Second door on the left."

"Great. Thank you."

Ally climbed the stairs, feeling the woman's eyes on her until she rounded the corner out of sight. With the steps creaking beneath her feet, amplifying the awkwardness of her ascent, she was seriously reconsidering the wisdom of coming here by the time she reached the third-floor landing. The second door on the left was ajar and Ally crept over to it.

Ben's small office was cluttered—mostly with electronics, but there were papers stacked haphazardly on various flat surfaces as well, including the only chair in the room that wasn't occupied. Ben's desk faced the door, but his attention was so wholly focused on his computer that she had a chance to study him. Dark brows pulled together in a frown of concentration. He rubbed at one eyebrow, as she'd seen him do the other day, and then typed furiously, his long fingers stabbing the keys.

Ally cleared her throat, and his hands froze mid-keystroke, his gaze snapping to hers.

"Hey."

"Hi there." *Too cheerful. Way too cheerful.* Ally ratcheted down the chipperness. "I brought you coffee. I feel like we got off on the wrong foot, and you said your machine was broken—though it occurs to me now you probably have coffee here."

"We don't actually," he admitted, still frowning. "There was an incident with a hot plate in the breakroom last year—old wiring—anyway, people usually bring their own."

Ally held up the cup. "Is that a 'yay, coffee'? Or did you already…?"

"Uh, yeah, yay coffee," he said, straightening from behind his desk. "Thank you. Sorry. I'm not used to people bringing me caffeine."

She extended one of the cups. "It's black, but I have cream and sugar packets. I wasn't sure how you took it."

"Black's great. Perfect."

"Great." He took the cup from her, and she realized she was blushing. She'd been hoping this would make her feel *less* awkward around him, not more. "I guess I should—" She waved toward the door.

"Actually, while you're here, I could use your help with something. I've been working on the newsletter, the Twelve Dogs feature, and I need a description of Partridge. All I've managed to come up with so far is 'impressively moist.'"

Ally released a startled laugh. "Probably not his most attractive feature."

Ben waved back toward his computer. "Do you have a minute?"

"Yeah. Of course."

He set down his coffee, quickly clearing a chair for her by redistributing the paper piles. He lifted the chair over the desk and set it beside his own, waving her toward it before resuming his seat. Ally came around the desk and perched on the edge of the chair, flicking stealthy glances around Ben's workspace. There were a few photos scattered around. One of an older couple she assumed were his parents. Another of Astrid with a smiling pair who must be her mom and dad.

On the computer screen, she saw a draft of the newsletter, complete with the photo she'd emailed him yesterday, but the block for text beneath was blank except for the words "Something clever here."

Ally grinned. "How about something like, 'Loyal, sweet-natured bulldog looking for a family to provide lots of cuddles'—or does it need to be Christmassy? Like 'On the first day of Christmas, Furry Friends gave to me a bulldog named Partridge who wouldn't fit in a pear tree'?"

Ben's teeth flashed white against his beard. "That's cute, but your first idea might be better. Talking about what owning him would be like, helping people picture it. What else does he like?"

"Treats. Naps. Belly rubs. Partridge is a big fan of belly rubs."

His fingers struck the keyboard, rapid-fire. "That's good."

"We should probably mention his age. And that he's neutered and house trained and up-to-date on all his shots."

Ben shook his head. "Leave that stuff for when you get them in the door."

"I feel like people want to know that he's not going to pee all over their carpet."

He grimaced. "The joys of pet ownership."

"Is that why you don't want a dog?"

"Who said I don't?" he demanded.

"You did. The other day. When I asked if you wanted to adopt."

"Right. Sorry. Sore subject. I just don't have space for a dog."

"Not all dogs need a lot of space."

"And not everyone needs a dog." He shrugged. "I've never seen the point."

"Of someone who loves you unconditionally and gets

euphorically excited every time you walk through the door? Yeah. That sounds awful."

He snorted. "They only love you because you feed them. I don't think that counts as unconditional."

"Feeding them definitely helps," she acknowledged, "but that's not the only reason they love you."

He leaned back in his chair, picking up the coffee she'd brought him. "Enlighten me."

"You're their person," she explained. "Dogs are just bundles of love, looking for someone to give it to. Why wouldn't you want that in your life?"

"Because they're messy and needy and they die much too fast."

"Wow. That got dark in a hurry."

"Don't you ever feel like you're setting yourself up for grief? Getting that attached to an animal that's only going to live a decade or two?"

"Knowing there's an end doesn't make it any less wonderful while it lasts. It just makes it that much more special when you have it."

He eyed her skeptically. "Let me guess, you're one of those 'tis better to have loved and lost people."

"Absolutely." She had to be. She'd lost the people she loved the most. "Aren't you?"

"I'm still making up my mind."

"You could always get a dog," she suggested. "Partridge is very affectionate, and he's only five—he's got lots of good years left."

"I'm good as I am. Thanks." He looked back to the screen. "Maybe we should add that. 'Has at least one or two good years left.'"

"Have you always been a pessimist? Or is this just a side of you that comes out around Christmas?"

Ben turned to her, affronted. "I'm not a pessimist."

"Really." Skepticism saturated her tone.

"I'm a realist. People don't think about the consequences of their choices. Everything has an effect."

"But just because there's a consequence doesn't mean you never take action. Life isn't about avoiding cause and effect. Sometimes the reward is worth the risk. Like with dogs."

"You really love them, don't you?"

"That surprises you?"

"I guess I expected you to be going through the motions since this is your grandparents' thing, but you're really into it."

"I guess I am," she admitted, grinning self-consciously. "Dogs make people happy—it's hard not to want to be a part of that. I wanted to update things, bring the shelter into this decade—which my grandparents weren't actually very excited about—but that was before we knew about the deadline. The funding."

He winced. "Yeah. Sorry."

"Not your fault. And maybe this feature will save the day."

He jerked his chin toward the text on the screen. "What do you think? Will that do?"

Ally scanned the words on the screen, smiling slowly. "It's perfect." Partridge sounded utterly charming. Someone was bound to fall in love with him. "Thank you, Ben."

"Thanks for the coffee." He lifted his cup in a toast.

"There's more where that came from if we can get these dogs adopted." Ally stood, gathering her half-full coffee and her bag. "When do you want the next pictures?"

"As soon as you have them. I'll put out one feature every few days until Christmas. Try to keep building interest. Do you want help with the photo shoots?"

"Um, yeah, if you want. Maybe just with some of the bigger dogs."

She didn't know why she said yes. She didn't need help. She was a professional. She could manage on her own—and she could always enlist her grandfather's help. But she didn't take it back as Ben nodded.

"I'll text you to work out a time."

"Great." She jotted down her number on a Post-it and handed it to him. "See you then."

Ally was smiling as she walked out the front door of the town hall building. Operation Fresh Start, complete success.

Chapter Eleven

The newsletter with the first Twelve Dogs of Christmas feature went out on Friday afternoon. All weekend Ally found herself straining her ears, listening for the sound of tires on the gravel driveway.

It was going to work. She knew it.

She and Ben had been texting back and forth, exchanging random ideas for the dogs. *I keep looking at these photos,* Ben had sent Friday evening. *You should send them to the news station in Burlington—see if they'll do the 12 Dogs feature with us.*

Ally had immediately replied to thank him for the idea—but why stop at Burlington? Tons of national morning shows had pet adoption segments, and she'd started researching all of them, trying to figure out how to get the dogs featured.

The next morning, her grandparents were discussing the town's Christmas parade when an idea popped into her head. She knew her grandparents would just tell her not to worry and to enjoy her vacation, but Ben would listen.

Do you think we could get some of the dogs onto a float in the Christmas parade? she'd texted. She knew he was busy. She hadn't expected an immediate answer, but his reply had come within seconds.

Good idea. I'll talk to the organizers.

She'd grinned at her phone like an idiot, irrationally delighted to have him on her team. Her grandmother had seen her smile and asked if she was texting with some beau. Ally had flushed as she denied it. There was nothing romantic there. Yes, he was objectively attractive, but she remembered Gram mentioning his fiancée. This was purely a friends thing, but it was still nice. Better than nice. She felt like she had a partner, someone working the problem with her, and it made all the difference.

She'd texted him to share her excitement when she found a box of adorable bandanas with ADOPT ME printed on them in the storeroom for the dogs to wear for the Christmas parade. And Ben tripped across an old Santa hat in the town's Christmas supplies and sent her a pic of it—so now they had one to use for the photo shoot for Jelly, which they had planned for later this afternoon.

Her grandparents didn't seem worried at all about the cut funding—they seemed to think everything would simply work itself out. And maybe it would, with Ben and Ally on the job.

Astrid and Kimber had shown up every day after school for the past week, spending a couple of hours playing with the dogs, walking them, feeding them, and working on their basic training commands. Their parents still hadn't been by the shelter, so Ally didn't think the girls had made any progress in convincing them to let them have a dog, but they were great with the animals. The dogs all seemed to adore the girls—possibly because they were a little free with the treats, but Ally couldn't blame them. All dogs deserved someone who wanted to shower them with Milk-Bones and liver snacks.

Dolce hadn't had her puppies yet, but she'd claimed the dog bed tucked into the darkest corner of the office as her own. She growled whenever Colby came over to investigate, adorable little rumbly grumbles, but she melted for Gram, who fussed over her constantly.

On Tuesday morning, Ally was going over the shelter's finances for the thousandth time—trying to figure out exactly how much they could slash adoption fees in an "everyone must go" special and still break even by the end of the year—when a car door slammed in the driveway.

Colby lifted his head at the sound, barks echoing through the kennels, and Ally perked up just as much as the dogs. "Maybe this is our first success story," she said to Colby, ruffling his head as she moved past him to the front door.

It had warmed up a few days ago, melting some of the snow and sending rivulets of water dripping off the eaves of the barn. Ally stepped out onto the damp gravel and smiled at the woman climbing out of a powder-blue vintage VW bug. "Good morning!"

"Hi!" The woman beamed as she approached, energy seeming to burst out of her smile. She looked to be in her twenties, with the kind of funky, eclectic fashion sense that would have made her a hit in Brooklyn. Her pink-streaked blond hair was barely long enough to be pulled into the ponytail that stuck up from the crown of her head. Lime-green leggings hugged the slim legs that appeared below the hem of her oversized winter coat and disappeared into fuzzy black boots. "You must be Ally. I'm Deenie."

"Nice to meet you." Ally clasped the hand that was thrust at her and immediately started trying to figure out which of the dogs would make this woman the perfect companion. On closer inspection, a heavy layer of glitter covered both of her cheekbones and the bridge of her nose. Maybe little JoJo? The papillon with her cute tufted ears would make the perfect accessory to this woman's funky style. "Are you looking for a dog?"

Deenie wrinkled her glitter-coated nose. "I sublet, so I can't have dogs in my apartment—and I have too much of a weakness for impromptu travel to be a good pet owner. But I was hoping you could still use me as a volunteer. I love animals, and I've helped out for Hal and Rita a few times. Expert dog walker, at your service." Her grin quirked. "Even Maximus listens to me."

"Seriously?" Ally held the door open, and they both retreated into the warmth of the barn.

Deenie reached out a hand to greet the giant wolf-hound mix in the nearest pen. "He's just a big teddy bear. Aren't you, baby? Yes, you are," she gushed in a high-pitched voice, before continuing to Ally in a regular tone, "I didn't realize you guys were in trouble until I saw in the newsletter that you'd lost your funding. Are you really going to have to close?"

Ally grimaced. "I'm working on getting us funding from other sources, but at the moment we have to assume we aren't going to get it and make arrangements for the dogs."

"That sucks. Freaking town council. We should start an online petition to save the shelter."

"I'll try anything," Ally admitted. "Though I'm not sure it'll help. I get the impression the town council doesn't have the money to spare. Something about the community center roof."

Deenie moved to the next pen to greet more of the furry residents. "It doesn't hurt to raise awareness. Get people fired up, maybe get them to open their check-books. I'd donate the money myself, but I'm always one month away from broke." She said it casually, so sure of who she was that the idea of being ashamed of trying to make ends meet didn't even occur to her.

Ally wished she could be so comfortable just saying things like that. She felt like she'd spent the last decade pretending she had her life more together than she did. "I'll take any help I can get."

Deenie straightened from where she'd crouched to coo at Fred and Ginger. She dusted off her hands, grimacing. "Sorry, I'm getting glitter everywhere. I just came from a gig."

"Are you a musician?" That certainly fit her style— and her confidence.

"No, I'm a princess."

A princess.

At Ally's blank stare, Deenie laughed. "I do princess parties for little kids. And I also design and create bespoke princess outfits for children of all ages. Honestly, the dresses are my biggest moneymakers, but the parties are way more fun. I get to dress up as Cinderella or the Little Mermaid and play with little kids all afternoon. All public domain princesses, of course, so the Big Bad Mouse doesn't come after me."

As soon as Deenie explained, Ally could see it. The energy, the enthusiasm—even with the pink punk-rock hair, she seemed like a Disney princess. Her smile radiated sunshine and sweetness, like the kind of person who could credibly have woodland creatures at her beck and call. "How does someone get into something like that?"

"I studied theater for the very young in school— which was awesome, but it turns out there's not a lot of demand for the arts aimed at preschoolers. Though there clearly should be. We're engaging their imaginations and building confidence and empathy—studies have shown all sorts of good things about children experiencing theater, but we're in the same boat you are. Always the first funding to get cut. So I started picking up whatever work I could and just sort of fell into the princess thing. Luckily, I love it. Hi there!" Colby came out of the office to investigate, and Deenie bent to greet him, still chattering cheerfully. "The best part is that I get to make my own schedule. Life's too short to live by someone else's rules, isn't it, baby?"

The last seemed to be directed at Colby, so Ally didn't bother responding. "If you've volunteered here before, have you met most of the dogs?"

"Only the longtime residents. I just got back from

backpacking across New Zealand for the last three months, so I haven't met any of the new arrivals. You're new, aren't you, baby?"

Colby flopped onto the floor, exposing his belly for her appreciation. "That's Colby. He's mine."

"He's a sweetie." Deenie obligingly rubbed his belly. "So where do you want me to start?"

Ally studied her build. Deenie had a good six inches on her, but she was thin, her wrists so delicate they looked fragile where they stuck out of her sleeves. "Can you really handle Maximus?" He looked like he would bowl her over in less than ten seconds.

Deenie grinned. "Just watch."

Deenie was a freaking dog whisperer.

By the time she left two hours later, every dog in the shelter was better behaved, and Ally was trying to figure out how to get Deenie on the float with the dogs in the Christmas parade. Apparently the princess had meant it when she said she didn't believe in schedules, so Ally had no idea when she'd be back, but Ally would take her whenever she could get her.

She was in the office, checking to make sure she hadn't missed any incoming applications, when Astrid and Kimber arrived at three forty-five, breathless from having run all the way from the school. Kimber shouted, "Hi!" toward the office before running to greet Captain America, the golden retriever who bounded to the edge of his pen to meet her.

"I think Kimber's found her favorite," Ally commented, joining Astrid where she was hanging her coat on one of the pegs that wasn't occupied by a collection of leashes.

"Do you have a favorite?" Astrid asked.

"Of the dogs up for adoption? I'm not supposed to. They're all wonderful in their own ways."

"But?"

Ally grinned. "I will admit I have kind of a soft spot for Partridge."

Astrid grinned back. "He's so squishy."

"That he is."

"Can I walk Cap today?" Kimber called, racing back to meet them.

"Sure. You can work with him on his heeling. Do you remember the training commands we talked about?"

"Sit, down, look at me . . ." Kimber rattled off. "He's going to be the best-trained dog in the whole place."

"He could be." Ally looked to Astrid. "Do you want to walk Cap with Kimber, or would you like your own charge today?"

"Can I have my own?"

"Sure. Who would you like?"

"Partridge?" Astrid smile shyly, and Ally grinned.

"Excellent choice."

After a slight delay in which Astrid and Kimber greeted every dog in the shelter, including Dolce, who was still holed up in the office, confirming to each and every one that they were good boys and good girls, Ally got the girls set up with their dogs of choice in the empty storeroom, where they could practice their good behavior. She watched for a few minutes until she had assured herself that everything was going smoothly. Cap and Partridge were such good dogs—though Cap was much quicker at picking up the training. She was hoping Partridge would pick up a few things through sheer repetition, since someone could be by to adopt him any second now that he'd been featured in the Twelve Dogs of Christmas.

The newsletter had to help. Ben was coming by after he got off work to help with the photo shoot for Jelly. They were going to find homes for all the dogs.

Then she just had to figure out what she was going to do with herself. But that was a problem for another day.

Ally had decided on the front porch of the house for Jelly's shoot, so she headed out to set the scene. Thankfully it wasn't quite as cold as it had been a few days ago, but her fingers were still stiff inside her gloves as she arranged Christmas garland over the railings, picturing Jelly sprawled adorably across the swing with the Santa hat on.

Before she knew it, Ben's SUV was pulling into the driveway. He climbed out wearing the Santa hat, and a startled laugh burst out of Ally. "I thought the hat was for the dogs."

"I'm trying to rehab my Scroogey image," he called out as he crossed to join her.

"It's working. Very festive."

"So is this." He climbed the porch steps, studying her handiwork. "It's like a Christmas card up here."

Ally bowed dramatically, grinning. "Thank you, sir." Then she sobered, glancing toward the already darkening sky. "But we need to hurry before we lose the light. I forgot how early the sun goes behind the mountains in December."

She started toward the barn and he fell into step beside her. "Who's up today?"

"I thought we'd do Jelly—he's just an eager bundle of love. A lot of people hear pit bull mix and assume he's aggressive, but Jelly Belly doesn't have a mean bone in his body."

"Did you ever hear back from the news station in Burlington about bringing some of the dogs into the studio?"

"I did. I was thinking maybe Fred and Ginger and a few of the older, calmer dogs would be good. Less likely to be rattled by the lights and the cameras and all the strange people."

"After you mentioned the parade, I thought we could also bring a few of them to the tree lighting in the town square on Friday. The whole town will be there, so it's the perfect chance to introduce them to as many people as possible—and prospective adopters will be able to interact with the dogs more than they will on a float in the parade."

"I love that idea." Another flood of optimism rushed through her. How could the townspeople help falling in love with the dogs if they met them in person?

Ben reached for the door to the barn, holding it open for Ally to precede him inside. She stepped into the warmth of the barn, the dogs barking excitedly in greeting.

"Hello, boys and girls!" She started toward Jelly's run with Ben on her heels.

"Ally!" Astrid called out from the back of the kennels. "Look what I taught Partridge to do!"

The girls rushed around the corner of the L-bend with Partridge waddling eagerly at the end of his leash between them and Cap heeling perfectly. Astrid looked up and stumbled to a halt, her eyes going wide—and fixed on a point past Ally's shoulder. Kimber jolted to a halt as well, horror flashing across her face.

Ally turned. Ben had also frozen in place.

The sudden tension in the air reminded Ally of two facts in quick succession—that her grandmother had said Astrid was Ben's niece the other day. And that she wasn't entirely sure Astrid's parents knew she'd been volunteering here.

Ally had completely forgotten the family connection— Ben and Astrid didn't look anything alike, and they didn't seem to have any nonphysical similarities, either. Astrid couldn't stop talking about how badly she wanted a dog and how much she was looking forward to Christmas—which didn't exactly fit Ben's reputation of grumpitude.

Her grandmother had assured her that it was all right for the girls to volunteer—and Gram knew the town better than Ally did. But Ally knew she should have reached out to Astrid's and Kimber's parents to make sure it was all right. She'd planned to, but she'd had a few other things on her to-do list, and she'd never thought of it when it seemed like a reasonable time to call. Part of her had rationalized that their parents must know by now— but that assumption wasn't looking terribly accurate as Astrid stared at Ben in horror.

"Uncle Ben," she said, her voice strangled. "What are you doing here?"

Ben's expression darkened beneath the Santa hat, which now seemed even more out of place on his head. "What am *I* doing here?"

Chapter Twelve

Ben had never grounded Astrid before. She was a good kid, thank God. A born people-pleaser. He'd never had to worry about her breaking the rules.

At least he hadn't thought he had. Now he was starting to wonder if he had any idea what he was doing with the whole parenting thing, because he'd been *sure* she was spending her after-school hours working on Pine Hollow Elementary's float for the Christmas parade. He'd pictured her properly supervised, armed with glue and papier-mâché.

She'd lied.

She'd flat-out lied to him. That had to be a groundable offense, didn't it? Of course, his parents grounding him had never done any good, but he had no idea what else to do if she was going behind his back. He was failing the parent test. Again.

"Would you like to explain what you're doing here?"

Astrid had frozen fifteen feet away from him, and she didn't move any closer. Kimber Kwan—whose parents also probably had no idea where she was—had gone statue-still as well with a golden retriever seated at her side, but Partridge strained against the end of the leash, trying to get closer to Ben. Neither of them paid him any heed.

"I wanted to surprise you," Astrid mumbled, barely loud enough for him to hear. "We've been learning how to take care of dogs. How to train them and stuff. I thought if you saw that I was really serious about taking care of my own dog—"

"We talked about this."

His voice must have been even darker than he thought because Ally shifted, putting herself between him and the girls. "Ben..."

"This isn't your business." He realized he was still wearing the Santa hat and swiped it off his head, shoving it at her as he moved toward Astrid.

"I don't see how it's your business, either," Ally argued, but he was already past her, closing in on Astrid. Partridge nearly tripped him with his greeting, but Ben didn't take his attention off his niece.

"So when you told me you were working on the parade float, that was a complete lie?"

"I did work on the float," she protested, though she didn't meet his eyes, adding reluctantly, "at first. I just didn't say anything when we finished..."

The kids had to be signed out by an adult. Pine Hollow was militant about stuff like that. "Did Aunt Elinor help you with this? Did you ask her to lie for you?"

She scuffed a shoe on the hardwood floor. "We told her we were walking home."

"So you lied to her, too."

She looked up, though she still didn't meet his eyes. "Technically we did walk home. We just didn't stay there."

"Astrid." Disappointment thickened his voice.

Astrid's gaze dropped again. "I just wanted to show you—"

"Get your things. I'm taking you home."

"Ben, come on..." Ally spoke from behind him, but he didn't spare her a glance.

"Now, Astrid." Ben glanced over at Kimber, who had been doing her best to fade into invisibility. "Do your parents know where you are?" She opened her mouth, her eyes wide behind her glasses, but no words came out. Ben grimaced. He used to be the cool uncle. Now he was the bad guy. "Get your things, too."

The girls turned toward the back of the kennels, hunched together. Astrid tugged gently on the bulldog's leash. "Come on, Partridge."

The girls and the dogs disappeared around the corner, and Ben forced himself not to turn and confront the woman who had also failed to tell him that his niece was sneaking around at the kennel behind his back. He just needed to keep his calm for a few more minutes.

"I won't be able to help you with the photo shoot today." His tone was rough, but he didn't try to soften it. "You can send me the pictures for the next dog, and I'll put them in the newsletter."

"I don't see why you're so upset." Her voice was closer, right at his shoulder, but he didn't look over.

"She was just volunteering. She's been very helpful, very responsible—"

"She's been lying."

She stepped into his line of vision so he couldn't avoid looking at her. "Okay, that's bad, but it's between her and her parents, isn't it?"

"I *am* her parent," he snapped, then forced himself to lower his voice so it wouldn't carry to Astrid. "Or her guardian, anyway. Her parents were in a car crash two years ago. It's just the two of us now. And I said she couldn't have a dog."

Ally's righteous expression crumbled with his second sentence. "Ben. I'm so sorry. I didn't realize—"

"It's fine," he said—which was probably the biggest lie of his life. It wasn't fine. It had never been fine. It was brutally unfair and wrong, and he could never let himself scream about the unfairness because he never wanted Astrid to suspect for a second that he wasn't unreservedly happy to have her in his life. He had to be strong for her. He had to show her that they were okay, just the two of them. So he had to make sure it *was* okay. Even if he knew nothing about being a dad. Starting with how to handle this situation.

She'd never lied to him before. Not that he knew of, anyway. How did he correct that? How did he punish her while still making sure she knew that he loved her unconditionally? He could listen to the parenting podcasts day and night, but it never made it any easier.

"She's a really good kid," Ally said.

"I know," Ben said, his voice a little rougher than

he'd intended. "But she still can't go around lying to me and going behind my back whenever I tell her no."

"Right. Of course not." She put a hand on his arm, and he had to fight the urge to shrug it off. "If I can help—"

"Send me those pictures," he cut her off. He didn't want help. This was his responsibility.

Ally pulled back her hand. Astrid and Kimber came back around the corner, wearing their coats and carrying their backpacks—and his chest tightened with the familiar pressure of trying to find the right answer in a sea of variables.

"Why didn't you tell me Ben West was Astrid's guardian?"

"Didn't I?" Gram paused on the threshold, where Ally had ambushed her grandparents as soon as they walked in the farmhouse door.

They stripped off their outerwear as Copper darted past her to check that everything was as he left it, and Ally held on to her patience, trying not to take her frustration with herself out on them.

"That was *necessary* context. Ben didn't know Astrid was volunteering at the shelter, and when he showed up today, Astrid and Kimber were here. Neither of them had permission to be."

Which she should have checked on. She couldn't believe she'd just taken Gram's word for it that it was okay. She knew better than that. No matter how confident

Gram sounded, she was always making the rules up as she went along.

"He was angry?" her grandmother asked, as if baffled by the concept.

"Of course he was angry. It looks like we were letting kids work at the shelter without checking with their parents—which we were."

"Don't worry about Ben," Gram soothed. "He always seems mad. That's just his way."

"No, it isn't," Ally argued. "He's been great all week." None of his texts or emails had been harsh or angry. They'd been fun. Friendly. She'd found herself looking forward to the buzz of her phone. "He was helping me arrange a segment with the local news in Burlington and talking about bringing some of the dogs to the tree lighting."

Gram perked up. "You know, that's a good idea. The parade folks offered to let us have our own float, with all the dogs we want, and your grandfather and I were saying we ought to do a pet fair up at the Estates— only the dogs under thirty pounds, since the Estates have that stupid size limit, but we have four or five small dogs that fit the bill. How's Dolce doing?" Gram flung off her scarf. "Do you think we should bring her into the house?"

"No," Gramps interjected firmly. "We're not keeping her."

"She's fine," Ally answered.

She was tempted to steer the conversation back to Astrid and Ben, but she knew futility when she saw it.

All her earlier optimism had drained out of her when

she watched Ben and Astrid drive away. She'd even missed the light for getting the photos of Jelly on the porch, and without someone to hold his leash, she had to make do with the less than picturesque setting inside his run.

She tried to slap on a fake smile, determined to keep her grandparents from worrying, but she couldn't stop thinking about Ben and Astrid. Reliving this afternoon, recalling the hard expression on Ben's face, and trying to figure out how to make things right.

Chapter Thirteen

"Y ou were volunteering, too. I don't see why it's such a big deal."

Ben clung to his patience as he spooned more penne onto his plate. He and Astrid were squared off across the kitchen table eating leftovers—and if he'd thought dinner would be peaceful after dropping Kimber off to face her own fate and grounding Astrid on the way home, he really should have known better. "It's not about the volunteering. It's about the lying."

"I didn't lie, I just didn't tell you."

Patience. "That's the definition of a lie by omission."

"If I'd asked you, you would have said no."

"Which is how you should have known that you shouldn't do it."

"Why not? You don't have a good reason."

It was so tempting to come out with *Because I said so*, but she was right—that was a terrible reason. "We don't have room in our house or our lives for a dog, and

I don't want you getting attached to some animal that's going to be someone else's."

"You were volunteering, too," she repeated.

"But I wasn't getting attached."

She narrowed her eyes, stabbing a piece of penne and changing tack. "If you have time for dogs at the shelter, why can't we have time for a dog in our house?"

"Adopting a dog is forever. Helping out at the shelter is four weeks, tops."

He realized his mistake when Astrid frowned. "Why only four weeks?"

Oh crap.

She was going to find out eventually. Frankly, it was a miracle Ally hadn't already told her. But this was not the moment he would have chosen if he'd been thinking straight. And okay, yes, he'd been lying by omission, but directly lying to her now *did* feel worse...and he wasn't going to look too closely at that double standard. Instead he braced himself and said, "The shelter is closing at the end of the month."

"What?" Astrid yelped, dropping her fork. "Why?"

"It's complicated—and that's why I'm helping Ally. Because it's a short-term commitment, not a lifelong one." And he felt guilty because it was partly his fault, but he wasn't going to give Astrid that ammunition. "We aren't dog people, Astrid."

"*I'm* a dog person. And if you would just give it a chance—"

"Astrid—" He forced himself to take a breath. "You already broke the rules. You lied to me. And now you want what? To be rewarded with a dog?"

"I wasn't trying to break the rules. I was trying to show you I can do this. I'm responsible!"

The last words were shouted, but he kept his response calm. "Responsible kids don't need to lie."

"This is so unfair! You never listen to me! Never!" She shoved away from the table, running from the room.

"Astrid!"

Her only response was the thud of her feet pounding up the stairs.

Ben swore, staring at the leftovers spread across the table. "Way to go, West," he muttered. "You're really killing this parenting thing."

And to think, they hadn't even made it to the teen years yet.

If Katie saw him now, would she regret her choice? He'd been a different person when she and Paul made their wills. Engaged. Seemingly on the same trajectory they had been, just a few years behind. When they'd asked him, it had been easy to say yes. Of course. But he'd never thought it would happen. Or that Isabelle would bolt the second he got custody. Or that he would lose his freaking mind trying to be everything Astrid needed when what she really needed was her mom and dad.

He stared at the door Astrid had fled through, wondering if he should go after her or let her be. Absently, he began boxing up the leftover leftovers. He was elbow deep in Mac's carryout baked penne when his cell phone rang.

He glanced at the caller ID and groaned, the inevitable feeling that he was about to disappoint someone else rising up in his chest. He caught the call before it could go to voice mail. "Hey, Levi."

"Hey, man, sorry to call so late."

It was seven thirty, but over the last two years he'd inadvertently conditioned his oldest friends to apologize every time they wanted something from him. Just another sign that he was winning at life. "You're fine. I was just cleaning up dinner. What's up?"

"It's about the game tomorrow. Connor can't make it—some business trip came up at the last minute."

Relief flooded Ben, chased by guilt that he was *relieved* he wouldn't have to see his friends.

Before he became Astrid's guardian, he'd had a standing poker night with his three oldest friends every Wednesday, but in the last two years he found himself postponing it more often than they actually played.

On the rare times they did manage to get a game going, he hosted in Paul and Katie's partially finished basement—which lacked basic amenities like walls, but at least Astrid could get to him if she needed anything. And he never let himself have more than one beer in case she cut off a finger and needed to be rushed to the hospital. Not that she ever had before, but he needed to be prepared.

Which meant hanging out with his friends wasn't the same. He never completely relaxed. But nothing had been the same since Katie and Paul died.

The poker night had become another thing he had to try to fit into his schedule, and he was always relieved when he wasn't the one who had to call it off.

"Mac and I can still make it," Levi went on—and Ben

cringed at the idea that he was still going to have to get through poker night, until his oldest friend continued, "but with the holidays and everything we figured maybe it was easier to just push it to next week."

Which would probably get pushed to the week after...and the week after that and before they knew it, it would be January. "Yeah, that's probably for the best."

A slight pause met the words, then Levi cleared his throat. "Will we see you at the tree lighting?"

"Probably. Astrid's grounded, but I'll have to make an exception for Friday since I have to be there for the council."

"You grounded Astrid? I thought she was the best kid on the planet. What'd she do?"

"Long story. I'll tell you next week."

"Right." Ben tried not to hear the skepticism in Levi's voice. "Well, let me know if you need me to throw her in a cell for a few days."

"Probably not necessary."

"Eh. The offer stands. Mi jail es su jail. See ya, Ben."

"See ya."

When he closed the call, he had three new text messages from his parents in Arizona.

Perfect. Just what he needed.

The terms of Astrid's grounding were that she couldn't use any electronics except for homework and to communicate with family. So she'd Skyped his parents. Of course she had.

His parents and Paul's always wanted to help—but they weren't retired yet, and they had their own lives in Arizona and DC.

And he'd told them over and over again that he was fine. That he had this. That Astrid was in good hands. Katie and Paul had entrusted Astrid to *him*, trusted him to keep her life as close to normal as possible.

He knew his parents were only trying to help, but every time they made a suggestion it felt like another person telling him that he couldn't do this. That he was screwing up. And that, worst of all, he was screwing Astrid up.

Their texts asked if he needed to talk. They asked if they should fly in earlier than planned for Christmas. They asked if perhaps they could pay for the dog or help Astrid train it—

Ben muted his phone, shoving it into his pocket. They were only trying to help, he reminded himself. They didn't *mean* to imply he was an unreasonable monster because he wouldn't let Astrid have a dog.

It just felt that way.

He trudged up the stairs, exhausted even though it was barely eight o'clock. The door to Astrid's room was cracked open, and it creaked inward when he rapped on it gently with his knuckles. "Astrid?"

A sniffle came from the bed. She was curled on her side, facing away from him. The purple dragon mural her mother had painted over her bed curled protectively above her, like Katie herself was watching him as he pushed the door open wider. Judging him because he'd made her daughter cry.

"Hey," he murmured. He perched on the foot of the bed, resting his hand on Astrid's ankle. She pulled her foot away from him, and he sighed, feeling like absolute trash. "You going to stay mad at me until Christmas?"

"Maybe," she muttered into her pillow without turning.

He nodded, folding his hands over his knee and looking around the room. The therapist he'd taken her to after the accident had told him that it was a good sign she was comfortable enough with him to get mad at him and trust he would still be there for her—but that never made it any easier. "You can't lie to me like that, Astrid. Something could have happened to you, and I would have had no idea where you were. I need to know where you are so I can keep you safe."

"The shelter isn't dangerous. Ally is super careful about which dogs we're allowed to help with. We're always safe."

"Even if you are, a meteor could strike or the zombie apocalypse could break out, and I need to know where you are so I can rush you to a bunker before you get infected and start craving brains."

She shot him a look over her shoulder so full of teen-age disdain he almost thought she'd aged three years in the last ten minutes. "That stuff doesn't happen."

"Maybe not. But I still get to worry about you. It's part of the job description. Even if part of me is proud of you for taking initiative and getting yourself a job there."

She sat up, turning toward him with red-rimmed eyes. "Then why am I grounded?"

"Because you hid it from me. Because of the sneaking around. We have to be able to trust each other."

She dropped her gaze to the comforter. "I'm sorry."

"Thank you. And I'm sorry I made you feel like you couldn't come to me. Like I wouldn't listen. I'm always listening. You're the most important thing in the world to me. You know that, right?"

She nodded, picking at a loose string on the comforter. A long pause stretched between them, then she looked up at him from beneath her lashes. "Am I still grounded?"

Ben pressed his lips together hard. Laughing right now would completely ruin the air of authority he was going for. "Yes," he said firmly. "For now. But that doesn't mean we can't do stuff together. We have to make that gingerbread this weekend—"

"Oh." Her gaze slid to the side again.

"What?"

"I signed us up for brownies instead."

Ben blinked. And tried not to think about the hours he'd already spent comparing online gingerbread recipes. "You did."

She shrugged. "I figured they were easier."

He took a breath. She wasn't wrong. "Brownies it is." At least he hadn't already bought molasses in bulk.

Astrid traced a pattern on the comforter. "Uncle Ben..."

"Yeah?"

"I really want to help Ally at the shelter."

His chest tightened. "I know. Me too."

"Do you think we could help just a little?" she asked. "Just until they close?"

She was such a good kid. He didn't want to reward the lying, but she wasn't asking for a dog. She was asking to help Ally. How did he say no to that? "I'll think about it."

She seemed to know better than to press the issue because she crawled over and hugged him as if that was all she'd ever hoped for. "Thank you, Uncle Ben."

"No promises," he warned—firm, even as his heart melted into goo. God help him if she ever figured out how much she had him wrapped around her little finger.

Chapter Fourteen

For the second time in as many weeks, Ally walked into town hall with both hands full of coffee. Thankfully, this time the woman who worked at the reception desk wasn't at her post, and Ally was able to slip upstairs undetected. Ben's door was open again, and she bumped it with her elbow to knock.

"Coffee?" she asked, lifting the cups when Ben looked up.

"Thanks." He stood from behind the desk—and at least he didn't look instantly pissed off by her presence. She hadn't been sure how he was going to react to her attempt to make amends. "This is a surprise."

"One black coffee." She handed over one of the cups, cradling the other between her hands. "I wanted to apologize for yesterday."

He grimaced, shaking his head. "I shouldn't have snapped at you like that."

"No, it was understandable. I didn't realize you were...I shouldn't have let Astrid volunteer without making sure she had parental consent. Or guardianship consent." She stumbled awkwardly over the words, but Ben didn't seem to mind.

"She does now," he confirmed. "Have my permission to help you after school."

"She does?" Her voice lifted, the words a little too high pitched.

"Yeah. Just as soon as I'm done grounding her." He took a drink of the coffee and made a face, staring at the cup like it was poison. "What is that? It's like drinking pure sugar."

"Whoops." Ally quickly exchanged the cup in her hands for his. "That one's mine. Peppermint mocha. I wasn't sure if you were going to hate me and figured I might want the chocolate to console myself."

"I don't hate you. It wasn't about you or the shelter." He grimaced, sitting on the edge of his desk, papers sliding precariously under him. "It was the lying. I can't have her—but I don't know if grounding her is actually going to do any good. I think it's harder on me than it is on her."

Ally was out of her depth, but she made her face as open and understanding as possible, silently urging him to go on.

"I feel like her jailer," he admitted. "I'm going to pick her up after school and work from home this afternoon so I can guard her. Keep her from sneaking off to help you. And how can I be mad at her if that's what she was doing? Volunteering at an animal shelter. Admittedly, she had ulterior motives, and she's definitely not getting a dog now, but I just hate this. I feel like such a hypocrite. I listen to all these podcasts and read all these articles about encouraging independence and raising responsible children. Free-range kids, they call it—as a countermovement to the helicopter parent thing where every second of a kid's day is scheduled and monitored. I want her to feel like she can do things herself, but the second I realized I didn't know where she'd been, I lost my mind. And the lying didn't help."

"It's understandable. You worry about her."

"Yeah." His gaze locked on his coffee cup, his voice low. "I'm just trying not to screw this up. This parenting thing...it's harder than it looks. You want to let her take risks so she's not scared of life, but how do you watch her do that? And when's the right time to let her?"

"I would never put her with one of the dogs who might be too much for her—"

"I know. It's not that." For a moment she thought he would stop there, but then he surprised her. "It's Katie and Paul. Her parents. It's like the stakes are higher, because I need to do it right for them. Because they would do it perfectly." His voice choked off and he cleared his throat roughly. "Though maybe the stakes would always be high if there was a kid involved. Maybe I'd always be scared out of my mind and convinced I was doing it all wrong. Maybe that's just what parenting is."

"For what it's worth, I think you're doing a great job. She's an amazing kid."

"Yeah, I don't think I can take credit for that. That's all Katie."

"I don't think that's all it is."

It was obvious how much he loved Astrid, visible in the affection on his face whenever he spoke of her and the way he agonized over doing the right thing.

"I figured out which dogs we're taking to the tree lighting on Friday," Ally said when the air in the room got too thick. "Deenie Mitchell's going to help out, but if you and Astrid wanted to come with us..."

Ben grimaced. "Let me see how this week goes. Astrid would love it, but I'm still trying to figure out how long to ground her for. If it even does any good." He glanced back toward his computer, and Ally took that as her cue to leave.

"I should let you get back to it, since you have to work from home later."

He looked up at her, frowning. "I was going to help you get those photos for the Twelve Dogs feature."

"Oh, don't worry. I can get my grandfather to help. I'll email them later this afternoon?"

"Perfect." His gaze caught hers, holding. "Thanks for the coffee. You really don't need to keep doing this."

"Maybe I just like seeing your smiling face."

Ben laughed like she'd made a joke, and Ally smiled to cover the fact that she wasn't entirely joking. She did like seeing him. Maybe more than she should with someone who was engaged.

But it was just coffee. Coffee and maybe friendship. There were worse things in the world.

🐾

On Friday afternoon, Ally was unloading the spoils of her latest Costco run into the barn's main storage room when Deenie burst in.

Today she was wearing jingle bells that rang whenever she moved and the world's ugliest Christmas sweater—which she somehow managed to make seem fashionable. She struck a pose in the doorway, her arms over her head. "Hear ye, hear ye! We have—drumroll please—an application!"

Ally nearly dropped the kibble in her arms, scrambling to set it down. "Seriously?"

Deenie had been volunteering regularly over the last few days, and Ally had given her access to the shelter email accounts so she could arrange permission for the dogs to attend various events around town. Deenie knew the people in town better than Ally did, so they'd agreed she was more likely to be able to wheedle them into agreeing.

Now she bounced over to Ally, grabbing her arms and spinning her in a circle. "A real, live adoption application!"

"Who's it for?"

"Captain America," Deenie announced.

"Is it the Kwans? Or someone who saw him on the Twelve Dogs of Christmas?" The golden retriever mix had been featured the day before.

"None of the above. They're from Burlington. Apparently they saw him on the news, and they're huge Avengers fans, and they couldn't resist. We should rename some of the others—see if they want an Iron Man or a Hulk to go with him."

Ally grinned at Deenie's enthusiasm. "Let's just make sure they're good candidates first."

Deenie danced toward the exit. "It's a start!"

"It is a start," Ally agreed.

The feature was working—but it was only one application, and they had so far still to go. She wanted to tell Ben about it, but she hadn't seen him since she brought him coffee on Wednesday. He'd responded when she'd sent him the latest round of pictures for the Twelve Dogs of Christmas feature, but there hadn't been any more texting back and forth. He had to be busy with Astrid—and she told herself it was silly to miss the texts.

She still didn't know if he was planning to join them for the tree lighting ceremony tonight.

When she finished unloading the supplies, Ally joined Deenie in the empty storeroom that had become their de facto training ground—and where Deenie was getting the dogs they'd picked for the tree lighting outing ready for their turn in the spotlight. Fred and Ginger scampered around the room, wearing the adorable ADOPT ME ribbons around their necks, while Deenie brushed JoJo to a shine.

Gram and Gramps had been helping earlier, but they'd gone to the house to feed Colby and Copper and get them settled before it was time to take the adoptable dogs to the town square.

Ally was inexplicably nervous about tonight. It was just a tree lighting, but it was her first big town event since she'd arrived, and now with the dogs needing homes, it seemed more important than ever that she make a good impression.

Still going Christmas crazy, Gram had hung jingle bells over the front door to the shelter, and they jangled as it opened, setting the dogs into a chorus of barking welcome.

"We're back here!" Ally shouted to her grandparents.

But it wasn't Hal and Rita Gilmore who appeared in the open doorway.

"Ben. Astrid." Ally stood up so suddenly she startled Partridge, who had been leaning against her knee. He tumbled onto his side in slow motion.

Astrid beamed, barely containing her excitement. Ben had his hand on his niece's shoulder and gave Ally a half smile as they entered. "Are we too late to help?"

Ally met his gaze, her heart thudding entirely too hard for a man she barely knew.

"Uncle Ben said you might be able to use us," Astrid gushed.

"Of course," Ally blurted, yanking her eyes away from Ben's when she realized she'd been silent too long. "We can always use an extra pair of hands."

Ben smiled, and she could almost swear his eyes *twinkled* before he glanced past her and gave a brisk nod. "Deenie."

"Hey, Ben. Astrid."

Partridge picked himself up from the floor and trotted over to greet the new arrivals, his bulk swinging pendulously as he snorted happily. "Don't drool on me," Ben warned, giving him a cautious pat on the head. Astrid was already kneeling on the floor, crooning at him as he snuffled at her fingers.

"Do you two want to handle Partridge?" Ally asked. "Since he's so happy to see you?"

"He's happy to see the treats he's convinced are in my pockets," Ben argued, but he picked up the end of the leash Partridge had been dragging.

"Hey. That's true love," Deenie argued from her position on the floor with JoJo crawling all over her lap. "The way to any male's heart is through his stomach."

Ally hadn't planned to bring the little papillon to the tree lighting. She'd mentally earmarked her as a perfect candidate for the Estates, but she'd noticed that Deenie the Dog Whisperer seemed to be particularly fond of the eager little dog with her tufted ears, calling her "princess" and putting little bows on her head—and if Deenie could somehow talk her landlord into letting her have a dog, it would likely be one that could fit inside a purse, just like JoJo.

She'd been wondering if they were bringing too many dogs—JoJo and Fred and Ginger and Partridge and Biscuit and Captain America, who was the best doggie ambassador of the group—approachable, placid, and sweet. Even though he had an application pending, he might bring people to the shelter to see the other dogs.

"I'm glad you came," Ally said to Ben, with a little too much feeling. She was just so happy to see them. Maybe too happy.

"Me too!" Astrid enthused.

Ben opened his mouth to speak, but the bells over the door jangled again, cutting him off.

"Merry Christmas! Ho-ho-ho!" her grandfather bellowed, and Ally grinned.

"Hold that thought," she murmured to Ben, moving past him to greet Gramps as he came down the aisle. "Everything okay at the house?"

"Yep. Your gram's checking on that preggo pupper again." He tossed an arm around Ally's shoulder, and she squished against his bulky winter coat. "She's smitten already. If I'm not careful, we're going to end up with that pooch and all her pups running around underfoot. Imminent foster fail."

"Maybe we should feature her on the Twelve Dogs," Ally suggested. "Get a family lined up for when she's ready so Gram doesn't get too attached."

"Who am I overly attached to?" Gram demanded as she rounded the corner to join them. "I love all my dogs equally and want each and every one to have a happy home." She wasn't using her sling again, and Ally resisted the urge to remind her that she was supposed to wear it even when she didn't think she needed it as a reminder not to overuse her arm. "Speaking of, I had the greatest idea when your Gramps and I went out to the Estates for bingo night—where I won five hundred dollars, thank you very much."

Ally gaped at her. "You won five hundred bucks at bingo?"

"Bingo is serious business at the Estates. It's a huge draw—which is why we should do our pet fair on a bingo day. Residents come in from all the patio homes to play." She frowned. "But then everyone who loses is bummed afterward. Maybe during one of the Christmas concerts is better. Less depressing. Hello, sweeties!"

She crouched to greet the dogs—and Ben and Astrid

and Deenie—and Ally hung back with her grandfather, dropping her voice. "Shouldn't she be wearing her sling?" Her grandmother had never been good at being cautious, but maybe Gramps could persuade her.

"She says it's too tight over her winter coat. Don't worry. We won't let her overdo it."

Ally tamped down her worry as they joined the others, but she couldn't get rid of it entirely. Gram was sitting on the floor with Astrid, playing with Fred and Ginger. Gramps walked over to her, never hurrying, and offered his hand to help her to her feet. They were so different at times that it was hard to imagine how they'd ever fallen in love, but then Gram looked up at him, putting her hand in his and smiling, and it was all right there on their faces. They were always there for one another.

Ally's chest ached with want. Her parents had been like that, but none of her relationships had ever come close. Was it her? Was she doing something wrong? Or had she just not found the right man yet?

"Hey." Ben appeared at her side as if in answer to the thought—and she flushed, quickly squashing the urge to reach toward him.

Engaged, remember? They were *friends*. Very platonic friends.

"Hey," she said back—clever as always, and relieved when her grandfather's voice rose over them, breaking the moment.

"Shall we get this show on the road?"

Chapter Fifteen

Ice crunched beneath their boots, and the dogs pranced at the ends of their leashes, sniffing everything as they passed. Pine Hollow was charming year round, but a special kind of anticipation seemed to hover in the crisp, cold air tonight as they walked toward the town square.

Twinkle lights were draped over picket fences and lining the eaves of every house they passed. Wreaths seemed to have appeared on every door. The town had that magical Christmas feel, and Ally felt herself smiling as Deenie and Gram kept up a lively running commentary on everything they passed.

This was why she'd wanted to spend the holidays in Pine Hollow. For moments like this. Feelings like this.

"Are you mad at me?" Astrid appeared at her side, her voice soft and hesitant, her gaze on her hands where she held Biscuit's leash.

Ally's chest tightened. "Oh honey, no. Of course not."

"Uncle Ben says I have to apologize to you. Since I let you think my parents said it was okay."

As apologies went, it left something to be desired, but Ally cared more about the why than a pretty I'm sorry. "Did you think you couldn't tell me?"

Astrid shrugged, still looking down. "Around here everyone knows. I guess...I don't know. It was nice to pretend it was like it used to be for a while."

"I can understand that." Ally tugged gently on the leash to get Cap to pick up the pace as he lagged behind to investigate a smell. "My parents were killed in a car accident when I was eighteen. I don't always tell people. It's like it isn't as real if they don't know."

Astrid looked up then, meeting her eyes for the first time since they'd started talking. "Was it someone texting?"

"No. Just bad road conditions and bad luck."

Astrid looked down, and when she spoke, the words were so soft Ally barely heard them. "Do you still miss them?"

"Every day."

Astrid nodded. They walked in silence for a moment, then Astrid looked up, worry in her eyes. "I love Uncle Ben."

"I know. I love my grandparents." Cap lagged again, and she gave the leash a little shake. "But it isn't the same."

"Yeah," Astrid murmured. Biscuit did a little dance, twisting himself in his leash, and a smile twitched around Astrid's mouth, fading as quickly as it had appeared.

"They said I could have a dog when I turned ten," she said softly. "My mom and dad."

Oh sweetie. Ally's heart ached at the unfairness of it. All the promises her parents wouldn't be able to keep. Just another thing that had been senselessly taken away.

"Come on, you two," Gram called. "Keep up!"

Ben looked over his shoulder from where he and her grandfather had been deep in conversation. Partridge waddled alongside. Ben's brow pulled into a frown, and Ally pasted on a smile.

They'd reached the main part of town, and the foot traffic was more congested here with all the townspeople gathering for the ceremony. Ally shortened up Captain America's leash to keep him closer, and Astrid did the same, mirroring her movements. Biscuit was one of the more docile dogs in the shelter, rivaling even Colby for laziness, but even he had perked up with all the new people around.

A stage had been set up to one side of the square, opposite the gazebo, which was strung with white twinkle lights until it glittered like an entire constellation of stars. A band played on the stage, filling the square with the sound of familiar Christmas favorites. Dozens of booths had been set up, hawking everything from cocoa to Christmas crafts—and the massive, darkened evergreen tree towered over it all.

The square was already packed, and the tree wouldn't be lit for at least another hour. Ally felt a little whisper of nerves as she looked at the swarm of strangers. She'd never been intimidated by the crowds in New York, but this was different. All of these people knew one another.

She was the outsider here. Suddenly she wished for her camera to provide a buffer between her and the world.

"Wait right here," Deenie instructed, picking up JoJo so she could navigate the crowds more easily. "The Friends of the Library said we could set up next to them. Let me see if there's enough space."

Deenie darted into the crowd. Seconds later, Gram perked up, tugging on her husband's arm. "Oh, look, there's Peg. Peg!" She waved, charging off into the crowd with Gramps and Fred and Ginger in tow.

"Can I go say hi to Neesha?" Astrid asked. "She thinks she can talk her parents into getting another dog, and she might like Biscuit." Ben frowned as he looked where she was pointing. The two of them began discussing whether Astrid could handle Biscuit on her own—and Ally glanced around the festivities, her anxiety increasing.

Around the square, people smiled and called greetings to one another—but Ally didn't know these people. She'd been here a month, and she was still as much of a stranger as she'd been when she only came for a few days around Christmas each year.

No wonder she wasn't finding homes for any of the dogs. She wasn't part of the community—

"You okay?"

Ally jumped at the sound of Ben's voice close to her ear. Astrid was a few feet away, showing Biscuit off to her friends. "What? Of course. I'm great."

Partridge and Captain America sat obediently at their feet. Cap alertly gazed at the people around them while Partridge alertly gazed at Ben's pockets, lest more treats fall out of them.

"You look kind of green," Ben observed. "I promise there's no ritual human sacrifice before we light the tree. You're safe."

"Says the man who's lived here his entire life." She glanced around nervously as someone called out Merry Christmas. "I don't know anyone. Who to talk to. Who to avoid."

"So ask me. I know all." He waggled his eyebrows, and she couldn't help but grin. "Omniscience is one of the benefits of living in one place forever. That's what I learned from *Groundhog Day*."

She randomly pointed toward the cocoa stand nearby. "Who's that?"

"That?" He followed her gaze. "Mac, owner of the Cup, best restaurant in town. Currently feuding with Magda, who runs the bakery. Something about a secret family cake recipe. Battle lines have been drawn. Sides have been taken. Mac's coffee is better, but Magda's pastries make you see God, so the teams are pretty even."

Ally smothered a smile. "And which side are you on?"

"Well, I went to school with Mac from K through twelve, and we still have a weekly poker game when one of us doesn't have to reschedule, so I'm pretty solidly Team Cup."

"Wait a second." Ally held up a hand in a stop sign as the rest of what he said clicked into place. "You prefer the coffee at the Cup? I've been getting it from Magda's this whole time because that's where you were getting yours the morning I ran into you. Why didn't you say something?"

"I'm a firm believer in never complaining about free

coffee delivery. And Magda's is still good. Mac's is just magical. But you can't go into the Cup without getting sucked in. It's a gossip vortex."

"Does Mac want a dog?"

Ben grinned. "You know, he might. He's sort of a lovable doofus himself. I've never seen him get mad at anyone but Magda. Maybe I'll borrow one of the dogs to bring to the next poker night."

"What's this about poker night?" a deep voice asked as a tall man in a dark wool jacket appeared at her side. "Are we actually having one this week?"

"Hopefully," Ben said, turning to clasp the hand of the new arrival, whose coat alone looked like it cost more than she made in a month. "Ally Gilmore, meet Connor Wyeth. Connor's another of my childhood friends and poker victims."

The tall, polished man grinned cockily, his teeth flashing in contrast to his rich brown skin. "I don't think it counts as victimization if I'm the one taking all your money."

"Funny, that's not how I remember it. If I recall, last time you were the one crying into your beer."

Connor turned to Ally, smiling smoothly as he took her hand. "Welcome to Pine Hollow, Ally. Don't let him fool you," he said, ignoring Ben. "He's the worst of any of us. Can barely hold his cards. It's pitiful."

"Just don't let my grandfather hear you have a game," Ally cautioned. "He's been fleecing the folks up at the Estates ever since I got here. He'd join you in a shot, and then you'd have to deal with the ego check of losing all your money to an eighty-two-year-old retiree."

Connor lifted his eyebrows. "Who do you think taught us to play?"

Ally looked to Ben for confirmation and found him smiling. "Seriously? You never said Gramps taught you to play poker."

"He taught all of us. Levi was always getting in trouble when we were younger, and his mom didn't know what to do with him. I don't know quite how it happened, but we all ended up out at the Elks learning about poker and blackjack—even bridge. Probably saved Levi from a life of crime."

"Which is really a shame," Connor said dryly. "The only reason I went to law school was because I thought I was going to have to defend him. All those wasted years."

Ben snorted. "Yeah, it's a pity law degrees are so useless."

"And where is this Levi now?" Ally interjected before they could get into trash-talking one another again. "A poker tournament in Vegas?"

"Nah." Ben jerked his chin toward the stage. "He's the chief of police. He's over by the homemade stocking station. Serving and protecting as we speak."

"You're kidding." Ally turned to look, and sure enough, a man with a police insignia on his coat stood about fifteen feet away, chatting with a curvy brunette.

"Welcome to Pine Hollow. We all get sucked back in. Just wait. If you stay here long enough, you will be, too. It's like quicksand."

Ally smiled at Ben's words, a laugh pressing up inside her chest. It wasn't even that anything Ben had said was particularly amusing, it was just that bubbly, helium-filled feeling of being with someone who made you feel lighter, like you could lift right off your feet.

Not that she was flirting. Obviously she wasn't flirting. They were *friends*. She just liked that she felt like she might belong here a little bit now. Like he'd opened a window into this world.

Though she was starting to think she really needed to meet his fiancée. The woman seemed entirely too theoretical. Ally needed the reminder that she was a real person.

Not that Ben had done anything inappropriate. He'd never even touched her. Their entire vibe was very Friend Zone. But she felt irrationally guilty when she got too comfortable around him. If she met his fiancée, maybe it wouldn't feel so wrong to enjoy his company as much as she was starting to.

"Hey." Deenie appeared at her side, flicking a glance up at Connor before speaking to Ally. "We're all set up over next to the library booth. You coming?"

"See you Wednesday, Ben. Nice to meet you, Ally." Connor gave a nod and moved into the crowd.

Ben extended a hand toward the gazebo side of the square, where Deenie was already disappearing. "Shall we?"

"After you." Ally shortened Captain America's leash, tightening her grip on her ridiculous crush on Ben while she was at it. She had a job to do—find these dogs homes—and she wasn't going to be distracted. She was far too mature for that.

Which was why she absolutely checked out his ass as she fell into step behind him. Maturity.

Chapter Sixteen

Suggesting the dogs come to the tree lighting had been a whim. A random idea off the top of his head. Ben hadn't expected it to be such a production. Or such a success.

Deenie had commandeered a tarp from somewhere and spread it out so they had a little patch of ground where people could play with the dogs without getting snow everywhere. That little patch quickly became the focal point of the square.

The dogs were a hit. Everyone wanted to pet the "celebrity" dogs they recognized from the Twelve Dogs of Christmas feature. Captain America lapped up the attention, but Partridge never strayed far from Ben's side, drool steadily darkening his bright blue ADOPT ME ribbon as he gazed optimistically at Ben's pockets.

Half the town seemed to stop by, called over by the shouts of laughter from Astrid and her friends as they played with Biscuit and JoJo, egged on by Deenie, who seemed just as comfortable rolling around on the ground as the kids. Ben introduced Ally to the butcher, the baker, and Joanie Pounds, who made her own scented candles. Then Mrs. Gilmore took over, pulling Ally to one side to meet her friends from the Estates.

Ben watched her, the smile on her face relaxed and natural—not at all the rigid grimace she'd had when they first arrived at the square. It hadn't occurred to him that all this might be overwhelming to an outsider until he'd seen that frozen face. But now she looked right at home. She'd probably be as up to speed on all the gossip as Linda Hilson by the time she went back to New York.

A little pang worked through him at the thought, but he brushed it aside. She was only helping her grandparents out with the shelter. As soon as her work here was done, she'd be back in the city being an important photographer again.

"Looks like this is the place to be."

Ben tore his gaze off Ally as Delia Winter appeared at his side. The mayor was his mother's age, with neatly styled bright white hair, a smooth brown unlined face, and strong opinions. One of the few things that had made his work on the council these last few years bearable had been her sense of humor. "We're very popular," he acknowledged, noting the crowd around them had only grown.

Delia crouched down to pat Partridge. "I love what you've done with the newsletter for these guys."

"It's sort of our fault they're closing. I figured we owed it to them."

"It's a smart solution. Doesn't cost the town anything, but helps them get the word out about the shelter closing and the dogs in need." She straightened, dusting off her hands. "Which is why I wanted to talk to you."

Ben instinctively braced himself for bad news. In his experience, people only wanted to talk to him when they wanted something from him, and right now he was maxed out.

"You know I'm terming out next year," Delia said. "We'll need a new mayor..."

It took him a moment to realize what she was driving at, and when the penny dropped he shook his head in horror. "No. Absolutely not."

"It wouldn't be that much more work than being on the council—and you'd actually get a stipend for it, so you wouldn't have to keep a full-time job. You already know how the town government works, and you're about the only person on the council I trust to look at things from all sides and try to find win-win solutions."

Ben shook his head. "I can't, Delia. I'm already counting the days until my term on the town council is over so I have one less thing on my plate."

"Okay." She nodded, not at all deterred. "Just think about it. The election's not for months."

He didn't need to think about it. He knew that no force on earth was going to make him run for mayor, but he liked Delia too much to tell her that to her face. He just nodded noncommittally and wished her a Merry Christmas as she took her wife's arm and made her way toward the platform in front of the tree to begin the lighting ceremony.

"You okay? You look like you're trying to murder the tree with your eyes."

Ben's glower cracked into a smile as he looked down at Ally. She had such a presence sometimes he forgot how small she was until she was standing right next to him. "I'm good. Just dealing with the usual ridiculous Pine Hollow ideas."

"Want some good news? Astrid says her friend's family is thinking of putting in an application on Biscuit. Counting the one we have pending on Captain America, that's two success stories, and we've only been at it a week. Now we just need to find homes for the other eleven. And the puppies." She groaned, laughing. "That sounded more optimistic in my head."

"We'll get there," he promised. "Have you figured out who you want to feature next?"

"I was thinking Maximus. He's so big, he's going to be hard to place. And Gramps and I were saying maybe we should feature Dolce soon—see if we can get some interest in her and her pups, but that might make more sense after we know exactly how many puppies we have."

"Maximus makes sense. Astrid and I have a bake-a-thon planned for tomorrow, but I could come by after to help wrangle him for the photos if you want."

"Actually, I might ask Deenie to help me. She seems to have the magic touch where he's concerned. If only she had an apartment that allowed dogs."

"He's awfully big for an apartment."

Ally shrugged. "I had Colby in New York, and my place was a glorified closet."

His eyebrows popped up. "You had a Saint Bernard in the city?"

"He actually makes a great apartment dog, because he's three-quarters area rug."

Ben snorted at the incredibly accurate description.

"Laziest dog ever. Though Partridge is giving him a run for his money tonight."

Ben looked down and found the bulldog sprawled on his back with all four legs flung in the air, fast asleep and snoring. "He's very dignified."

"It's his gift." Ally glanced over at Astrid and her friends. "So a bake-a-thon, huh? Is that a family tradition?"

"More like forced labor inflicted on us by the town. It's for the annual Pine Hollow Elementary Christmas Fair. All the children are required to bring enough baked goods to feed a battalion. Then they sell them to one another and their parents, and the proceeds go to fund after-school activities for the rest of the year. We're on brownie duty this year."

Ally cocked her head, her dark eyes studying him. "Why do I get the sense you aren't excited by brownie duty?"

He grimaced. "My sister was Supermom. She would've done something that would have sold out for sure. I told Astrid we could do some kind of fancy gingerbread or something, but I don't think she trusted me to pull it off, so she signed us up for brownies instead."

"You can do a lot with brownies. I bet they'll still sell out."

He cringed. "Yeah...Astrid's concern about my culinary abilities may have been warranted. I'm best when I just follow the instructions on the box."

"I could help you," she offered. "I mean, after all you've done for the shelter, I definitely owe you a few hours of brownie baking."

Ben opened his mouth to decline her offer, but Astrid appeared out of nowhere, bouncing from her cocoa-induced sugar high. "You're gonna make brownies with us?" she exclaimed. "That's so awesome!"

"You don't have to," Ben assured her. "You really don't owe me."

"Please," Astrid wheedled. "We need your help. You don't even know how much we need your help. Uncle Ben is, like, the *worst* cook in the world."

"Hey. I'm standing right here."

"I wouldn't want to intrude." Ally met his eyes uncertainly. "You must have someone else who would be more appropriate."

"Like Martha Stewart? Normally she'd swing by to help out, but her schedule's so busy this time of year."

"No, I meant—" A crackle of feedback from the PA cut her off as the mayor stepped up to the microphone.

"Merry Christmas, Pine Hollow!" Delia's voice boomed across the square—and everyone chorused "Merry Christmas!" back at her.

Ally turned toward the stage, tipping her face up toward the tree. Ben must have seen the ritual lighting of the tree twenty times, and it always seemed kind of silly to him—all of them gathering to watch the mayor flip a switch. As if there was anything magical in that. Ally must be even less impressed, coming from the land of Rockefeller Center. Pine Hollow's holiday traditions must seem pathetic by comparison.

But then she looked back at him over her shoulder, bouncing on the balls of her feet and grinning as the mayor went through her speech, and he realized she was loving this.

"I wish I'd brought my camera," she whispered, turning her face back toward the tree.

He couldn't imagine what she would want to take pictures of. It was just a small-town square, full of small-town people, making a spectacle out of something ordinary.

But then all the lights around the square dimmed, the choir that had taken the stage after the band began to sing "Home for the Holidays," and the townspeople grew quiet, every eye in the square turned toward that one point as the mayor flipped the switch.

A gasp went through the crowd, followed by a cheer. Thousands of twinkle lights in every color illuminated the tree, casting their glow on all the faces turned up toward the spectacle. He glanced down to see Ally release a sigh and bite her lower lip—and when he looked back at the tree, it did look a little bit magical. He'd never gotten choked up at a tree lighting before, but Ben's throat tightened, and he looped one arm around Astrid's shoulders, tugging her against his side. She leaned into him, the weight of her seeping into him along with the warm glow of the tree.

He'd considered skipping the event tonight to start a load of sink laundry, since the washer was still out of commission, but now he was glad they'd come.

The choir finished their song to another cheer and launched into "Rudolph the Red-Nosed Reindeer." Astrid pulled away from him, and the moment was over—but when he looked down, Ally was smiling up at him, and something seemed to catch in the air between them, holding and building, twisting tight—

"Aunt Elinor!"

Ally jerked like she'd been hit by a Taser, yanking her gaze away from Ben's at Astrid's shouted greeting. Ben turned to greet his sister's best friend, accepting her hug hello. "Hey, E."

"Hi. Who's this?" She turned toward Ally with a smile.

"Ally Gilmore!" Ally's voice was too loud, her smile almost manically bright. "I run the animal shelter. Ben and Astrid have been helping me. It's so nice to meet you!"

"You, too," Elinor replied, though her smile was cautious. "I'm Elinor, spelled the *Sense and Sensibility* way, so I had no choice but to become a bibliophile."

Ally laughed as if the comment were a fabulous joke. "So have you two known each other long?" she asked cheerfully.

Elinor cocked her head at him, as if trying to think back that far. "Since kindergarten? Right?"

"Yeah. Elinor and I were in the same grade back then. Before she started skipping grades and left us all in the dust."

"Wow! That's awesome!" Ally gushed.

Ben's brows pulled together at the jarring enthusiasm.

"Thanks." Elinor looped an arm around Astrid's shoulders. "So are you guys all set for the Christmas Fair?"

"We haven't even *started* baking yet," Astrid groaned,

but then she perked up, beaming. "But Ally's going to come over and help us tomorrow, aren't you, Ally?"

"I—" Ally froze, doing her best impression of a deer in headlights, her gaze flicking from Astrid to Elinor to Ben and back again. "I mean—not if—I could—unless you wanted to help instead?"

"Me?" Elinor laughed. "I'm no help whatsoever in the kitchen. But I'm glad these two will have guidance. We all suffered through Ben's attempt at scones last year."

"Hey. They weren't that bad." Elinor arched a brow at him, and he relented. "Okay, they were, but in my defense the quinoa flour was right next to the regular flour."

Elinor laughed. "Save them, Ally," she urged. "You're their only hope."

"You really don't have to," Ben argued. "Don't let the emotional blackmail sway you."

Ally's face had gone strangely stiff. "I mean, I..."

"Do you want to meet JoJo, Aunt Elinor?" Astrid interrupted. "She's *so* cute."

Elinor grinned down at Astrid. "Absolutely."

The two of them moved to the other side of the area Furry Friends had claimed, leaving Ben alone with Ally—or at least as alone as two people could be standing in the middle of a crowded town square.

"It's okay if you don't want to come," Ben said. "Astrid and I would love to have you, of course, but you don't owe us anything."

Ally frowned up at him. "You still want me to come?"

"Of course. If you want to. You really don't have to—"

"No. I...I'd like to. If it's okay."

"Yeah. Absolutely. You wanna come by around

three? After the shelter's afternoon hours? I'll text you the address."

"Great," she said, looking more confused than excited, though he couldn't figure out why.

"Is everything okay?" He was sure he'd missed something in the last ten minutes, but Ally just shook her head.

"No, yeah. I'll see you tomorrow. Three o'clock."

Chapter Seventeen

Ben's fiancée was gorgeous. And a genius, apparently, since she'd skipped however many grades. And wonderful with Astrid, if the tree lighting ceremony and the fact that Astrid already called her "aunt" was anything to go by. She was freaking perfect and she was *real*.

Which was why Ally was only going to Ben and Astrid's to bake brownies as a *friend*. Because they were friends. Because men and women were perfectly capable of being friends. And because Ben's gorgeous perfect fiancée sanctioned the get-together. Because she was obviously not in the least threatened by Ally and completely trusted her fiancé, who hadn't said a single non–Friend Zone thing to Ally since they met.

That moment by the tree when she'd looked at him and he'd looked at her and everything had seemed to slow down, the lights illuminating the angles of his face, and something inside of her went quiet and still with anticipation...that wasn't anything. That wasn't real. Reality was the perfect fiancée. And the Friend Zone—where she was very happy to be. She *liked* Ben and Astrid.

And she really did owe him for all his help with the dogs.

Captain America was officially being adopted by the family in Burlington, just as soon as his adoption fee cleared. And there were two more applications just in the last twenty-four hours. Kimber Kwan had managed to talk her parents into putting in an application for one of Dolce's puppies, and an online application had come in for Daisy.

Today's visiting hours at Furry Friends had been so busy her grandparents had decided to extend them into the evening just in case anyone else dropped by to see the dogs after hours, but they'd encouraged her to go over to Ben and Astrid's when she'd offered to stay and help. Even Deenie had practically shoved her out the door when she'd discovered Ally had plans to go help them.

Ben's culinary efforts must really be legendary in the town if so many people were encouraging her to save him.

The cloth straps dug into her fingertips as she carried the two bulging reusable grocery bags up the walkway of the cozy little house on Maple Street. Before she'd known about Astrid, she wouldn't have pictured Ben in a place like this—so homey and family-centric, with a glider on the tiny front porch and a sensible crossover in the driveway. She couldn't help but wonder where he'd lived before, because she had the distinct feeling this was his sister's house.

Ally adjusted her grip on the bags and pressed the doorbell, her lips twitching as the sound was greeted by a delighted shriek and the rapid thunder of footsteps that sounded far too loud to be coming from a ten-year-old girl.

Astrid flung open the door, beaming. "You came!"

"Of course I came."

Ben appeared in the hallway behind Astrid, his eyebrows arching as he took in the bulging shopping bags. "I did tell you I already bought the mix, didn't I?"

"You did," Ally confirmed, stepping across the threshold. "These aren't mixes. These are my secret ingredients."

Ben eyed the bags as he lifted them from her hands so she could remove her coat. "Is it vanilla? My mom says the secret ingredient is always vanilla, but this feels like a *lot* of vanilla." He did a biceps curl with the bags, the muscles in his arms jumping against his soft gray sweater.

Ally forced her eyes off the display—*engaged, dummy*—and turned to hang her coat on a peg. "Patience. All will be revealed."

Ben snorted. "Come on. Kitchen's this way."

"I am *so* excited you're helping," Astrid gushed, dashing ahead of them through a narrow archway.

Ally fell into step behind Ben—and nearly took him out as her toe caught on the edge where the flooring shifted from hardwood to tile. She tumbled against his firm back and he twisted to steady her, though she was already back on her feet, her face flaming.

"Careful," Ben warned too late. "I should have mentioned the floor's kind of uneven there."

"Our kitchen has character," Astrid announced proudly.

"Most character in Pine Hollow," Ben added dryly.

He wasn't wrong. The kitchen was small and decorated in the height of seventies chic. The appliances all looked like they'd seen better days, and there was something about the island that made it seem like it was in the wrong place, giving the entire kitchen a lopsided feel. But it was also cheerfully cluttered. Lived in. And Ally smiled. It reminded her of her grandparents' place—badly in need of an update, but utterly charming. "I love it."

"It's a fixer-upper," Ben said. "And someday we'll actually have time to fix it up."

"I like it how it is," Astrid insisted. Ben didn't say a word, but the way he looked at the back of Astrid's head made Ally think the fact that Astrid didn't want to change it was a big part of the reason the kitchen hadn't been updated.

"So what is all this stuff?" Ben asked, heaving the bags onto the kitchen table.

Boxes of brownie mix and all of the materials for making them had already been neatly laid out on the island. Ben and Astrid had gone to the trouble of getting everything ready for her, and Ally felt a flicker of misgiving that she'd gone overboard. She'd remembered what Ben had said last night about how Astrid's mom would have made something amazing that would have sold out, and she'd wanted to do something special—especially since Ben and Astrid had been such a help—but now she worried that it looked like she was trying to take over.

She reached for the bags, suddenly self-conscious. "I knew you already had the brownies covered, but I figured some special toppings could help them stand out." She began pulling goodies out of the bags. Pretzels, marshmallows, caramels, milk chocolate, white chocolate, candy canes, sprinkles, and gummy worms. "I used to live next to a sweet shop in New York, and their brownies were never just brownies. I figured we could steal that idea..."

"Wow." Ben was staring at the bounty spread over the table.

"Too much? I shouldn't have—"

"No, this is great," Ben interrupted.

"This is *awesome*," Astrid squealed. "These are going to be the best brownies ever in the history of brownies!"

Astrid bounded around the kitchen and Ben met Ally's gaze over her head. He mouthed, *"Thank you,"* and she smiled, the pleasure of the moment shimmering down into her chest and wrapping around her heart.

"Shall we get started?"

Three hours later, Ally bent over the counter, pressing crushed candy canes into the layer of melted white chocolate coating the latest batch of brownies before it could cool and harden. Ben stood beside her, his shoulder brushing hers as he did the same with pretzels and caramel to another tray of brownies, while Astrid worked at the island, perfecting her own creation, which included layers of graham crackers and gooey marshmallows. He had a little smudge of flour on his neck that Ally kept eyeing, though she couldn't bring herself to brush it away.

"We need to taste-test them," Astrid announced.

Ally's lips twitched. "Quality control is important."

"After dinner." Ben didn't look up from his tray.

"We could have brownies for dinner," Astrid suggested hopefully.

Ben snorted. "Nice try." He glanced toward the clock and then at Ally. "Though we should probably feed you after you spent all afternoon helping us. How do you feel about pizza?"

Her stomach growled. "Very positively."

"I'll order!" Astrid shouted, bounding off the step stool she'd been using and grabbing Ben's phone. "Do you like pepperoni and pineapple, Ally?"

"Uh...absolutely."

Ben leaned closer, lowering his voice. "You're allowed to say no to her, you know. We can get more than one kind of pizza."

His face was close to hers when she looked over, the dark fringe of lashes around his eyes making her knees wobble, though she told herself that was just because she'd been standing too long with her knees locked. "I happen to love pepperoni, and I may not have had it with pineapple before, but I'm willing to give it a try."

Ben arched a brow. "Get some cheese bread too," he said to Astrid, louder, though his gaze stayed locked on Ally's.

"Do you think we have enough?" Astrid asked after she'd called in the delivery order. She bounced around the kitchen, counting the different varieties of brownies they'd made. Once the last group cooled, the individual treats would be wrapped in cellophane, tied with ribbons, and added to the half-full basket on the table.

"We have plenty," Ben insisted. "It's about quality, not quantity. And thanks to Ally, our quality level is high. Though I still think the ones with the milk chocolate and the gummy worms are weird."

"Just wait," Ally insisted. "Those are going to be the most popular. You'll see. They're delicious."

"I'll take your word for it."

"They're perfect," Astrid praised, still bouncing around the kitchen, though Ally was reasonably sure she hadn't actually ingested any of the sugar. "Instagrammable."

Ally arched a brow at Ben and he winced. "One of the moms Instagrams her kid's lunches and posts the pictures to the class parents' Facebook group. Just in case you're ever feeling like you might be doing okay with PB&J, there's always someone there to ask you whether the peanut butter is organic and imply you're trying to give your kid diabetes if the jelly has more than two micrograms of added sugar."

Ally cringed. "Ouch."

"It's a cutthroat business, parenting."

She eyed their bounty. "I'm pretty sure none of this is

organic, and all of it has enough sugar to have the kids bouncing off the ceiling."

"It's a Christmas treat. There will be vegan and organic and gluten-free options at all the other tables." He cocked his head toward her. "We'll be the sinful, decadent ones."

His deep voice made the words sound even more sinful and decadent. Ally focused on her hands, fighting a blush. *Engaged. Taken.* She closed her eyes, mentally picturing Elinor the Great.

"We ate all that crap when we were kids, and we're still here."

Kids. Focus on that. That was platonic. She opened her eyes, poking more candy canes into the top of the white chocolate. "It sounds like you were quite the troublemaker when you were younger."

"Me? Nah. I was just always getting pulled into Levi's schemes. He was the ringleader. And yet somehow he never seemed to get caught. Unlike the rest of us. I think I would've been grounded every other week if Katie hadn't covered for me."

Ben's hands went still, and the energy in the room shifted. He glanced over at Astrid, who was pretending to be preoccupied with her brownie creation, but leaning closer to catch every word.

"What was she like?" Ally asked softly. "When you were kids?"

"*Funny.* In a really sarcastic way. Smart and good in school—good at everything. Which I thought was horrible, of course, because how do you follow that? But also *mean*," he said with a laugh. "She could be vicious—

though that was mostly just when she was hungry or I'd done something stupid to piss her off. The usual little brother stuff. She loved to read, but she hated reading around other people. She said she could hear me breathing and it distracted her—so, of course, I mouth off that I can't very well stop breathing, and she threatens to make me..." Ben studied his hands, pressing pretzels gently into place. "Everyone liked her. More than they liked me, but I didn't mind, for some reason. Maybe because I liked her, too. It was weird when she went away to college. She wasn't one of those kids who came home a lot or wrote every day. We'd get a few emails, a few phone calls, but then it was Christmas, and she was back and making everything... She really threw herself into it. Christmas was..." He trailed off, his throat working, and shook his head sharply. "Ugh. Don't know why I started talking about that."

"Because you miss her?" Ally murmured.

"Yeah." Ben swallowed, pressing his lips together.

The doorbell rang and Ben coughed, shaking himself. "That'll be the pizza."

He was out of the kitchen before Ally could blink. She brushed candy cane slivers off her hands and turned to study Astrid. "You okay?" she asked softly.

"I remember that, too." She met Ally's gaze, her small face working to contain her emotion. "How she hated if you made any noise at all while she was reading. I forgot, but she did. There was this one time, I was chewing gum and she was all, 'I brought you into this world, I will take you out of it.' But you always knew, like, she didn't mean it. She just said stuff like that, like jokes. And then she'd chase me out of the room and tickle me until I couldn't breathe."

"I bet she loved that you were there. Chewing gum and all."

Astrid's grin was faint and lopsided. "Yeah."

"Pizza!" Ben announced, stepping back into the kitchen with his arms full of the boxes. "Make a space."

Ally and Astrid quickly set about clearing enough of the table for the pizza box, the previous moment gone, but lingering in the air with the sweet poignancy of memory.

Chapter Eighteen

I'm glad you came tonight." Ben shoved his hands into his pockets, burrowing down against the cold. "And not just for the sake of the brownies. Though they're infinitely better than they would have been if we'd been left to our own devices."

The night air pressed against his face, heavy with the promise of snow, as Ben walked Ally back to Furry Friends. As soon as they finished the pizza, when he realized she'd walked all the way from Furry Friends with those bulging bags of groceries, he'd offered to walk her home, but Astrid had begged her to stay. And none of them had really wanted her to leave.

They'd watched *Elf* after dinner while waiting for the last brownies to cool so they could package them up. Ally had stayed until he'd sent Astrid to read in bed, his neighbor Mrs. Fincher available if Astrid needed anything while Ben walked with Ally.

It had been a good night. The best night he'd had in a long time, if he was honest. It was weird. He felt like himself again. Like the vise of stress that had closed around him had opened, if only for a little while.

"I had fun," Ally said as their boots crunched the ice on the sidewalk. "And I definitely owed you for all your help with the dogs."

Guilt dug into him. "You don't owe me anything." He flexed his hands in his pockets. "If anything, I owe you. That was *fun* today. I think I forgot what that felt like. For Christmas not to be work. And Astrid loved it. You always seem to know what to say to her." He grimaced. "Unlike me."

"Hey." She bumped his arm with her elbow. "Don't give yourself such a hard time. You're doing a lot better than you give yourself credit for."

"Yeah, but that stuff tonight about Katie...I don't know why I started talking about that." They passed the town square with the tree glowing cheerfully from the center. "In some ways it's easy not to talk about it, because everyone already knows, you know? That's the good and the bad of a small town. Everyone knew Katie and Paul. It's weird talking to someone who didn't. Good weird," he clarified quickly. "But strange. Everyone misses them, but we don't talk about it. I don't know if that makes it easier or harder."

"If it's any consolation, I think Astrid liked hearing you talk about her mom."

Ben grimaced, hunching his shoulders against a gust of wind. "I wish there was someone who could tell you when you were doing it right and when you were getting it wrong. There are lots of people with opinions and no way of knowing if you're actually being a good parent. You never know when you're letting her down, so you always feel like you are."

"Ben." She took his arm. "You're a good guardian."

"Am I? Probate was a lot. This parenting thing is a *lot*. I feel overwhelmed all the time—I can't even keep a washing machine working."

"I don't think a broken washing machine counts as bad parenting."

"I know. I just used to be the fun uncle, and I loved her like crazy, but I didn't know the routines. I didn't know the day-to-day. Her pediatrician's name or that she still slept with HopHop or that Katie had just started her on Harry Potter, reading them aloud together one chapter at a time..."

After the accident, Astrid hadn't wanted to read them with him. The books sat on a shelf in her room, gathering dust.

"How are you supposed to know when you're doing this *right*?" he asked. "Elinor said this thing to me the other day about stress changing the way your brain is wired if it goes on for too long. I feel like I've been in stress brain for two years." Ally dropped his arm, and he glanced over at her, groaning. "And now I'm unloading all of this onto you. I'm sorry. First-world problems. So many people have it worse."

"Just because it's not the worst-case scenario doesn't mean it isn't hard. Hard isn't relative. It doesn't get easier because someone else has it worse. It's just *hard*. You don't need to make your hard seem smaller than someone else's." She glanced up at him, lightening the moment with a quick flashing grin. "Just don't make it bigger."

"What's your hard?" The words were an impulse, and he immediately wanted them back. "Sorry. I didn't mean to pry."

"No, it's fine. The shelter, I guess. Though mostly I worry about my grandparents. They're the last family I have, you know?"

They'd reached the edge of the driveway that led up to Furry Friends and Ally's house, but Ben slowed his steps, not ready for the walk to be over. He'd known, in some vague, distant way, that Hal and Rita had a granddaughter but no living children, but he'd never really put it all together that Ally was all they had left. And vice versa. "Your parents..."

"Car accident. When I was eighteen. Freshman year of college. I was living in a dorm, and it felt like any roots I'd ever had were yanked up, and I didn't belong anywhere anymore—but I always knew I had my grandparents. It meant a lot, just knowing I wasn't alone. It means a lot to Astrid, too. Having you."

"I don't know."

"It does," she insisted. "Are your parents around?"

"Arizona. They'll be here for Christmas. Astrid's other grandparents are based in DC. They help when they can, but the everyday stuff, the decisions, that's on me."

"That's a lot of responsibility to hit all at once."

He shook his head, rejecting the idea that it was too much. "I wanted it. I wanted her. I still do. And in some ways it's easier when it's just us. My parents want to help when they're here, but then you have to accept the help the way they want to give it—which is sometimes more work than just doing it yourself. And then if it is actually helpful, you start to rely on it, and then it's gone and it's that much harder to adapt again. It's better—"

"Not to rely on people?"

"To do it myself." He glanced down at her. "But I worry all the time. I'm always trying to make the right choices for her. And I know I'm probably overthinking...everything. I never used to analyze every little thing, but with Astrid I can't seem to stop myself. It's like—cell phones. How old is old enough for a phone? Some of her friends already have them. And social media—can I stop her from having Twitter and Instagram and TikTok and God knows what else before I think she's ready for it? Our parents never had to think about screen time and organic, human-growth-hormone-free whatever. If you put something in a plastic container, are you trying to kill the environment? Everything has a ripple effect now, and there's no conventional wisdom. There's no right answer. I'm just going to keep doing things wrong in new ways."

"No, you aren't. Even if you are making mistakes—and everyone does, it's called being human—you're also doing things right. You're there for her. She knows that."

They'd reached the edge of the porch, and Ally stepped onto the first step, turning to face him as the first fat snowflakes began to drift down around them. The twinkle lights on the porch railings cast a gentle light in the snowy night, but inside the house was dark.

"Your grandparents asleep?"

"Yeah. They aren't exactly night owls."

He studied her face as she looked toward the house. "You worry about them?"

"Constantly," she admitted. "I know they're adults and they've taken care of themselves for decades, but that doesn't stop me worrying. Gram is so reckless—she never thinks of the consequences of walking a dog that's too strong for her until her shoulder has to be surgically repaired. Maximus tried to chase a bunny while she had his leash wrapped around her wrist—dislocated her shoulder, tore a bunch of ligaments, and now she thinks it was a fluke and it'll never happen again. That she doesn't need to wear her sling or worry about reinjury. Gramps tells me not to worry, but how do you not worry? They're in their eighties. At least he seems good. He's healthy and his mind is still sharp, but any day something could happen and... they're all I have left."

Snow had begun to fall in earnest, making the entire world feel hushed. "That's why you came up here."

"Part of it. They hadn't even told me about Gram's accident because they didn't want me to worry. I was supposed to have a shoot in the Bahamas, and I'd already planned to bring Colby up here so they could watch him while I was away, but then my shoot got canceled and I found out about Gram's accident, and I just... I needed to be here. Helping out at the shelter was a good excuse to watch over them."

"What are you going to do when the shelter closes?"

She huffed out a humorless laugh. "I'm not even letting myself think about it. Just living in the present. Find homes for the dogs, look after my grandparents, worry about the future when it comes." She took a step up onto the porch, but he stayed below, leaning against the railing. Ally turned back, eye-to-eye with him as she stood on the top step. "What did you mean you can't keep a washing machine working?"

He grimaced. "It's been busted for weeks. I was supposed to have a technician come out and fix it a week ago, but he keeps rescheduling, and we are getting desperately low on clothes."

"Why don't you just bring them here? We have a washer and a dryer. You're welcome to them whenever you want."

He frowned. "I'm not bringing my laundry to your house."

"Why not? If you're coming over to the shelter anyway, why not just throw in a load while you're at it? Get those coffee stains out. It doesn't cost us anything—"

"Water, electricity."

"I think we can handle a few extra gallons this month. And I owe you at least one load for dousing you in coffee." Ally folded her arms, frowning at him. "Are you too good for my laundry? Or just stubborn?"

"Neither. I just—"

"Have to do absolutely everything yourself and can't ask for help?"

It was a startlingly accurate analysis for someone who'd only known him a couple of weeks—and it made him wonder how obvious he was.

"You're making your life harder than it has to be," she insisted.

"I'm not *making* it anything."

"Tell you what. My grandmother desperately wants to put Christmas lights up on the eaves of the barn. I did the ones on the porch here, but I haven't gotten around to those, and I'm afraid one of these days I'm going to come home to find my eighty-one-year-old grandmother on the top of a twenty-foot ladder stringing lights with one good arm. You come by and help me with those one evening this week, and you can do your laundry at the same time. Win-win."

He studied her face. "I feel like you just made that up."

"I would never make up one of my grandmother's crazy schemes. Are you in?"

"Sure. I guess. Friends don't let friends decorate alone."

Something shifted in her smile, distance seeming to expand between them even before she took a step back. "I'll see you this week then."

"Right." He shoved off the base of the porch railing, taking a step out from under the eave. Snow instantly coated his shoulders. "Good night, Ally. Thank you for the help tonight."

"You, too."

She disappeared inside without another word.

Snow continued to fall around him as he made his way back through the peaceful stillness of the town. People were starting to turn off their Christmas lights for the night, but the town still looked like a postcard. His steps slowed as he moved through the square. When was the last time he'd done this? Walked somewhere without worrying about when he would arrive, without thinking of the twelve other things he needed to be doing at that moment.

Had Ally done that? Or was it something about the afternoon, about spending hours decorating brownies and hanging out with Astrid and Ally, that had shifted his perspective, reminding him that life didn't have to be about doing the responsible thing one hundred percent of the time? Sometimes you could enjoy yourself.

He needed to do poker night again. No more excuses.

He climbed the steps to Katie and Paul's house, wondering what Ally had seen when she walked in. He'd left all their half-finished house projects half-finished and told himself it was because he didn't have time. Which he didn't. But if he was honest with himself, he'd also been afraid of wiping away the last traces of their presence.

Not that he still saw them when he looked at the uneven flooring. Sometime over the last two years, he'd stopped seeing Katie and Paul in the house. It was hard not to be sad about that, even though Katie wouldn't want them living in the past. She'd wanted the big house with the yard. The two-year plan.

A crack of light still shone beneath Astrid's door when he reached the top of the stairs, and Ben gently knocked on the door. When she called for him to come in, he opened it a crack, leaning against the frame.

"I'm back."

"Okay." She was sitting in bed in her pajamas with a library book on her lap.

Ben's gaze moved past her to the bookshelf—and the row of Harry Potter books neatly lined up on top. He nodded to the shelf. "Did you ever read those? The Harry Potter ones?"

She followed his gaze. "Not yet," she admitted. "I didn't want to read them without my mom. Is that weird?"

"No, sweetie. It's not weird."

"I thought I might...my friends are all reading them now. They're on the Battle of the Books list."

"It's okay if you want to," he murmured. "It's okay if you don't. Though I hear they're pretty good."

She cocked her head. "You haven't read them?"

"Nah. I've just seen the movies."

She rolled her eyes. "That so doesn't count."

He grinned. "Okay. Maybe I'll check 'em out."

Astrid glanced to the shelf. "Maybe we could read them at the same time."

He didn't know when the last time he'd made time for reading for pleasure was. "I'd like that." She looked down at the book in her lap, tugged downward by the story, just like her mom used to be, impatient to get back to the world between those pages. "Don't read too late," he cautioned, starting to close the door before his eyes could get wet.

"Uncle Ben?"

He paused. "Yeah, kiddo?" He cleared his throat.

"Thanks for today. It was a good day."

"It was," he agreed. "I love you, you know that?"

"Yeah. Love you, too."

Ben closed the door with a click, swallowing around the tightness in his throat.

It felt wrong to be grateful for any moment since Katie and Paul died, but he was grateful for today. And every other day he got with that kid. Half the time he didn't know what he was doing, and one hundred percent of the time he was scared to death, but sometimes his chest squeezed with a feeling he'd never had before he became Astrid's guardian. A feeling of love so big it actually hurt—and maybe as long as they had that, he wasn't doing such a terrible job. Maybe.

Chapter Nineteen

Fresh powder swirled around Ally's ankles as she headed toward the barn, calling out morning greetings to the dogs who came to the outdoor portion of their runs to see her. Last night with Ben and Astrid had left her feeling more optimistic about the world—and the two new email applications that had come in this morning had only solidified that feeling.

"We have some interest in you, Jelly!" she called to the peanut butter–colored Lab–pit bull mix who bounded to the end of his enclosure, trailed by his buddy Biscuit, who was carrying Jelly's dog bed in his mouth.

"How did you get that through the dog door?" she asked him. The bed was as big as he was and dragging through the snow as he trotted proudly toward her with his offering. Ally bent to pet the two of them through the fence as Biscuit dropped Jelly's bed at her feet. "The least you could do was move your own bed if you were going to start redecorating."

Biscuit leaned into her hand, gazing up at her with

adoring black eyes as Jelly wiggled in every direction simultaneously, too excited by the attention to contain himself. "What do you think? You guys want to live in Massachusetts? There's a family down there with a huge fenced yard for you to run around. Does that sound good?"

She decided to take their wriggles of excitement as a yes.

Last night's snow covered everything in sight. It was only a few inches deep, coming up just past her ankles, and easy enough to drive through—thank God, because after the last big snowfall and the way her arms had ached after wrestling the ancient snowblower up and down the driveway for hours, she wasn't looking forward to tackling it again.

Tire tracks cut down the driveway from her grandparents' Subaru. They'd gone up to the Estates for brunch with friends—and to talk to the administrators about the dog fair. Ally was grateful for the quiet and the chance to think after her conversation with Ben last night.

She entered the barn, going through the morning routine of taking care of the dogs, making sure everyone was fed and cuddled before retreating to the office to process the applications with Colby's head resting on her feet. Captain America would go to his new home tomorrow, but there were now applications waiting for four of the others.

She wanted all the dogs to find homes—but they had to be good homes. So she read essay answers about where the dogs would sleep and where they would be kept when the family wasn't home, scheduling home visits and worrying that she wasn't being thorough enough. She had a crick in her neck from hunching over the laptop, and her eyes were starting to blur from staring at the screen when the jingle bells above the door rang and her heart leapt in Pavlovian response.

She should be hoping to see more prospective pet parents, but if she was honest with herself, she was hoping it was Ben.

As friends. That was the only reason she was excited to see him.

Ally pushed away from the desk, Colby lifting his lazy head to watch her. "Who do you think it is?" she asked him, as the Saint Bernard heaved himself to his feet with a sigh. She pushed open the door, but didn't immediately see anyone. "Ben?"

She stepped farther into the kennels with a chorus of barks—and found Deenie sitting on the floor of JoJo's run, playing fetch with the tiny papillon. She looked up, beaming when Ally and Colby appeared. "Hey! I was looking for you."

"Inside JoJo's run?"

"Who's a good girl?" she cooed to the dog as she brought back the toy. "She just looked so desperate for someone to throw Squeaky Mouse. How could I resist? Right, sweet baby?" Deenie stood, brushing off her leggings. "Did you want to go together?"

"Go…?"

"To the Christmas Fair. Did your grandparents leave already?" Deenie slipped out of the run.

"They're up at the Estates."

"Oh." Deenie frowned. "Aren't you going to the fair?

After making like two million brownies for the thing, you should at least see what it's all about."

"I thought it was just for the families of the kids. Won't it be weird if I show up?"

"Nah. It's a town thing. Everyone goes. Come on. I'll leave my car here, and we can walk together. You have no idea how bad parking can get—you wouldn't think it, since there aren't that many people in Pine Hollow, but when everyone is trying to cram into the school lot— nightmare. Where's your coat?"

Ally opened the door to the office to grab her coat, and Colby padded past her to throw himself down on his dog bed with a sigh. Dolce had gotten comfortable enough with him that she didn't even lift her head, her feet twitching with puppy dreams. "Should we take any of the dogs?"

"Not this time. Only service animals allowed."

On impulse, Ally grabbed her camera off the corner of the desk as she left. She hadn't taken many pictures— except of the dogs—in the last week. She tucked the camera into her bag, slinging the whole thing over her shoulder and following Deenie out into the snow.

"Have you heard of My Forever Home? That segment on that one show? The one with the guy?"

Ally smothered a grin at Deenie's oh-so-clear descrip- tion as they followed the path Deenie's tires had left in the snow down the long driveway to the street, where the sidewalks had already been cleared. It was a winter wonderland. The kind that never lasted for more than a few hours in New York before everything started to turn dirty gray.

Ally pulled out her camera to capture the Currier and Ives perfection of the town, covered in snow, the afternoon sunlight glistening off it like crystals. She aimed and shot as Deenie kept up a running commentary about her—currently failing—attempts to get them featured on another national morning show's pet adoption segment.

By the time they reached the school, she felt centered, in the zone as she snapped pictures of the town. But the second the door opened to the gymnasium a wall of sound hit them, assaulting that sense of calm with an aural sledgehammer.

"Come on!" Deenie shouted over the din. "Let's start with the hot apple cider booth!"

Ally kept her camera in her hands, clinging to it like JoJo clung to Squeaky Mouse. The gym had been decked out in holiday regalia, chains of red and green construction paper draping from the high ceiling. Dozens of booths manned by kids of all ages crowded into the space. Ally automatically scanned the booths—only realizing she was looking for Ben when she spotted Elinor instead and flinched.

It wasn't like she'd done anything wrong, hanging out with Astrid and Ben yesterday. Elinor had even encouraged her to do it. But it still felt slimy somehow. Like if she was honest with herself, she had to admit that she had *wanted* something to happen. Which wasn't her. She didn't have crushes on men who were taken.

Except apparently she did.

"Ally! I was hoping I'd run into you."

Ally jumped, greeting Elinor with what had to be

the world's fakest smile. "Elinor! Hi. It's so great to see you!"

"You, too. I thought I might come out to your shelter later this week. I've been thinking about getting a dog."

"You have?" Ally blinked, momentarily thrown. Ben was so vehemently anti-dog. Did Elinor not know that? Should Ally tell her? She hadn't even considered encouraging Elinor to adopt one of the shelter animals because of Ben.

"I figure once Christmas break starts this Friday I'll have the time to actually train one and get them used to me and the house. So maybe I'll stop by then?"

"I . . . yeah. Yeah, that would be great."

"Excellent." She beamed. "And can I just say, kudos on the brownies. Astrid's booth has been *the* place to be this afternoon, and we all know that wasn't Ben's doing."

"He actually did a lot," Ally protested, feeling strange defending him to his own fiancée. Elinor really did seem amazing, but Ally was having a harder and harder time picturing them together.

"I'm sure he did, but still, on behalf of all our stomachs, *thank you*. Jeremiah, *put down that icing*." Elinor moved off quickly to save one of the students from having frosting shampoo applied to his hair by an overly helpful friend.

Deenie appeared at her elbow a moment later, carrying two cups of spiced apple cider. "I lost you." She handed one cup over. "What happened?"

"I ran into Elinor," Ally said, as if it was totally normal to befriend a woman on whose fiancé she was developing a very problematic crush. "Apparently she's considering adopting a dog."

"Yeah? That's great. We'll have them all adopted by Christmas at this rate."

Ally took a sip of the cider, the flavors of cinnamon and clove blending sweetly on her tongue. Nerves whispered through her as Ben's question from last night floated through her mind. Then what would she do?

When the shelter wasn't there anymore, she would need a new excuse to stay in town and look after her grandparents, because she was starting to think her future wasn't in New York anymore.

"Come on. I want to see these infamous brownies everyone is talking about." Deenie linked her arm through Ally's, towing her through the crowd and forcing Ally to focus on her cup so she didn't spill hot cider on random passersby—because dousing people in hot beverages was her thing with Ben.

She was so focused on her cup, she was practically on top of Astrid's booth before she looked up—and spotted Ben standing a few feet away, supervising.

He grinned as soon as he spotted her and came around the table to her side. "You were right."

Deenie had dropped her arm, pressing forward among the kids crowded around Astrid's table to check out the remaining wares and leaving Ally alone with Ben in the middle of the crowded gym.

He looked good, so good in a snug gray sweater with a red-and-white-striped candy-cane scarf draped around his neck in a nod to the season. With his neatly trimmed beard, the look was very mountain-man chic—and it was working for him. She wanted to raise her camera and snap a picture, but somehow that felt too intimate. "I was?"

He gestured to the booth. "The gummy worm brownies were the first to go. Remind me never to bet against you when it comes to baked goods."

"I know my desserts."

"Astrid insisted we save one of each kind for quality control. You should come by and help us compare them."

It was tempting to say yes, but guilt whispered through her and she found herself dropping his fiancée's name into the conversation. "I was just talking to Elinor. She's thinking of adopting a dog."

"Yeah? That's a great idea."

Ally frowned, trying to figure out how Ben could be anti-dog in his own house but want his fiancée to adopt. Weren't they planning to live together when they got married? Was the engagement a long-term thing?

"She has a nice fenced yard, maybe she'll want one of the bigger dogs. Or Harry? Smart dog for a smart woman." He grinned at Ally. "I'm starting to get into this puppy matchmaking thing."

"That's . . . great," she stammered, unsure how she was supposed to respond. She loved his help—and Deenie's. It was purely platonic help. And if his fiancée wanted a dog and he didn't want one, it was none of her business.

"I scored the last caramel pretzel brownie!" Deenie appeared so suddenly at her side that Ally jumped, spilling warm cider onto her hands. "Whoops. Sorry. Didn't mean to startle you. Hey, Ben."

"Hey, Deenie."

"You're looking very festive today," Deenie commented, flicking his scarf.

Ben grimaced. "It's my attempt to keep people from noticing I'm wearing the same sweater for the third time since my washer broke."

"When are you going to come use the washer and dryer at my place?" Ally demanded.

"Ours is supposed to get fixed on Wednesday, but I promise I will take you up on that if this repair guy reschedules again. And I'm happy to help you hang those lights either way."

"Uncle Ben! We're out of change!" Astrid called, and he grinned.

"Duty calls." He nodded to them both and rounded Astrid's booth to help her.

Ally only realized she was watching the pair of them when Deenie conspicuously cleared her throat. "So...Ben seems more relaxed."

Ally wiped the smile off her face. "What?" she asked, as if she hadn't just been ogling another woman's fiancé.

"Nothing," Deenie singsonged. "Come on. I hear there are made-to-order s'mores around here somewhere."

"Didn't you just buy a brownie?"

"That's for later. S'mores are for now."

Deenie linked her arm with Ally's, and she let herself be led along, refusing to look over her shoulder at Ben and Astrid.

Chapter Twenty

W e're finally doing this," Mac marveled as he watched Connor expertly flick cards onto the felt of the poker table. "I thought poker night was officially dead."

"It hasn't been that long," Ben protested.

"Four months," Levi grunted, shielding his cards with one hand as he lifted the corners to study them.

Ben shot him a look. "It can't have been that long."

"No, it was August," Connor confirmed. "Astrid was about to start school. You complained so much about back-to-school shopping I still have her school supplies list memorized."

Since Connor had a tendency to memorize everything he heard, Ben tried not to take the comment personally, until Levi added dryly, "Me too."

"We've had poker night since then. I distinctly remember planning one in October. I bought extra beer..." And then Astrid had gotten the flu and he'd canceled, and all that beer was still sitting in the basement fridge beside the onion dip that had probably gone bad. Did onion dip go bad?

Levi's grin was evil. "The extra beer is in there right now, isn't it?" He leaned back, tilting his chair on its hind legs until he could snag the fridge door handle and pull it open. "Who wants?"

Connor and Mac both gave an affirmative, and Levi somehow managed to load both hands with beer without tipping over and falling on his ass. When he flicked the door closed and tilted back upright again, he dropped four beers on the table, one in front of each of them, including Ben.

"I shouldn't drink tonight. Astrid..."

"If you don't want it, Connor'll drink it, but I somehow doubt you having one drink and relaxing for the evening is going to hurt Astrid. It might even do her some good if you learn to unwind a little."

"Are you implying I'm wound too tight?"

"Yes," they all said in unison, and his jaw snapped shut on his retort.

"I have a lot on my plate." He reached for the beer, taking a defiant swig. "Is someone betting or what?"

To Connor's left, Mac started the betting, and for a few minutes they all focused on the game. Poker was serious business in this group—but so was trash-talking, so he wasn't surprised when Levi eyed him a few minutes later and commented, "You been spending a lot of time out at that shelter. How's Hal and Rita's granddaughter looking these days?"

Ben narrowed his eyes. "It's not like that. We're friends. I feel responsible for getting the shelter shut down, so I'm helping her find new homes for the dogs. Speaking of which, you looking for a new police dog? There's this massive wolfhound mix named Maximus who would probably scare the ever-loving shit out of any criminals."

"I think Pine Hollow might be a little on the small side for a K-9 unit. Besides I wouldn't know how to train one."

"So you hire someone for that. What about you, Mac?"

Mac flipped two cards onto the table to be dealt two more. "Health code violation. Magda would use any excuse to shut my ass down."

Connor frowned at him. "You allow your customers to bring dogs into the restaurant."

"Yeah, but not into the back. My kitchen could double as a surgical suite it's so clean, but one dog back there and Magda will have the health inspector so far up my ass I'll feel them when I cough."

Ben snorted. Mac's language always got more colorful when he was tipsy, and he was a total lightweight—one more beer and he'd be singing show tunes.

"You know I won't let her shut you down," Connor said. "I can bury her in specious lawsuits until she can't so much as sneeze without an attorney present, and she'll back off."

"Relax, Dirty Perry, I've got this."

They all stared at Mac. Finally Levi drawled, "Dirty *Perry*?"

"Like Perry Mason? Dirty Harry Perry Mason?" At their expressions he rolled his eyes. "Shut up. I hate you all."

A laugh burst out of Ben as Levi tipped back in his chair and Connor shook his head, both of them chuckling. They were right—it had been too long since they did this.

The unfinished basement at Paul and Katie's wasn't nearly as nice as Connor's palatial house overlooking the ski resort or even Mac's apartment above the Cup, but what it lacked in walls and flooring it made up in amenities. Ben's things that hadn't landed in storage had wound up down here: a dartboard, the massive fridge that contained beer and guac and Ben's not-so-secret junk food stash, the gorgeous poker table with its brushed felt, and a worn, overstuffed leather couch. Mac had crashed on that couch more times than he could count after he'd passed show tunes and transitioned into "I love you guys."

"Uncle Ben!" Astrid's feet thundered down the basement steps. She tumbled into the room, breathless with excitement. "Dolce's having her puppies! Can I go over to Ally's? Mrs. Gilmore said I could be there."

Ben glanced at the time on his phone—they'd started poker night early since all of them had early mornings the next morning, but it was still nearly eight o'clock. "I don't know, Astrid. It's a school night. And I don't want you walking over there by yourself in the dark. I'll take you to see them tomorr—"

"Deenie's going, too! She said she could pick me up. *Please*, Uncle Ben? I'm never going to ever have another chance to see newborn puppies ever in my life and this could be a formative experience for me. I could put it in my college application essays—"

Connor snorted, and Ben shot him a *You're not helping, asshole* look. "You still have school tomorrow—"

"I'll be back before nine! I promise! If I'm not, you can take away all my Christmas presents and ground me until I'm ancient. *Please? Please-please-please?*" She clasped her hands together, looking downright pathetic.

Ben glanced at his oldest friends, wondering what they thought of the show, and what they would think when he gave in. Because he'd just realized he was going to give in. "Okay," he said finally. "But I want you back home, in the door, shoes off, before nine o'clock. It's still a school night."

"Yes!" Astrid leapt into the air, clapping her hands, and then raced around the table to fling herself against his shoulder, hugging him tight. "Thank you, thank you, thank you! You're the best, Uncle Ben!"

Then she was up the stairs in another rumble of footsteps.

"I love that kid," Connor commented as soon as she was gone. "Her emotional blackmail is top-notch. That thing about the college essays." He lifted his fingertips to his lips for a chef's kiss. "Magnificent."

"Who's Deenie?" Levi asked, frowning. "I thought I knew everyone in town."

"Deenie Mitchell? Pink hair? Twenties? Does all those princess parties?"

"I'm sorry, does what now?" Connor interrupted.

"Princess parties," Ben explained. "Little girls all dress up as princesses, and a woman dressed up like some cartoon princess leads them through a tea party. It's a whole thing. Astrid's group was super into it a couple of summers ago, and Deenie was *the* person to get if you wanted a successful princess party."

Connor looked mildly horrified. "I'm never having children. No offense."

"None taken. You can get a dog instead. May I recommend Partridge?"

Mac handed Connor his empty and accepted another beer from Levi—show tunes imminent. "How is it you know everyone in town and we don't? Levi polices them, and I feed them. You would think we'd know everyone..."

"Yeah, but they complain to me. Join the town council. You'll see. You meet *everyone* when they want to make sure you know exactly what you're doing wrong." He didn't mention the mayor's suggestion that he run for her office. He wasn't sure which would be worse, their surprise or their support.

"That Twelve Dogs feature is cool," Connor said, flicking his ante into the center of the table. "Which one are you and Astrid adopting?"

"None of them," he insisted. "Not until I fix up this place, sell it, and move somewhere with a yard."

"So you invited us here to con us into adopting dogs, but you aren't even willing to get one yourself?"

"I just think they'd be good for you," Ben defended.

Connor arched an eyebrow. "With as much as I travel? I can't have a dog."

"They have these amazing inventions. They're called pet sitters."

"Ha."

Ben shrugged. "You were the one who was saying

your house was too quiet. Wouldn't it be great to have someone who was always happy to see you when you got home?"

"Unlike Monica?" Connor drawled—and Ben realized too late he'd veered a little too close to the Subject Which Must Not Be Named. Connor's ex had been the female version of himself—a type-A superachiever with a five-year plan and a color-coded sock drawer. They'd been two weeks away from their wedding when she declared that she wasn't *happy* and ran off to India to study yoga.

Connor had burned her copy of *Eat, Pray, Love*.

Now he lived alone in the four-thousand-square-foot modern masterpiece he'd bought for the two of them, and the echoing emptiness of the place was a sore point.

"I just thought a dog might be nice," Ben offered.

"You thought that? Or you thought you might score points with the pretty shelter lady if you help her find homes for all her dogs."

"I'm not trying to score points. It isn't like that." He hadn't even thought of her that way. Not really. Yes, he liked spending time with Ally, and yeah, she was cute, but it was as if his brain acknowledged those truths and then put them in a box along with all the other things he didn't have the mental bandwidth to deal with.

"No?" Connor challenged. "So you wouldn't mind if I asked her out?"

"I don't think she's your type."

"Maybe I need to date someone who isn't my usual type," Connor argued.

Ben couldn't tell if he meant it or if he was just

arguing to win—but it was annoying as hell. "Just leave her alone."

"Why?" Connor goaded. "Because you called dibs?"

"She isn't a piece of pizza. You can't call dibs on a person."

"You know what I mean. Bro code shit. If you were into her, I would back off, but if you aren't, there's no reason why you shouldn't want me and your new *friend* to be very happy together—"

"Maybe she deserves better than you."

"Maybe," Connor acknowledged. "Someone like you, perhaps?"

"She's moving back to New York," he snapped.

"I'm in New York for business all the time—"

"Connor." Levi's voice was deep and hard, cutting across the table.

Connor's always-arguing mouth snapped shut and he shrugged. "Just sayin'."

"You know..." Mac swayed in his chair, fumbling one of the poker chips from his rapidly diminishing supply between his fingers. "When you guys were all engaged and I wasn't, I always thought you were going to go off and leave me and it was going to kill poker night, but look at us now. Four single guys."

Silence hung hard over the table as they all stared at Mac.

Open mouth. Insert foot. That was Mac.

Mac opened his mouth again—and "Oh, What a Beautiful Mornin'" from *Oklahoma!* burst out.

Levi chucked an empty beer koozie at his face. "No singing at the table!"

Two hours later, Ben shushed Mac again as he slung his friend's arm over his shoulder and heaved him up the basement steps. Astrid had arrived home at five minutes to nine, gushing about the newborn puppies, and was currently two stories above them—hopefully soundly asleep in her bed, since tomorrow was a school day. But she wouldn't stay that way for long if Mac kept singing.

"I'm s'glad we did this," Mac slurred happily as they staggered upward. "I love you guys. You know that?" He twisted in Ben's grip, trying to see behind him where Connor and Levi were ready to catch him if he started to take a header downward. "I love you guys," he bellowed. They all shushed him, and he nodded sagely, shout-whispering, "I love you guys!"

"We love you, too," Ben assured him.

"How does anyone get that drunk off three beers?" Connor marveled.

"I used to think he was faking it," Levi commented from his position taking up the rear. "But if so, he's been conning us consistently for fifteen years, and I don't think Mac has that kind of endurance."

"You should date the dog lady," Mac blurted, swaying as Ben opened the door at the top of the stairs and tried to shove him through. "We can all see that you like her. It's okay to like somebody. You just gotta say, 'Dog lady, I like you.' And maybe she likes you, too."

"I'll keep that in mind," Ben promised. Now that they were on the main floor they had a little more room to maneuver, and Connor appeared at Mac's other side, taking half his weight.

"It's not a bad idea," Connor chimed in helpfully. "Though you might want to consider calling her Ally rather than Dog Lady. Just a thought."

"I'm not going to call her anything. We're friends."

"Uh-huh," Connor agreed skeptically.

"I like friends," Mac declared with drunken sincerity.

"Does it bother anyone else that he doesn't even get hungover when he's like this?" Connor asked. "How is that fair? All the fun of being slap-happy-drunk and none of the morning-after consequences? Where is the cosmic justice?"

"Yeah," Levi drawled. "That's one of the real injustices of the universe that's going to keep me up nights."

"Hey. Fair is fair."

"We really should do this more often," Ben said dryly—but he actually meant the words.

Levi seemed to sense the truth behind his comment, meeting his eyes and giving a wry twist of his lips. "Yeah. I've missed you assholes."

"Language!" Connor gasped with mock horror. "The little ears might still be awake."

"Don't think I've forgotten the time you tried to teach her to swear," Ben growled.

Connor shrugged. "It was British swearing. Bloody bollocksed isn't even really a thing in this country." Ben glared at him and Connor grinned. "You're just jealous you didn't think of it first. Or you would be if you loosened up on the reins a little bit. She's a good kid, Ben."

"She is," Levi confirmed. "And you know you can call us, right? Anytime you need anything?"

"Yeah. Of course."

He just didn't do that. He didn't ask for help. And Levi's look said he knew it.

"Idiot," Levi said softly, clapping him on the shoulder and stepping out into the cold night air.

Ben closed the door behind the three of them to the sound of Mac winding up for a rendition of "Memory." He headed toward the kitchen to rinse the empty bottles for recycling and realized he was smiling.

They did need to do that more often. When he made time for the people who knew him best, he felt more like himself again—and like he could manage all the other ten thousand things he had to do. It shouldn't make any sense. He'd wasted three hours tonight, playing poker and talking about nothing with his friends. But he felt like he'd gotten time back. Gotten himself back.

He wanted to tell Ally about it.

His hands stilled on the bottles. *Did* he have feelings for her that weren't friendship? He hadn't even let himself consider the possibility, but he'd hated the idea of Connor asking her out. The thought of Connor asking out Elinor didn't bother him in the slightest. Elinor was his friend. Ally was his friend. But Ally was also...

He didn't know. He didn't know what else she was. He just knew she couldn't be whatever that was. Because she was leaving. She had a life in New York to get back to. This was temporary. The shelter. This season. And he couldn't do temporary. Not with Astrid in the picture. He had to be smarter than that. He had to put Astrid first. Always.

Chapter Twenty-One

"W"ho's ready for a Christmas parade? Is JoJo ready? Is the sweetest most precious little girl ever ready to be a parade star?"

Ally watched Deenie cooing over JoJo as she put tiny red ribbons on her ears. She arched an eyebrow. "You really should just adopt her."

Deenie looked up, laughing at herself. "I know. But I really can't have pets in my place, and you never know when wanderlust is going to hit."

Ally turned her attention back to Partridge, sobered by the reminder that Deenie wouldn't always be there. This last week and a half had been wonderful. They'd failed to get the national pet adoption segment they were hoping for, but with Astrid and Ben and Deenie and her grandparents all strategizing ways to get the word out, she didn't think they even needed it.

In a couple of hours she and Deenie would be loading the dogs onto the Furry Friends pickup, which had been decked out in Christmas cheer for the parade, but now they were putting ribbons on the dogs and deciding who would get to wear the Santa hat and who would wear the reindeer antlers.

The reindeer antlers had been Ben's latest addition. He hadn't been by to do his laundry, but he had swung by with Astrid a couple of times this week, lingering in the office to chat with Ally while Astrid played with the dogs. Partridge still followed him around like a duckling wherever he went, and Ally was starting to think he might not be quite as immune to the lopsided bulldog as he wanted everyone to think.

"Will Ben be at the parade?"

Ally jerked guiltily. "What?" Had Deenie seen something on her face? Had she somehow known that Ally was thinking of him? "I don't know. I mean, isn't the whole town going to be there?"

"He didn't tell you?"

"Why would he tell me?"

Deenie grinned. "I don't know. I just thought you guys have been hanging out together a lot. Doing 'shelter stuff' together." Ally had no idea what the air quotes around "shelter stuff" meant, and she definitely wasn't going to ask. "Last weekend at the fair, I thought maybe I sensed a vibe."

"A vibe?" She laughed, hoping it didn't sound as artificial to Deenie as it did to her own ears. "What kind of vibe?"

"You know. Like a 'you, me, mistletoe, let's do this' kind of vibe."

"Deenie! Nothing's going on. We're just friends. He's nice."

"Right..."

"What?" Ally demanded.

"Nothing," Deenie insisted, but at Ally's look she capitulated. "It's just he doesn't exactly have a reputation for being nice. He's *nice* to you."

Ally couldn't wrap her head around it. How could anyone fail to see how kind Ben was? How utterly self-less? "What kind of reputation does he have?"

"You know. Grumpy. Impatient. Brusque." Deenie paused her grooming efforts. "I love that word. Brusque." Her hands started moving again. "I mean, we all under-stand why. He got hit with a whole boatload of grief and never got out from under it, but he's still the town grumpus."

"Grumpus?"

"Grinch. Grouch. Whatever. I know—I spend too much time around five-year-olds, and it's affecting my vocabulary, but you know what I mean. And I'm just saying that Ben isn't known for nice, but when he's around you, he's different. Happy. I guess I just wondered if something was going on."

"No. Absolutely not. Our friendship is purely pla-tonic." And if she said that often enough, she would force herself to believe it.

"That's a bummer."

"Deenie! He's *taken*."

Deenie blinked, looking up from JoJo's bows. "He is?"

Ally shot Deenie a look. "Elinor? His fiancée? Ring-ing any bells?"

"Elinor Rodriguez? Like *Elinor* Elinor?"

"Yeah."

Deenie's jaw dropped. "You thought she was engaged to Ben *West*?"

"Yes?" Deenie's shock was corroding Ally's confidence, and she frowned, suddenly not so certain she'd read the situation correctly. But her grandmother had *said* Ben was engaged. And Astrid called Elinor her aunt. And they'd seemed so comfortable with one another...

Deenie snorted a laugh. "That's one I've never heard before."

The jingle bells above the door jangled, and Elinor appeared like she'd been conjured by the conversation— or, more realistically, like she'd already told them she'd be arriving on Friday afternoon when she was done with school so she could meet the dogs and decide which one might be right for her.

Ally jolted to her feet. "Elinor!"

The librarian smiled, as always slightly wary of Ally's overenthusiasm. "Hey." She glanced at the dogs currently being beautified. "Is this a bad time?"

"No! Of course not! Would you like to look around and see if anyone catches your eye?"

"You know, this explains so much," Deenie said conversationally. Ally shot her a *let's-keep-this-conversation-to-ourselves* glare, but her psychic powers must have been on the fritz, because Deenie kept talking. "I was wondering why you kind of spaz out around Elinor—I even wondered if maybe she was the one you were into, but if you thought she was with Ben, it all makes sense."

"Ben?" Elinor repeated, pausing in the act of looking in one of the dog pens. "Ben West?"

Her surprise was the final nail in the coffin of Ally's belief. "You aren't engaged to him?"

"To *Ben*? No. God, no. Not that he isn't lovely—"

"Oh, she knows," Deenie put in helpfully. "Ally has a thing for him."

"You do?"

Elinor's gaze lasered in on her with intense focus, and Ally wished for a hole to open up and swallow her. "I really don't."

But Elinor didn't seem to hear her, a slow, knowing smile spreading across her face. "You know that does explain a lot. You get this sort of manic look in your eyes whenever you talk to me. Honestly, I thought you were just desperate for female friends. It was sort of adorable. Unnerving, but adorable."

"Oh God," Ally groaned, hiding her face behind her hands. "I'm sorry. I was trying so hard to be normal."

"Well, there's your problem," Deenie chirped. "Normal is the worst."

"You really thought I was engaged to Ben?" Elinor repeated.

Ally felt her face heating and knew it must be seven shades of scarlet by now. "My grandmother said he was engaged, and then Astrid called you Aunt Elinor, and you two are so natural with each other..."

Realization dawned on Elinor's face, and she released a soft laugh. "Astrid calls me Aunt Elinor because her mother, Katie, was my best friend in the whole world. Ben and I grew up together. And then I made the mistake of dating one of his best friends in high school, so we were pretty much forced to see each other even more.

And yes, Ben *was* engaged. Past tense. Isabelle left him as soon as the custody papers came through, and Ben hasn't looked at another woman since. But he has been spending a lot of time at this shelter."

"He's helping with the dogs."

Elinor nodded. "Uh-huh."

"It isn't like that," Ally insisted.

But a voice in the back of her brain whispered, *Is it?*

She'd thought Ben was taken. She'd been so sure. So she hadn't even let herself consider that he might be interested in her, but now she couldn't help but think of everything they'd done together in the last couple of weeks and wonder if she'd been wrong about more than his relationship status.

Had he been flirting with her? That night when he'd walked her home after brownie baking and the snow had started to fall so peacefully around them, making her feel like she was inside a real-life snow globe—had that been a *date*? Had he been thinking about kissing her?

Were they dating and she hadn't even *known it*?

"Uh-oh. Looks like someone just took the blinders off." Deenie grinned gleefully. "How's that platonic relationship looking now?"

Ally shook her head, denial running strong. "He hasn't done anything—held my hand, kissed me, he hasn't made a single move." Even if she might like him more than a little bit, that didn't mean her feelings were reciprocated.

"He wouldn't with Astrid around," Elinor put in. "I'm not sure he's been on a single date since he became her guardian."

"Two years?" Deenie asked incredulously. "That poor boy and his blue balls."

Ally snorted, startled out of her confusion by the dry comment from the bubbly princess who always seemed to have glitter somewhere on her body. In the run next to them, Harry perked up and rushed to the gate, sitting her best sit with her long fluffy tail sweeping the ground behind her in an eager wag as she gazed fixedly at Deenie.

"Not that kind of ball," Deenie told the Aussie, repeating her favorite word and sending her into even more determined good-girl behavior. "No ball, Harry. Sorry, baby."

"He knows the word ball?" Elinor eyed the gorgeous Aussie, who still sat with her ears pricked forward, just in case a game of fetch was about to materialize.

"She, actually. Harry for Harriet. And yeah, she knows a lot of words, and she'll play fetch until your arm falls off if you let her."

Elinor frowned at the complicated padlock system on her run. "What's all this?"

Ally grimaced. "Harry, also for Houdini. She knows how to open doors. Our own little explorer."

Elinor chuckled. "Should we call you Dora, sweetheart?"

"See? I'm not the only one who spends too much time around children," Deenie said while Harry cocked her head at Elinor.

"If you adopted her, you could rename her whatever you want. The trick, we learned, is to lure her back rather than chase her. When you try to catch her, she thinks it's a game of keep-away, and just when you think you have her cornered she'll leap over something you were sure she couldn't leap over, and it all starts over again. But if you grab a piece of cheese and ask her to come, she'll behave like a perfect angel."

"She's pretty," Elinor commented, eyeing the merle Aussie, who was still doing her best good-girl routine, as if she knew she had a receptive audience in the librarian. And maybe she did know. The dog was scary smart.

"Would you like to play with her? We have her in the biggest run, but even with that much space, we bring her to the paddock to get her zoomies out a few times a day, or she starts trying to climb the walls of her run." Literally. Ally had never seen a dog try to scale a fence before, but Harry could do a lot of things normal dogs didn't even try. "You'd be doing us a favor."

Elinor grinned to let her know she'd been laying it on a little thick, but she still nodded. "Sure, I'd love to help."

Ally got Elinor set up in the back paddock with Harry and her favorite squeaky ball, then returned to the grooming station, leaving Elinor laughing at Harry's antics.

"I think we might have a match," she whispered as she picked up Peanut for a cuddle. "Ben said he thought Harry might be good for Elinor."

"Did he?" Deenie asked, layering the words with extra meaning. "So you and Ben *have* been spending time together..."

Ally groaned. "We're *friends*," she insisted. "He doesn't see me as anything else."

"That doesn't mean he couldn't with the right push,"

Deenie suggested. "Sometimes males are stupid and have to have their faces shoved in what's good for them before they realize what everyone else knew all along. Look at Maximus."

Ally snorted. "Did you just compare Ben to Maximus?"

"He's a lovely dog with a huge heart, and he desperately wants to please everyone. He just can't seem to figure out what you want from him unless you shove it in his big, dumb face. That sounds a lot like Ben." She cocked her head. "Actually it sounds like most of the men I've dated, too." She frowned, then another sunny smile burst across her face. "On second thought, you probably shouldn't take dating advice from me. I'm the worst."

She said it as cheerfully as she said everything else, without an ounce of negative feeling, but Ally was starting to understand that was Deenie's way of keeping anyone from trying to dig too deep. She had some experience with that. "It must be hard to find something long-term when you're always traveling."

"It is," Deenie agreed brightly. "Luckily, I'm not looking for long-term." She held up two different ribbons. "What do you think for Trapper, red or green?"

Ally considered pushing, not letting her change the subject, but Deenie seemed determined to keep her secrets, and there would be time. At least she hoped there would be. She was enjoying this life in Pine Hollow that she'd started to build. With Deenie and Astrid and Ben...

Her thoughts seemed to keep circling back to him. If he wasn't taken, had he thought *she* was Friend-Zoning *him*? Was that why the little moments that felt like stretchy taffy between them had all fizzled? Because she'd given him a stop signal? Could there actually be something there?

He was a great guy. He loved Astrid like nothing else. He tried to do his best for the town, even when they all seemed to think he was a Grinch. He missed his sister so much he wouldn't update his own kitchen. And more than anything else, he had a good heart. That was hard to resist.

And if he wasn't engaged...

"Ally?"

"Green." She made a snap decision on the bow, blushing at the direction of her thoughts—again. "Definitely green."

She would see him at the parade. She would know soon enough.

Chapter Twenty-Two

Ben knew gossip flew around Pine Hollow faster than Santa's sleigh on Christmas Eve. He knew how little it took for a story to gain traction in a town their size. He just wasn't used to all the speculation being about *him*.

In the last week, word had gotten out that not only had he and Astrid been helping at the shelter and attended the tree lighting with Ally, but that she'd also brought him coffee at work and helped make the brownies that had been such a hit at the Christmas Fair. This was, apparently, tantamount to an engagement announcement. The town was in a frenzy.

Ben was used to his neighbors stopping him on the street to complain about whatever business was in front of the town council—stopping him to ask about his love life was something else entirely. The smiles, the winks, the friendly claps on the shoulder—all of it was freaking him out.

After the third "I hear you've been spending time with

Hal and Rita's granddaughter" and the fourth "Have you seen Ally yet today?" Ben was ready to snap at the next person who smiled speculatively at him as he and Astrid navigated their way toward the school, where the floats were assembling for their procession through town.

Luckily Astrid seemed oblivious. Thank God.

The last thing he needed was to be spotted with Ally and fan the flames of the gossip, but Astrid and Kimber had asked if they could ride with the dogs on the Furry Friends float instead of on the Pine Hollow Elementary float, so he was going to have to be seen with Ally at least long enough to drop his niece off.

Astrid and Kimber had helped decorate the shelter's old pickup until it was dripping with Christmas cheer—and Astrid shrieked when she saw it, lined up near the back.

"It looks so good!"

Kimber was already there, and Astrid raced over to greet her friend and the dogs, tumbling around with them behind the back of the truck.

"I'll pick you up right here after," Ben called to Astrid, eager to make his escape before Ally appeared and the gossip exploded.

"You aren't riding with us?"

Too late.

Ben turned to face Ally as fifty pounds of bulldog planted itself on his foot, leaning against his shins. "Hello, Partridge."

Ally stood a few feet away from him, smiling—and his brain kicked into fight-or-flight overdrive. Was she standing too close? Smiling too much? Was that why the entire town thought they were together? Was she smiling with intent? Did *she* think they were together? She looked adorable in her purple coat and white scarf—just like the first time he'd seen her, and that night he'd walked her home in the snow—but just because he always remembered what she was wearing didn't mean he had feelings for her. He didn't have room in his life to have feelings for her, no matter what his poker buddies and half the freaking town might think.

"Ben?"

"No," he blurted, realizing he'd missed a question. "No, I figured—uh—I figured the bed of the pickup would be too crowded with all the dogs and you and your grandparents and the girls."

"Well, Gramps is driving, and I think only Gram is going to be riding in the bed. The rest of us are walking alongside with the dogs so the crowds get a closer look at our adoptable wares. And when the dogs get tired—or the girls get tired—they can ride in the truck with Gram until they get a second wind. So there's plenty of space if you don't mind a very slow walk through town."

"No, I, uh, already told Levi I'd watch the parade with him."

It was a lie, but she smiled. "Oh, well. Maybe next time. My grandparents are determined to make this a yearly event for the shelter if we can somehow keep our funding going."

Ben frowned. He would have expected her to have one foot out the door already. He'd known it was inconvenient to have to place all the dogs so quickly, but he hadn't realized they were trying to keep the shelter open. "You're looking for more funding?"

"We're looking everywhere we can think. We have a GoFundMe page, and Gramps and I have been filling out grant applications every spare minute. I'm not going down without a fight."

"I would've thought you'd be impatient to get back to your life."

Her brow furrowed, but before she could reply a shout interrupted them.

"Ally! We have a problem!" It was Deenie's voice, and Ally grimaced.

"Duty calls. We'll see you after the parade—unless you've changed your mind?"

"No, I...Levi, you know."

"Right. Have fun! Wave to us! C'mon, Partridge!" And then she was gone, taking the fifty-pound bulldog with her, off to deal with whatever last-minute catastrophe had befallen the Furry Friends float.

Now he just had to find Levi and convince him to watch the parade.

It felt weird, walking away from the float. But that was just because Astrid was there. It wasn't like he belonged there. He was only helping out because he felt guilty. Not because seeing Ally was the best part of his day.

A yearly event...

Was she really thinking of staying?

He hadn't even considered she might stick around— which, if he was honest, was probably why it felt so easy talking to her about his inadequacies as a parental figure.

She was temporary, and when she left she could take all his secret insecurities with her. But if she stayed...

God, the rumors would be impossible. Everyone would think she was staying for *him*. The town would have them married by Valentine's Day. Just what he needed.

He was halfway to the town square that was the middle of the parade route before he remembered he needed to be looking for Levi.

"Ben!" Delia waved him over, and Ben waved back, climbing to the top of the stands where the mayor and her wife would be watching the parade, along with several of the town councilors and their families.

Ben greeted everyone in a quick round robin of Merry Christmases, making his way to Delia's side. "Have you seen Levi?" he asked after the pleasantries were accomplished. "I'm supposed to watch the parade with him." *Even if he doesn't know it.*

Delia frowned. "Levi Jackson? Isn't he driving Santa's car this year?"

"Right." *Damn it.* "I must have misunderstood."

"Watch right here." She patted the bench at her side. "I want to talk to you about something, and the show's about to start anyway. Hold on while I get this sucker rolling."

Delia clattered up to the top of the stands, where a podium with a microphone waited. She made a quick speech, welcoming everyone to the fifty-third annual Pine Hollow Christmas parade, and then declared it officially open, her voice booming across the square. A cheer went up—and the high school marching band began to play a ragged rendition of "It's Beginning to Look a Lot Like Christmas" as they marched into the square.

The Pine Hollow Christmas parade was no Macy's Thanksgiving Day Parade. There weren't any balloons, and the floats were all low budget—but the cheers were just as loud. This year's Miss Teen Maple Syrup rode through town behind the marching band, perched on the back seat of a shiny red convertible. She was trailed by a float from the local dentist, who was—rather incongruously, in Ben's opinion—throwing candy canes to the crowd. He wanted to text Ally about it—and then kicked himself for the impulse.

No wonder half the town thought they were dating.

The dentist was followed by a float from Summerland Estates—the only group likely not to be bothered by the roar of the local Harley Club that rumbled down the street behind them. There was a float from the ski resort, another pageant queen, and then the middle school band struggling through a valiant attempt at "Santa Claus Is Comin' to Town."

Then came the Furry Friends float.

The old green pickup had never looked better, draped in garland and a giant Furry Friends banner. Hal sat in the driver's seat, wearing a Santa hat and waving out the window as the truck rolled slowly down the street. Rita perched in the truck bed like one of the pageant queens, beaming and waving and lifting the paw of the little chihuahua she held so he could wave, too.

There were a couple of other dogs in the bed of the truck, including Partridge, who had apparently reached his endurance limit for the day before they got to the square, but Astrid, Ally, Deenie, and Kimber walked alongside with a dog each. The girls looked so proud. Deenie had worn elf ears and glitter and worked the crowd like a pro, but it was Ally he couldn't stop looking at.

She was smiling shyly and waving at the crowd, the city girl who was uncomfortable at the center of attention but loved being part of it all. There were so many contradictions in her, and he found himself trying to puzzle them all out. She seemed so hungry for community but so nervous whenever they were at the town events. She told him he was too hard on himself, but she never gave herself a break, constantly doing things for her grandparents and the shelter and him—always putting her own needs last. She needed someone to tell her to slow down. She needed—

"So you and the dog lady, huh?"

Ben's attention snapped to the left, where Delia was watching him with a smug little smile. "Not you, too. This town is ridiculous. We're *friends*."

"Uh-huh," Delia agreed, still smiling. She craned her neck to watch the Furry Friends float move around the corner. "She seems nice. Good with Astrid."

"She is. Very. And also going back to New York." He hadn't dated anyone since Isabelle left—and he wasn't about to start thinking that way now. Especially not with someone who wasn't sticking around. No matter what the town thought.

"That's a shame. You two would have been cute together. Davis heard she was a big-shot photographer and wanted to see if she'd be interested in snapping a few shots for the tourism website." They both applauded as the bakery float appeared.

The bakery float was always one of the biggest in the parade, thanks to Mac and Magda's ongoing cake feud, which had now spilled over into all aspects of town life. The Cup's float was bound to be just as spectacular.

"Did you think any more about that mayoral run?" Delia asked, her voice deceptively light. "The election isn't until March, but you need to file the candidacy paperwork by the end of the year..."

Ben groaned. At least now he knew why she'd wanted him to sit next to her. "Delia, I'm not running for mayor. I don't need the headaches, and no one would vote for me anyway. I'm the most despised member of the council."

She turned to face him fully, forgetting about the ongoing parade. "Why on earth would you say that?"

His eyebrows popped up, surprised by her surprise. "I'm the one who gets yelled at in line at the Cup because we won't raise the budget for the tree lighting. And I'm the IT guy for the town, so I can see who is getting the most complaint emails of anyone on the council, and it isn't you, and it isn't anyone else. It's me."

"Which means people think you're *listening*. Because you *are*. Half the members of the council will never change their minds about anything, so why waste time bugging them at the Cup or writing out long thoughtful emails they'll never read? You read them. You pay attention."

"I'm the town Grinch."

Delia laughed. "Ben West, if you're the Grinch,

you're the Grinch after his heart grows three sizes. You can be as gruff as you want on the outside. We all know you've got a gooey center. Anyone who's ever seen you with Astrid can see that."

It sounded nice, but he didn't believe a word of it. "You can't flatter me into running for mayor, Delia."

"I'm not flattering you. But if you really don't want to do it, I'll let it go. Even if you would be the best."

He eyed her. "You aren't going to let it go."

She grinned, unashamed. "Probably not. Though I will drop it for now—after I leave you with one last thought. If you don't do it, think of who will and how much it will annoy you to watch them do it wrong for a four-year term."

Ben shook his head. "You're evil."

"I get the job done."

"We should just vote to remove term limits and let you keep going."

"Nah. Margaret's ready for me to be home more. And I've been promising her a trip to Europe for two years now. Time to pass the torch." She nudged him with her elbow. "Just think about it. You'd be a good mayor."

"I'd rather be the town Grinch."

She laughed and they both turned back to watching the parade, but her words kept shifting around in his brain, just like she'd intended them to. Machiavellian, his boss. But maybe she wasn't entirely wrong...about more than just the mayor's position.

Chapter Twenty-Three

By the time the parade ended, Ally's feet were aching and she was no closer to figuring out whether Ben thought they were dating. Not that she'd been obsessing about it as she walked. Much.

She'd been pretty good at putting him out of her mind until Astrid had come right out and asked her, "Are you dating Uncle Ben?"

They'd been walking along beside the Furry Friends float, and Ally had nearly tripped over her own feet. She'd stammered something about the two of them being just friends, which she really hoped was believable, because even if there was something starting with Ben, it wasn't her place to talk to Astrid about it, and she certainly wasn't going to talk to Ben's niece before she talked to him.

But the conversation hadn't helped the whole put-it-out-of-her-mind plan. Especially when Astrid kept hinting that if they *wanted* to date, she'd be totally fine with that. Luckily, Astrid was easily distracted by the dogs.

Ally felt awkward walking in the parade, an imposter waving to all the townspeople who were probably wondering who the heck she was and what she was doing there, but she focused on the dogs and on Astrid and Kimber, and before she knew it the parade was over.

The breakdown area was a madhouse, with marching band members running in every direction, so Ally texted Ben and Kimber's mom that she would bring the girls back to the town square and meet them at the gazebo.

Astrid and Kimber walked two steps in front of her, whispering excitedly to each other the whole way. The square was still crowded, but at least there weren't dozens of teenagers running into one another with brass instruments. Ally didn't immediately spot Ben, and she followed Kimber and Astrid up into the gazebo.

"Over here, Ally," Astrid urged. "We can see best from right here."

Ally moved where Astrid indicated, looking over the railing, but she still didn't see Ben.

"There are my parents." Kimber waved, but made no move to join her mom and dad, who waved back and continued their conversation with a couple Ally didn't recognize.

"Where's Uncle Ben?" Astrid asked, bouncing with impatience, as if she suddenly couldn't wait to get home.

"He'll be here," Kimber assured her, and Ally frowned at the odd interaction—then she saw Ben weaving his way through the townspeople, half-jogging as he crossed the square.

"Sorry. I was halfway to the diner when I saw your text," he explained, trotting up the gazebo steps.

"Oh, sorry." Ally started to move away from the rail to meet him, but Kimber was suddenly blocking her way. "I just figured it would be easier to meet here."

"No, this is great." He was breathless and smiling as he clapped a hand on Astrid's shoulder. "I forgot what a zoo breakdown is. You about ready to go, Astrid?"

"Can I spend the night at Kimber's?"

His eyebrows popped up. "Has anyone asked Kimber's parents?"

"We'll ask now." Astrid held up both hands in a stop sign when he would have turned to leave the gazebo. "You stay here. We'll be right back."

Ben frowned suspiciously, but he didn't move as the two raced off. Ally leaned against the railing behind her. "They were really great during the parade."

"I'm glad they didn't give you any trouble."

"They're angels. Though I should probably warn you, Astrid was talking about coming to the shelter every day while school is out, and I'm pretty sure Gram invited her to help us with the pet fair at the Estates tomorrow."

"Is that tomorrow?"

"Two o'clock."

"I'm sure we can make that work. If you don't mind having us underfoot..."

"Of course not. All help gratefully accepted." She tamped down the smile that wanted to consume her face. "Everything okay with town business? It looked like you and the mayor were having a pretty serious conversation when we spotted you in the stands."

Ben grimaced. "She wants me to run for mayor. Which is ridiculous. I don't know why she picked me. I can't be mayor."

Ally cocked her head. "Why not?"

"I'm not...I don't know, I'm not mayor material. I'm not..." He shrugged, folding his arms across his chest, the posture all defensive little boy. "Delia seems to think I'm this great person. Like I'm Bob Cratchit instead of Ebenezer Scrooge."

"Ben..." Ally shook her head, baffled. Was that why he'd been so sensitive to the Scrooge jokes? Because he was scared it was true? Did he really not see himself as a good person? "How many people are on the town council?"

"Six. Plus the mayor."

"And how many of them are out at the shelter helping me and adding new features to the town newsletter to make sure my dogs find homes before the funding dries up?"

He shook his head. "You don't understand. I was the swing vote. It was my call."

"It doesn't matter. You didn't make it alone, but you were still the only one to show up. You've shown up for me. You show up for Astrid. You drive yourself crazy trying to show up for everyone in this town. So don't be telling yourself you aren't good enough to be mayor. You're the best person I know."

The words hung between them, more impassioned than she'd intended.

He *was* the best person she knew.

And she had feelings for him. A lot of feelings. Her

crush had swollen until it pressed against the inside of her chest, making her breath go short.

"Look, you two! You're under the mistletoe!"

Ally looked up at Astrid's shout and there it was—the fateful sprig dangled right above where Astrid had coached her to stand. Ben looked up too, and Ally's heart began to pound.

This was it. The moment of truth.

All he had to do was kiss her.

Ben stared up at the offending branch with the sinking feeling that he was the victim of a conspiracy.

He *liked* Ally. Everyone already seemed to think they were a couple, so it was easy to think maybe they should be. She was sweet and smart and fun to be with—and the lush curve of her lower lip made him think a thousand impure thoughts. Not that he needed to be thinking that way five feet away from his niece.

He didn't need to be thinking *any* way five feet away from Astrid.

She was already attached. He wouldn't be surprised if Astrid was pulling for them to fall for one another—probably picturing a house full of dogs. It was one thing to start a new relationship when it was just his heart on the line, but if Astrid got her hopes up, if Astrid loved her and then things fell apart with Ally down the road...if she moved back to New York...

He had to think of Astrid. He always had to put Astrid first.

In a different world, he might have kissed Ally. They might have been good for each other. But this was the world they lived in. This was his life.

It didn't matter how perfect the moment was. Or how pretty she looked with her face tipped questioningly up toward his. Or how badly he wanted to just lower his head, close the distance between them, slide his arms around her—

A cymbal crashed as one of the kids in the marching band dropped it, the sound echoing across the square, jerking him out of his thoughts and reminding him of how public they were.

"No." He rocked back. Ally turned her face to the side, flushing with embarrassment, and he held out his hands, afraid to touch her, but needing to make her understand. "Sorry. I'm sorry. I—"

She shook her head, backing away. "No, it's fine. It's just a silly—"

"It's not that I—things are complicated—"

"No, I understand. I should..." She dodged around him toward the exit to the gazebo. "I need to get back to my grandparents before they send out a search party."

"Ally..." He reached out a useless hand.

She was already clattering down the gazebo steps, smiling a huge, false smile for the girls as she passed them. "See you later, girls!"

Ben stared after her, a pit settling hard in his chest. He hadn't wanted to start something that had no future, especially not in full view of the town, but he hadn't meant to hurt her, either.

Way to go, West. The looks on Astrid's and Kimber's

faces when he met their eyes confirmed he was, in fact, the most useless of men.

"What did you do?" Astrid asked him, appalled.

"Nothing. Let's go home."

He'd done the right thing. Ally was moving back to New York. His life was here with Astrid. He couldn't get involved with her. He just had to keep reminding himself of that.

Chapter Twenty-Four

Public mortification: 1. Mistletoe: 0.

Ally rushed through the crowded town square trying not to wonder how many people had seen Ben reject her right there in the heart of the town.

He'd had an explanation—because of course he did. It was complicated. Sure it was. But she really didn't want to stick around to learn all the reasons he didn't want her. She shouldn't have listened to Deenie and Elinor and Astrid and everyone else who had seemed to be silently speculating on the two of them.

They were *friends*. And if she'd been hoping it could be more, that was obviously one-sided.

That was all it was. No big deal.

She probably didn't even like him as much as she thought she did. It wouldn't be the first time she'd latched on to a guy because she was lonely and he was convenient. She'd promised herself she wasn't going to do that anymore. She'd been lonely in New York, but she *liked* Pine Hollow. She liked working at the shelter and going to town events. It felt good to be a part of something, and she was probably mixing all those feelings up in what she thought she'd been feeling for Ben. That was it.

The chaos around the diner had cleared out by the time she got back to the Furry Friends truck. Her grandparents had loaded all the dogs into their crates, and she jogged the last twenty yards to meet them. "Sorry that took so long!"

Just busy having my self-esteem crushed.

"Not to worry," Gramps assured her. "You have perfect timing. The last truck blocking us just moved."

"Did you find Ben?" Gram asked, a gleam in her eye—which Ally studiously ignored.

"Yep. And Kimber's parents, too. They're all set. Did Deenie take off?"

"She had another engagement."

"Great." She clasped her hands together. "Let's get these dogs home."

The dogs. The shelter. That was what she needed to be focusing on. She had more important things to think about than Ben West and an abandoned mistletoe kiss.

"You two make such a sweet couple."

Ben gritted his teeth through the same patient smile he'd been using all day and repeated the same phrase he'd uttered at least twelve times already. "Ally and I aren't a couple, Mrs. Kowalski."

The sound of barking echoed off the walls of the

Summerland Estates common room as the white-haired octogenarian leaned forward, one hand held up to her ear. "Hmm?"

"She's just a friend!" Ben clarified at a half shout.

"Of course she is, dear." Mrs. Kowalski beamed. "And what a lovely girlfriend!"

Ben gave up—as he had every other time he'd had this conversation in the last twenty minutes. He almost hadn't come today. He'd told Ally he and Astrid would be here, but after the botched mistletoe moment, it had been tempting to skip the pet fair.

Not that he'd botched it. He definitely shouldn't have kissed Ally in the middle of the town square, but he might have been able to handle the dismount more smoothly. Astrid had spent the night at Kimber's, so he'd had plenty of time to think about what he should have done. He owed Ally an apology, but for now he was trying to keep his distance as much as he could in the Estates common room. For all the good that was doing.

Every senior Ben spoke to had another comment about how wonderful it was to see him and Ally together. What a "charming couple" they made. He could talk himself hoarse explaining that they weren't actually together, but the Summerland residents simply smiled and patted his hand—either not hearing him or not believing a word he said.

At least the pet fair seemed to be a success, though he couldn't take any credit for that. When he and Astrid had arrived at Furry Friends this afternoon, Deenie and the three Gilmores were already loading the dogs into their crates.

They'd brought all the dogs who were under the weight limit—the dachshund mixes Fred and Ginger, the papillon JoJo, the chihuahua Peanut, the one-eyed Jack Russell terrier Trapper, and one scruffy little black mutt of indeterminate breed named Daisy, who might be a tiny bit bigger than thirty pounds, but there wasn't a scale around, so they were fudging it. And even Daisy—who had an unfortunate tendency to pee when she was nervous—seemed to have found a fan club among the Summerland residents.

Though not as much of a fan club as Ally had.

She'd brought her camera and moved around the room, smiling and snapping shots of the seniors with the dogs. Ben watched her, admiring how effortlessly she charmed everyone—just as she'd charmed the whole town.

"Lilian, look at this little angel!" Mrs. Kowalski called, holding Peanut up for her companion's appreciation, and Ben took the opportunity to step back and let Peanut work his wiles on the women. The ancient chihuahua seemed to be the biggest hit with the residents, even though he was completely deaf. He had giant bug eyes and always seemed to be shivering, but he was fast on his way to becoming the Summerland Estates unofficial mascot.

Trapper was currently ensconced in the basket of Mrs. Walker's walker, making the rounds and being cooed over by one and all. Deenie was nearby showing another resident all the tricks she'd been teaching JoJo. Daisy had tucked herself close to Astrid's side but was peeking out from behind her leg and being coaxed onto the lap of another resident.

No one seemed to be paying him any attention, so

Ben took the opportunity to weave through the crowd toward Ally.

"Hey," he murmured as he came up beside her. "Getting some good shots?"

Ally flicked a glance at him without lowering her camera. "Yep."

Not exactly encouraging. But he didn't know if he'd have another chance. "I wanted to apologize about yesterday. That thing with the, you know."

Her cheeks flushed. "It's fine. We don't need to—"

"It's just there were some rumors going around, about the two of us. You and me."

Her lashes lowered. "I've heard them, too."

"I know mistletoe doesn't mean anything romantically, but I didn't want to fan the flames. I hope you weren't offended—"

"No, of course. That totally makes sense—"

"I have to think of Astrid—"

"Right. Absolutely." They both spoke quickly, the words folding over one another—until Rita Gilmore's face suddenly appeared between them.

"If anyone asks, Trapper is now Hemingway," she whispered urgently. "Bob Blake is *this* close to taking him, and he used to be a literature professor, so I made a little fib about *Hemingway*'s name to seal the deal. Those two are perfect for each other. Both so ornery you can barely stand them. How are you two doing? Any luck?"

Ally's face was still rosy and she wouldn't meet his eyes, but she spoke to her grandmother as if they hadn't just been having one of the most uncomfortable conversations of his life. "Peanut's a crowd favorite."

Mr. Gilmore approached, leading Fred and Ginger. "Any ideas about who might be good for the lovebirds?" he asked. "Everyone adores them, but no one seems willing to consider adopting two dogs."

Ally crouched down to cuddle the matched pair. "Maybe if they were each adopted by someone here they could visit one another regularly?" she suggested.

"Try Verna and Lyle Johnson," Mrs. Gilmore said suddenly, tugging Ally's arm and pointing to a couple across the room. They weren't crowding around the dogs like some of the other residents, just sitting along the sidelines, watching and holding hands. "Those two haven't spent a night apart in sixty-five years. If anyone understands why Fred and Ginger need to stay together, they will. You two both go."

Ben barely had time to react before a leash was thrust into his hands, and Rita Gilmore gave him a surprisingly hard shove in the middle of the back.

Ally frowned at her grandmother but seemed to decide against protesting. She met his eyes. "Shall we?"

"After you."

Ally crossed the room, excruciatingly aware of the man at her back and trying not to fuel the rumors already swirling around them. She hadn't expected him to come today, but she should have known Ben West never forgot a promise—even one as casually given as his offer to help with the pet fair had been.

She focused on the Johnsons as they approached,

determined to find the perfect home for Fred and Ginger. Just like the dachshunds, the Johnsons were a matched set, both on the short side with neat, close-cropped white hair and glasses, and each wore engraved name-tags pinned to their shirts, as most of the residents at the Estates did.

"Hello," Ally greeted them cheerfully. "I'm Ally. And this is Ben."

"We know, dear." Mrs. Johnson smiled. "You're Hal and Rita's granddaughter. And you are the councilman everyone can't stop talking about."

"I'm not sure that's a good thing." Ben shook the hand Mr. Johnson extended.

"Lyle and Verna Johnson," Mr. Johnson offered, before bending down to extend his fingers to Fred. "And who are these little hot dogs?"

"That's Fred, and this is Ginger," Ally explained. "They're a bonded pair. We think he's twelve and she's thirteen."

"Aren't they sweet?" Mrs. Johnson murmured.

"We weren't expecting dogs," Mr. Johnson explained. "We're just here for the Christmas concert. We always come early to get the good seats."

His wife patted his hand. "We're so glad you brought the dogs here, though. It's so good to see everyone enjoying them. What a treat."

Ben sat on the chair beside Mr. Gilmore, but Ally ignored the one opposite and sank down into a crouch, patting Ginger. "It was my grandmother's idea."

"Rita's such a doll. She fits right in here already."

Ally smiled at the common misconception. "I know

they're out here a lot, but my grandparents don't actually live here. They're just visiting friends."

"Of course, dear. I only mean when they move in next year."

"They aren't..." Ally trailed off, looking to Ben for help.

Conversations had a tendency to take unusual turns when there were multiple hearing aids involved, like a very creative game of telephone. She knew Mrs. Johnson was confused, but thankfully Ben caught her look and leaned forward, his next words loud and crisp. "Have you lived here long?"

"Fifteen years." Mr. Johnson sat up a little straighter, proudly. "We were among the original charter residents. Before they built all those patio homes."

"And you like it here?"

"We *love* it here." Ginger leaned against Mrs. Johnson's ankle, her tail rhythmically thwacking Ally on the shin, and Mrs. Johnson smiled. "Aren't you a sweetheart?" she asked Ginger, stroking her head. "I know there are some folks who don't adjust well—the ones who feel like they've been put here rather than made the choice to come on their own. Like poor Bob Blake. But for us, this was how we maintained our freedom, rather than giving it up. We have the help we need, and we don't have to be dependent on our children and grandchildren if we don't want to."

"It's a community," Mr. Johnson went on, seamlessly picking up his wife's thread. "The best thing about Summerland Estates—heck, about all of Pine Hollow—is the community. But you get out of it what you put into it. You have to reach out to your neighbors to feel them reaching out to you."

Ally frowned. She'd never thought of it that way. She figured you either fit or you didn't.

"You two make such a sweet couple."

The words jerked her back to attention.

"Oh, no." Ally protested. "We aren't . . ."

"I'm just helping with the dogs, until we can get them all adopted," Ben explained.

"Ah," Mr. Johnson smiled. "I remember those days. Verna worked in a soda shop, and I'd go in for malts every single day just to see her. I was lucky she didn't work out at the dairy or I'd've been out there bothering the cows."

Ally flushed, hurriedly changing the subject. "Is it true you haven't spent a night apart for sixty-five years?"

"Sixty-six. Not since the day we got married," Mrs. Johnson said proudly. "When Lyle had to go in for his heart surgery, they didn't want to let me in the recovery room—"

"But I just told them my heart wasn't going to beat right if she wasn't with me."

Mrs. Johnson met her husband's eyes. "None of the doctors had the heart to tell us no after that."

Ally's throat tightened, heart aching for that kind of connection. The kind her parents had, and her grandparents. That person who was there for you. No matter what.

She bent down, gently ruffling Ginger's ears. "That's like these two," she commented. "Initially when they came in, we tried to separate them, but they just cried and cried. They're always touching." Mrs. Johnson's hand was still tucked into her husband's, but Ally didn't look at it, trying not to lay it on too thick. "They like to burrow underneath covers, so we put a blanket over their dog bed, and half the time when I look in their run, there's just one long lump under there from the both of them."

"You said they were twelve?"

"And thirteen. She's a little older than he is."

"How old is that in people years?"

"They'd be about in their sixties—so retirement age. They don't act like puppies anymore, though they still love treats, and Fred has a chew toy he likes to carry around like a prize. He loves to bark when there's company coming, but we think his first owner must have worked with him on that, because if you tell him to hush he usually does. Ginger has some back problems sometimes, so she does best in a place with no stairs, and if she's allowed up on the furniture, it's best if she has a ramp rather than needing to jump up and down."

"We know all about bad backs." Mr. Johnson smiled. "Don't we, little lady?" He reached down to pet Ginger, moving slowly, and the little dog delicately licked his fingertips.

"And we don't have any stairs..." Mrs. Johnson commented, giving her husband a sideways look.

"Oh ho." Mr. Johnson chuckled. "It looks like we might be getting a ramp for our sofa before too long. Whatever makes my Verna smile like that." Mrs. Johnson smiled and he winked at them.

Ally looked at the paper-thin skin of their interlaced

hands—what must it be like to spend sixty-six years with someone and still want to hold their hand? To have that kind of connection? Those shared memories.

To be loved that much.

Ally forced her gaze away from the link, focusing on talking up Fred and Ginger until the members of the local choir started filtering in and it was time to take the dogs home so they didn't add their own chorus to the upcoming concert.

She caught Ben's eye, and they said their goodbyes to the Johnsons.

"I'll go round up Astrid," he offered, his hand brushing the small of her back as they crossed the room—though she might have imagined the touch it was so brief. Then he was gone, collecting his niece as she headed toward her grandparents and Deenie.

Gram took Fred and Ginger's leashes, freeing up Ally's hands so she could pick up the camera hanging around her neck. She felt more comfortable as soon as she had it in her hands. Turning at the door, she lifted the camera for one last shot of the room. Lyle and Verna Johnson leaned toward one another, smiling and whispering—and still holding hands.

"You coming?" Deenie spoke from beside her as she snapped the picture.

"Do you think that's still possible?" Ally asked as she lowered her camera, her eyes still on the Johnsons. "Sixty-six years with the same person?"

"If I live to be ninety-five and my husband doesn't kick it before then. Note to self: Add *longevity DNA* to my dating wish list."

Ally shook her head. "You know what I mean. Do you think that's even out there anymore in a world of apps and instant gratification? Have we lost the ability to stick it out for sixty-odd years and still want to hold hands at the end of the day? Are there still men out there who even want that?"

Deenie glanced over her shoulder pointedly. "One or two."

Ally followed her gaze.

Ben. Crouching down to put a tiny little dog sweater on Peanut and tuck him inside his coat against his chest so the chihuahua wouldn't get cold outside.

Everything inside of Ally went gooey, but she quashed the emotion. He'd made his feelings clear, even if it still felt like something was humming beneath the surface every time he looked at her. "It doesn't matter how much I want him," she whispered to Deenie, keeping her voice low so it wouldn't travel. "He has to want me back."

Ben looked up at that moment, catching her eye.

"Yeah…" Deenie grinned. "Somehow I don't think that's going to be a problem."

Ally wanted to argue. She wanted to point out that heated looks were no guarantee. He'd rejected her beneath the mistletoe. There might be something between them, but if he wasn't willing to take that risk, nothing was going to happen.

She wanted a partner. She wanted sixty-six years. It didn't matter that she could see it. Ben had to see it, too. And until he did, she was just holding her breath.

Chapter Twenty-Five

Astrid chattered about the dogs the entire way home, then immediately begged to go back to Furry Friends to play with the ones who hadn't come to the pet fair. Ben texted Ally to get her consent, then dropped Astrid off, not even getting out of the car.

His parents were arriving in two days and the washer repairman had rescheduled again. He was too busy to help out. At least that's the excuse he gave himself.

The next day, Astrid wheedled her way over to the shelter first thing, and he didn't see a trace of her until after dark—which at least gave him time to catch up on all the work he'd been falling behind on. He was starting to get a little jealous of Furry Friends by the time the front door opened Sunday evening, announcing her return.

And then he heard the other voice with hers in the foyer. He knew he should stay away, but Ben came out of the kitchen, catching Astrid and Ally just inside the door with their coats on.

"Still need homes for the puppies—" Ally broke off midsentence when she saw him. "Hey."

"Hey," he replied ingeniously.

"It was getting dark, so I wanted to walk Astrid home," Ally explained, fidgeting with her scarf.

Astrid glanced between him and Ally. "Aunt Elinor adopted Harry. She invited me to go over there and help her get settled. If it's okay?"

"Um..." Why couldn't he think of an answer? "Have you eaten dinner?"

"Not yet. Mr. Gilmore made us all these super awesome calzone things for lunch, so I'm barely hungry."

Ben jerked his chin toward the kitchen. "Eat something. Then we'll talk about whether you can go help your aunt." After he texted Elinor to make sure the help would be welcome.

Astrid flung off her jacket and boots, hurtling past him into the kitchen before popping her head back out again. "Thank you for today, Ally. It was the best day ever."

She disappeared into the kitchen, leaving Ben and Ally alone with the awkwardness in the air between them. "Best day ever?"

"She pretty much played with the dogs all day." Ally bit her lip, hesitating, discomfort thickening the air between them until she broke eye contact. "I should get going. My grandparents..."

"Right. Thanks for bringing Astrid back—if you text me when she needs to come home, I can come get her next time. I don't want to put you out."

"It's no trouble. I like walking her. And it's such a nice night."

"Do you want me to walk you...?"

"No. No, of course not. I know the way. Who knows what people would think, right?" She released a nervous laugh. "G'night, Ben."

"Good night, Ally."

She closed the door behind her and Ben slumped against the wall, groaning. "Nice, West. Very smooth."

"You should go over there."

Ben jumped a mile at the voice behind him. "Astrid! Make some noise."

"I *did*." She gave him her newly developing teen-age stare.

"Right. What did you need? Dinner?" He ushered her back into the kitchen, trying to get his brain to reboot properly.

"I don't see why you're pretending you don't like Ally," she complained as she followed.

Please let us not have this conversation right now. "Of course I like Ally. She's a good friend."

"Is it because of me? Because Isabelle left because of me?"

Ben slammed to a halt so fast he nearly gave himself whiplash. "Who told you that?" He faced her. "Why would you think that? Astrid, Isabelle leaving had nothing to do with you."

She shrugged, her mouth twisting to one side. "Except it kinda did. You guys were supposed to get married and then..."

"Hey." He bent down, grasping her narrow shoulders between his hands. She acted so grown up that it jarred him sometimes to realize she was still so small. "Isabelle leaving had to do with her and with me. It wasn't about you. You are the best thing in my life."

She met his eyes. "I heard you tell Ally you have to think of me—"

Shit. "That just means you come first, and I don't want to do stupid things that might affect you down the road."

"Being with Ally would be stupid?"

"She isn't staying in Pine Hollow, Astrid. I know you like her. I like her, too. But if we get too attached, it's only going to hurt that much more when she has to go back to her regular life." He gave her shoulders a gentle squeeze. "You and me. We do okay, right? I know I'm not always the best with the bake sales and the Instagrammable lunches, but we're good, right?"

She bit her lip. "Yeah."

"Good." He hugged her, releasing her and moving to the fridge to see what he could scrounge up for dinner, reiterating, "Ally and I, we're just friends."

"I guess."

He sent her a look over his shoulder. "What does that mean?" He wasn't sure he wanted an answer.

"Only that you seem awfully scared to be seen with her if you're just friends."

"It's this town. Trust me. Someday you'll understand."

"Uh-huh."

He shook his head. Was the female of the species born knowing how to cut the legs out of an argument with a dry *uh-huh*?

He threw together some sandwiches, texted Elinor to make sure she wanted Astrid's "help," and pulled on his jacket to walk his niece over to Elinor's cute little Craftsman bungalow with the big yard. When Elinor opened the door, Harry zoomed out—but after a speedy lap around the porch she raced back inside, the sound of her paws retreating into the depths of the house with Astrid hot on her heels.

"Shoes!" Ben called after her, cringing as she trailed snow down the hall. "Sorry."

"I'll get her to clean it up," Elinor assured him. "I'm still working on getting Harry to stop long enough for me to wipe her paws, so my floors are already a disaster."

"Thanks for letting her come over. She was so excited."

"That is one dog-crazy kid. You have more willpower than I do—I would have caved and let her have one months ago."

Ben stiffened, bracing himself against the judgment, and Elinor, who never missed anything, noticed.

She stepped out onto the porch, pulling the door closed so Astrid wouldn't hear. "Ben, I didn't mean—"

"No, you're right. She should have a dog. And a house with a yard and a tire swing. Katie had it all planned out. Did you know she had a vision board with all their ideas? The two-year plan. Everything Astrid should have by now."

She grimaced. "Katie showed me the vision board, but no one expects you—"

"To be able to do what Katie did? Because she was Supermom and I'm Ebenezer?"

Elinor snorted. "Katie never thought of herself as Supermom."

"We all know she was amazing—"

"She was *human*," Elinor insisted. "You know they started that two-year plan when they moved into the house, right? When Katie was still pregnant with Astrid? She used to joke that it was a rolling two years."

Ben frowned, shaking his head. That couldn't be right.

"She wasn't perfect. She was making it up as she went along, just like the rest of us. Do you know she used to call me crying because she was afraid she was the worst mom ever?"

Ben jerked, the words a shock to his system. "What? Why would she...?"

"Did you know Astrid got stitches when she was two? She tripped over something Katie had left on the floor and took a header into the fireplace. I think Katie cried harder than Astrid. She was so sure it was all her fault."

Ben shook his head. "She never told me that."

"Why would she? She was your big sister. She always wanted to live up to your idea of her. But she didn't have to be perfect to be a good parent, and neither do you. You don't have to be on the PTA board or the most dedicated member of the town council to honor her memory. And you don't need a house with a yard to prove you were the right person to raise Astrid."

Ben eyed Elinor's house with its big fenced yard. "Did you ever want to be the one to raise her?"

"Of course I did." Elinor smiled, though her eyes were sad. "But you were Katie's choice, and I knew Astrid would be surrounded by love regardless of which one of us had her. Though you could let her sleep over here from time to time. I have a very nice guest room."

It wasn't the first time Elinor had offered—and he'd always said no before. He'd always thought she was saying she didn't think he could handle being the primary parent, but now he wondered if he'd been so busy trying to prove he was the best one for Astrid that he hadn't done what was best for Astrid.

"We didn't bring pajamas or a toothbrush, but if you wanted she could stay tonight," he offered on impulse.

"Yeah?" Elinor grinned, the sadness leaving her eyes. "That would be great. I have some stuff she can borrow."

"She'll probably want to be over here all the time now that you have a dog."

Elinor shivered, reaching for the door. "I should probably get in there before Dora starts bouncing off the walls."

"Dora?"

"Dora the Explorer. I'm trying it out. Ally says she's smart enough that she'll probably learn any name I throw at her, but I haven't made up my mind yet."

At the mention of Ally, Ben took a step back. "I'll let you get to it. G'night, Elinor."

"G'night. And Ben...thanks."

He nodded, though he was the one who should probably be thanking her. He shoved his hands deeper into his pockets and ducked his head against the cold as he started down her front walk.

Paul and Katie's house was abnormally quiet when he let himself in and paused in the foyer, silently cataloguing all the projects he'd meant to get to. The same ones Katie had never finished.

The uneven stair. The break in the flooring. The out-dated kitchen.

Maybe he wasn't failing her quite as much as he'd thought. He was starting to convince himself he was do-ing all right—until he stepped into the mudroom and saw the broken washer. Irritation flashed through him, not just at the laundry machine, at the whole damn town.

He was so sick of living his life under the judgmental eyes of every single person in Pine Hollow. Constantly worrying if he was doing the right thing. Why should he have to avoid Ally so people wouldn't gossip? Why shouldn't he be able to walk her home without everyone in town speculating about them?

He was so freaking *tired* of not being able to do anything just for himself.

Ten minutes later the car was loaded, and five minutes after that he pulled into the Gilmores' driveway, realiz-ing after the fact that maybe he should have called first, but he was here now.

It was barely past seven, but the house was completely dark, illuminated only by the twinkle lights wrapping the porch railing. The floodlight in front of the kennel was still on. Ben headed that direction, pulling out his phone to belatedly text Ally. He bent over his phone as he walked, trying to figure out how to explain the impulse visit, when a voice spoke behind him.

"Ben. Is everything okay?"

Ben spun to face Ally as she and her Saint Bernard tromped toward him through the snow at the edge of the driveway. "Yeah. Sorry. It just occurred to me I should have called."

"It's fine. I was just walking Colby. My grandparents are up at the Estates for some Christmas party. You all right? Where's Astrid?"

"She's at Elinor's. Helping Harry get settled in. I may never see her again."

"She does love dogs." Ally smiled softly as she and Colby came to a halt a few feet away from him. A safe distance. An unnatural distance.

He'd put that distance between them.

He wanted to be friends again, but he felt like he'd screwed everything up, overreacting to the mistletoe thing. Reaching for some way to put them back on friendly ground, Ben glanced over his shoulder at the barn. "You still need help with those lights?"

Her eyebrows arched skeptically high when he looked back at her. "You sure you want people seeing your car parked in front of my house?"

He shrugged, thrusting his hands into his pockets. "They're gonna gossip either way." And he was tired of feeling like he had something to prove. He never felt that here.

She glanced at his car, spotting the row of overflowing laundry baskets in the back seat. "You're only here because that washer repairman never showed up, aren't you?"

"Maybe," he acknowledged lightly, before sobering and answering honestly. "Or maybe I just miss the company."

A slow smile spread across Ally's face and she shook her head. "All right, Ebenezer. Let's get your first load in, then I'll show you where the lights are."

Chapter Twenty-Six

"D id you test any of these?"

Ally grimaced, handing over yet another dud strand of lights to be tossed into the how-the-heck-do-we-recycle-these box and reaching for the next candidate. She and Ben sat side by side on the floor in the living room, trying to find enough working lights to decorate the barn, while Ben's laundry rumbled away in the washer.

After two days of avoidance and awkwardness, they were safely back in the Friend Zone, and Ally wanted to stay there. She'd missed being able to talk to him. It was comfortable again, going through the lights together. Unfortunately, they only had one working strand so far—and even that one flickered ominously.

"Gramps says these are the ones he always used, but I'm not sure he's actually put any lights up on the barn in the last few years."

"Try the last decade." Ben held up a cord, eyeing the

ancient wiring. "How badly does your grandmother want lights on the barn?"

"It's hard to tell," Ally admitted, plugging the next contender into the power strip. "She's so enthusiastic about everything that sometimes the degrees of enthusiasm get lost in translation. But this year she seems to be really going all out for Christmas." The lights lit—then made a sparking, popping noise that had both Ally and Ben racing to unplug them.

"Enthusiastic enough that we want to risk electrocution?" he asked, holding up a smoking cord.

"Probably best not to burn down the house," she acknowledged.

"Or the barn," Ben added, winding up the lights to toss them in the failure box.

"Not with the dogs inside. Though if we had somewhere to put them, I might risk it," she joked. "We could use the insurance money. Right now I'd try just about anything to keep this place open."

He reached for the next tangled strand. "I thought you'd be getting excited about going back to New York. With so many of the dogs finding homes, you can get back to your life without worrying about the shelter."

Ally shrugged, her eyes on the knot in her hands. "I'm not sure I am going back."

His hands stilled on the lights. "You aren't?"

"I don't know. Everyone talks about my life in New York like it was glamorous and perfect, like I've made this huge sacrifice, but part of me was already looking for a reason to leave. That was why I didn't have another lease lined up."

Ben frowned, shaking his head. "I thought you wanted to go back. You said you miss it…"

"I said I miss feeling like I know what I'm doing. I didn't know the first thing about running the shelter when I came out here, but now…I don't know. I feel like I'm getting the hang of it. Right in time for us to close."

He stared at her, the lights in his hands forgotten. "I thought you loved being a photographer."

"I do, but it's…" She fidgeted with the lights, not meeting his eyes. "It's lonely. My work is all freelance. I'm traveling all the time. I don't see the same people every day. Even the ones I work with most regularly, we may only see each other every few months. I applied for a job with this company with a reputation as one of the best places to work in the city—Spectrum, where the work is more stable and I'd be part of a team—but I haven't even gotten an interview."

"Maybe they just haven't called you yet."

"Maybe." She flicked a glance at him. "I just haven't made any connections there, you know? I feel like I've been looking for this thing ever since my parents died. Like I'm homesick, but I don't have a home to go back to. It wasn't just the house. My parents were the people who knew me best. *That* was home. And it was hard for my friends to understand, hard to connect with my peers when it felt like I was dealing with this massive thing that was too big for any of them to handle. So I kind of retreated. Photography was the only thing that felt right. And I was good. I worked through holidays and landed an amazing internship that led to jobs I never dreamed I would get. I was so busy chasing success it took me a while to realize how alone I'd made myself."

Ben was silent for a moment, then he nodded. "I did that, too. Not for the same reasons."

Ally frowned, studying his face. "You did?"

"Right after college. I went to work for a tech start-up in Silicon Valley."

"Really?"

"Don't sound so surprised. I wasn't always Pine Hollow's most notorious councilman. My sister and I both went out of state for college, and then my parents moved to Arizona. I never expected to come back here. When I got that job, I thought that was it. That was my life. But then Katie and Paul moved up here. They wanted their kids to grow up like we had, with that community. A couple of years after Astrid was born, I came to visit. Just randomly. Using up a bunch of vacation I'd built up. I'd been working insane hours, and I was totally burned out. I think I slept for the first two days I was here, but then I started talking to Katie, playing with Astrid. I reconnected with Connor and Levi. And I realized all I had was work. And that wasn't what I wanted."

"Exactly." Ally nodded, her eyes locked on his. "I don't even know what I would do if I stayed here, especially with the shelter closing, but right now I can't imagine going back to New York. I never really built a life there. The one time I tried to...I was dating this guy—Matthew. Smart, successful, checked all the boxes. But I think I was so scared of being alone I latched on to the first halfway decent guy I found and bent over backward trying to make things work with him. It took me way longer than I should probably admit to realize we wanted completely different things. I just really *wanted* to want the things he wanted. Does that make sense? He loved New York. He wanted penthouses and park views, and I told myself I wanted that too, but whenever I closed my eyes and dreamed about the future I saw porch swings and a big old dog lying on my feet."

Colby thumped his tail in his sleep, as if he knew he'd been mentioned, and she leaned over to rub his head. "And then I realized the other thing missing from all my future visions was Matthew. He never belonged on that front porch. I don't think he even knew I wanted that. I never told him. I never disagreed with him. Which meant every time we had an argument, I would give in because I didn't want him to leave. The only thing I ever really fought him on was Colby. He didn't want a dog, and I wasn't willing to give him up. I think it surprised him when I put my foot down. He was always telling me he loved me and that I was exactly what he'd been looking for—his unicorn—but I was only that person because I always let him win. And that's what it felt like—winning and losing. Not like we were a team. Not like we were both trying to get to the same goal. My grandparents—they're partners, you know? It doesn't matter how different they are, they're best friends and they want each other's happiness as much as their own. That's what I want."

She looked up and caught him watching her, her gaze snagging on his winter-blue one as her heartbeat suddenly accelerated.

Ben met Ally's eyes, trying to remember all the reasons he'd thought getting involved with her was a bad idea and coming up with nothing.

"Yeah, I, uh, I didn't have that, either," he admitted when the silence stretched too long. "With my ex." He didn't talk about Isabelle—but the usual rules didn't seem to apply with Ally. "I felt like she was just one more thing I had to manage." He grimaced. "Astrid asked me today if Isabelle leaving was her fault."

Ally winced. "Ouch."

"Exactly. It wasn't. I mean the timing lined up, and maybe in a way everything that happened with Paul and Katie and having Astrid suddenly be the most important thing in my life, maybe that all put things with Isabelle in harsh perspective. I don't know, I just—it's like you said, we weren't a team. It's good it ended when it did."

"And you haven't dated anyone since?"

"No. I've been so overwhelmed—" He cringed. "Don't tell anyone that. I don't want people to think—"

"You're essentially a single dad. It's okay to ask for help."

"I've never been good at that. And now I just—I don't want to give anyone a reason to think I'm not fit to take care of Astrid. I used to have these dreams, these recurring nightmares that a social worker with a clipboard would show up at our door and tell me I'd officially failed at parenting and they were confiscating her."

"Ben." Ally put a hand on his arm, her palm warm through his sweater. "You're a great uncle. A great *dad*. But you're allowed to ask for help. You don't have to do it all yourself."

"I know," he insisted, but the words rang false. "Elinor said this thing today about how Katie wasn't perfect either, but I want to be perfect for her. Everything she dreamed of for Astrid, I want to be able to give her. They had this two-year plan—which I guess was actually a ten-year plan, but I still feel like I'm letting Katie down because I haven't managed to fix up the house like she dreamed and move Astrid out to a big place with a lot of land where she can have a dog."

Ally's hand still rested on his arm and she squeezed gently. "You know you don't have to live Katie's and Paul's lives just because they can't."

His shoulders tensed. "I'm not trying to live their lives." Even if he had moved into their house. And taken over Paul's town council seat. And Katie's position with the PTA.

"I know, but…all the photos in your house are of them. It's like you don't even live there."

"I'm just busy. I haven't had a lot of time to get new photos taken." He heard the defensiveness in his own voice. Because she was right. It wasn't his place. He'd moved into the guest room, not the master. He'd put the Christmas tree up in exactly the same place they'd had it—and told himself it was because he wanted to hold on to their traditions for Astrid.

"Of course." Ally dropped her hand, letting him off the hook. "I know how that is."

He couldn't meet her eyes, his gaze catching on the framed prints above the mantel—not the typical family photos, but gorgeous cityscapes of New York. Central Park. The Brooklyn Bridge. Even the candid family photos that were scattered around the room were classy, black and white and elegant. He jerked his chin at the mantel. "Did you take those?"

Ally followed his gaze, a small smile tipping one side of her mouth. "Yeah. Back when I first moved to the city. I used to go for these long walks with my camera, trying to see *everything*. The world made more sense through my lens."

He heard the wistfulness in her voice. Did she really think she didn't miss it?

"You sure you don't want to go back?"

"I don't know," she admitted. "I don't have a career here. But I want to be here for my grandparents. And I feel like I'm closer to that porch-swing vision of the future here than I would be in the city."

"Maybe. Or maybe your city guy would have wanted the front porch someday. I never thought I would want the things I want now. People change."

"When they suddenly become guardians to wonderful little girls?"

"Or just when they decide they want to. People always act like I gave up my big dreams to move back here, but I just changed them." When he realized Ally was watching him, he shrugged and turned his attention back to the lights in his hands. "Maybe your guy would have changed, too."

"Maybe," she acknowledged. "Or maybe the front porch guy is already here."

He met her eyes and the moment seemed to stretch, the air suddenly thick. Her dark eyes seemed to see right through him. He'd been so certain she was leaving. If she wasn't...

Bzzzzzz.

The washing machine's timer sounded like an alarm clock, buzzing loudly to shatter the moment.

Ally jolted away, averting her face.

"Time to change loads," she said, too brightly, scrambling to her feet.

Ben was slower to follow. "What about the lights?"

"I think they're officially a lost cause. I'll tell Gram we didn't have enough working strands." She wouldn't look at him. "I should go check on the dogs. Unless you need help with the laundry?"

"No. No, I've got it. Thanks."

"Anytime," she chirped, grabbing her coat and bolting toward the door.

Chapter Twenty-Seven

She'd nearly kissed him.

Right after she'd told him her entire life story and what she wanted most in the world.

Ally jogged across the driveway, grateful for the bracing wake-up call of the cold. She was failing miserably at this whole keeping-it-friendly business. Everything had been going so well. They'd been chatting, sorting lights, and then suddenly she'd been telling him things she'd never told anyone. It was so easy to be honest with him. She didn't know where the trust had come from, but she did trust him, with her innermost secrets apparently.

And then he'd looked at her and it felt like the world went into slow motion, like there was something linking her to him and tugging the two of them closer together. Like the connection they'd built was pulling them toward a kiss.

God, she'd wanted to kiss him—but he'd said he didn't want that. He'd said he had to think of Astrid. Of course, Astrid wasn't here, but still.

Was it different now?

The dogs barked greetings as she entered the kennels, the sound thinner now with fewer dogs than had been there a week ago. There were still plenty to adopt, but the Twelve Dogs of Christmas plan was working, and she was happy about that, happy for the forever homes, though she kind of missed Jelly's exuberance and Harry's zoomies and even Biscuit's attempts to redecorate.

She checked on the puppies and then moved through the kennel, taking the time to give each dog the attention they craved. She was in Partridge's pen, the bulldog sprawled on his back with all four legs splayed for a belly rub, when the dogs began barking again, announcing Ben's arrival.

"Ally?"

"Back here," Ally called.

Partridge immediately abandoned her belly rubs, rolling to his feet and waddling to his dog bed to collect his favorite toy and bring it as an offering to his deity. When Ben appeared in the open door to his run, Partridge was ready with the slightly-the-worse-for-drool stuffed purple monkey. The squeaker had long since stopped working inside, but Partridge didn't seem to mind. He dropped the soggy monkey on Ben's feet.

"Charming." Ben gingerly nudged the toy aside.

"That's true love right there, bringing you his favorite toy."

"He loves everybody," Ben argued, but he crouched down, rubbing Partridge's fur rolls.

"True," Ally agreed as she refilled his water dish and tidied up his run. "I'm amazed he hasn't been adopted.

He's always been my favorite. A big ole droopy love machine. He's Astrid's favorite, too."

Ben's arched brow said he wasn't swayed. "Why don't you adopt him yourself?"

"It's a slippery slope. I promised myself I wouldn't try to save them all myself. It's way too easy to end up the crazy dog lady."

He ruffled Partridge's ears. "It must be tempting."

"You have no idea. I already had one foster fail with Colby—he was supposed to be temporary, but I fell in love. I'm pretty sure that's what Astrid is hoping for— that if she gets you to spend enough time around the dogs you won't be able to resist."

"Yeah, I figured that much out. But she's going to be unpleasantly surprised. I'm a master at resisting temptation."

The words hung in the air between them, tangled up with double meanings.

Ally cleared her throat, her face flaming. "Did you get the next load of laundry started?"

"Yes. Thank you. My parents will have clean sheets to sleep on after all."

His parents. Safe subject. "When do they get in?"

"Tomorrow afternoon."

"Astrid must be excited."

"She is."

Ally met his eyes at the distinct lack of enthusiasm in his voice. "But you aren't?"

"I am. Or I would be if I wasn't two weeks behind on Christmas." Ben rubbed at his eyebrow. "I hate the pressure of trying to find something everyone will like."

"You know, no one is going to punish you for not getting the perfect gift. The holidays shouldn't be stressful."

He laughed humorlessly. "And yet they always are." She stepped out of Partridge's pen, heading toward Fred and Ginger's, and Ben followed. "I just want everything to be perfect. So Astrid doesn't feel like she's missing out on anything. I still have no idea what I'm going to get her for Christmas. She's only asked for one thing."

"You could always get her that one thing," Ally suggested cautiously.

She opened the gate, and Ben knelt beside her, extending his fingers to Fred and Ginger. "They're still here."

"The Johnsons are picking them up tomorrow. And we got an application for Daisy. Hopefully this one sticks."

"Successful pet fair."

"Very." She studied him, returning to their earlier subject. "Astrid's really good with the dogs, Ben. I think she'd take really good care of one."

"I know she would. I just—we don't have a yard. The goal was to fix up the house, sell it, move to a bigger one with a yard, and *then* get a dog. I'm just not there yet. But ever since her birthday, it's like dogs are all she can think about."

"It makes sense." Ally rolled Fred's ball, sending him scampering after it. "Since her parents told her she could have one when she turned ten."

Ben's hands went still on Ginger's ears. "What did you say?"

Ally looked up, the stunned expression on Ben's face freezing her heart in her chest. "She didn't tell you. Oh, Ben, I'm sorry..."

"Katie and Paul told her she could have a dog?"

"When she turned ten. Apparently that was when they thought she'd be old enough to take care of one."

Ben sank from his crouch to sit on the floor. Sensing his distress, Ginger climbed into his lap, giving his fingers little licks of comfort. "Why didn't she say something? Did she think she couldn't tell me?"

"She probably didn't want to upset you." *So I did that with my big mouth.*

"I don't want her to think she can't talk to me about Katie and Paul. She's already missing out on so much—"

"Ben." Ally knee-walked across the space separating them to kneel at his side. "Something is always going to be missing at Christmas because her parents aren't here, but that doesn't mean she isn't happy. That doesn't mean you aren't doing an amazing job. Part of her will always be sad they're gone—of course, she's sad—but she loves you. And I think in some ways she tries to protect you as much as you try to protect her. She's a great kid."

"She is." He looked over at her, meeting her eyes from a distance of inches.

For the second time that night, the weight in the air seemed to grow heavy with the things they'd said. And those they hadn't. "Thank you," he murmured. "Since you've been here..."

"I didn't do any..." The protest trailed off when his gaze dropped to her lips.

"You did. You do." His pupils seemed to have doubled in size in the low light of the barn.

They were just friends, of course they were, but tonight it felt like they'd been dancing on a tightrope, never more than an inch away from falling into a kiss. If she could just will it to happen—

Ben leaned closer and her focus narrowed to his lips and the inch separating them from hers. He moved slowly, slow enough for her to stop him—but that was the last thing she wanted to do. One large hand cupped her jaw and her eyelids fell shut a fraction of a second before his lips brushed hers.

She'd wondered if the Friend Zone thing was because they had no chemistry. If she would feel nothing when he kissed her.

Turned out, chemistry was *not* a problem.

After the first questioning touch, Ben made a sound low in his throat and tilted his head, deepening the kiss. Ally leaned into him, only the pressure of his lips and her grip on his lapel keeping her from falling over. His beard was soft against her skin, and every cell of her body hummed to life. He slipped one arm around her—

And tiny paws scrambled over her lap, rough little tongues lapping at her hand where it rested on his arm.

They broke apart, a slight smile curving Ben's lips as a pair of dachshunds climbed all over them. Ally grinned, that bubbly helium feeling back.

"We should probably..." She tilted her head toward the house.

"Good idea." Ben climbed to his feet, offering his hand to help her up. As she came to her feet, Maximus groaned in the next run, but Ally didn't look away from Ben—

Until a noxious odor wafted in their direction.

"Ugh." Ally cringed, trying not to breathe. *"Maximus."*

"Wow." Ben held one hand over his nose and mouth.

The moment officially dead, Ally hurried toward the pen door so they could escape, her eyes watering. "The Force is strong with that one."

"No interest for the big guy yet?" Ben asked through his hand as they evacuated from the smell zone—and he clasped her hand in his.

Ally tried not to float right off the ground. *Be cool, Gilmore.*

"Not yet. Though maybe someone who saw his Twelve Dogs feature will still decide to come in."

"It seems to be working." He nodded toward one of the empty runs as they passed it.

"It is. Though we have a ways to go. And I still don't know what I'm going to do with Dolce and her puppies. Gram is trying to convince Gramps to keep Dolce, but we still have to find homes for the pups once they're weaned."

"How many were there?"

"Astrid didn't tell you? She's obsessed with them, especially little Lulu. There are four—three boys, one girl. All with the most adorable little squishy faces. Kimber claimed one of the boys, but I need to add the others to the website and get them up on Petfinder. Especially since I think we're pretty much out of Pine Hollow Christmas events we can crash with the dogs to try to convince people to adopt them."

They'd reached the front of the barn, and Ben dropped

Ally's hand so she could slip on the coat she'd left on a hook there.

"There's always the pageant," he commented as he shrugged into his own jacket.

"The what?"

"The holiday pageant on Christmas Eve. Don't tell me you've never gone with your grandparents?"

"I can't say I have."

"It's sort of a nontraditional thing," he explained. "Half town talent show, half Christmas story, culminating with a very bizarre nativity scene. Every year it gets a little stranger—I can't imagine adding dogs to the mix would raise many eyebrows. Let me talk to the committee and see if they'd be willing to include the dogs who haven't been adopted yet."

"That'd be great."

The *Jaws* theme music played from Ben's pocket, and he groaned, reaching for his phone. "Sorry. I'd silence it, but I want Astrid to be able to reach me."

"The *Jaws* music is your ringtone?"

"Actually that's my email alert for the council email."

"Seriously?"

"Can you think of a better signal of doom? 'The Imperial March' from Star Wars is too long."

She eyed him as she lowered the lights in the kennel, the dogs curled up in their beds. "You know, I'm not sure you hate the council stuff as much as you want everyone to think."

"Oh no, I hate it more."

"No…" Ally shook her head. "You could have given up your seat, but you never did."

"Too stubborn for my own good." He held the door open for her, and she paused, shaking her head.

"Nope. I think you like helping people. I think you, Ebenezer, are a closet softie. People talk in this town, you know. I've heard about some of the initiatives you put through. Programs at the community center..."

"It can't all be closing shelters and crushing dreams."

She laughed, stepping out in the wintry softness of the night, and turned to face him, hooking one finger into the lapel of his coat. "You can pretend to be as curmudgeonly as you want. I see you, Ben West."

He met her eyes—and that thing came alive again, that spark that always seemed to be lingering between them, waiting to be ignited. "I see you, too."

The cold night air made her feel every inch of her skin as her face heated. His gaze had dropped to her lips again, but she kept her eyes on his, willing him to close the distance. His chin lowered, his eyes going heavy-lidded.

Headlights panned across them. Ben stepped hastily back, and Ally resisted the urge to groan aloud. "That'll be my grandparents."

At least they hadn't caught them kissing in the driveway. This thing between her and Ben, whatever it was, felt too fragile to withstand the gauntlet of the Pine Hollow gossip mill.

The car continued up the driveway, and moments later Gram and Gramps clambered out of the Subaru.

"Ben!" Gram yelled cheerfully. "We weren't expecting to see you here tonight!"

"His washer's on the fritz, so I told him he could use

ours," Ally called as her grandparents crunched across the snowy gravel.

"Of course he can." Gramps clapped him on the shoulder as they met at the base of the porch steps, Ben keeping a careful distance from her, though her grandparents seemed oblivious to the lingering tension in the air. "Our washer is your washer. You want some fruitcake? Rita won a fruitcake, and I can't stand the stuff."

Gramps ushered Ben into the house, and Gram followed, waving a hand for Ally. "Hurry up, Ally girl. It's cold out here."

It was nearly two hours later when Ally helped Ben carry baskets full of clean, folded laundry out to his car. Her grandparents had gone up to bed a while ago—after stuffing them both with fruitcake—but neither she nor Ben had said a word about the kiss, even when it was just the two of them, folding laundry side by side, the distance between them seeming to grow larger by the second, the silence an oppressive weight.

He regretted it. The kiss. She could feel the remorse radiating from him.

She set the last basket beside the others in the back of Ben's car and stepped back, wrapping her arms around herself. She hadn't worn a coat, so at least she could pretend the defensive posture was from cold and not dread. "So…"

Ben met her eyes. "So."

She liked him. She really liked him. But if he

regretted kissing her, if it had been an impulse brought on by loneliness . . . she understood that. She really hoped it wasn't the case, but he'd been so quiet . . .

"I can't . . ." Ben's voice was low even though they were alone in the middle of the driveway. "I don't think I realized how hard Astrid took it when Isabelle left. I didn't expect her to blame herself. And I . . ."

He stopped to clear his throat, and Ally waited, dreading what she knew was coming.

"I need to be careful. She's already so attached to you. This can't be . . . I like you, Ally, but, um . . ."

But you regret it. "I understand. You don't want—"

"Any misunderstandings. Exactly. We have to be on the same page. The way this town gossips . . . and you aren't even sure you're staying. I just think it's best if no one knows that we . . . and if we don't . . ."

"Right. Of course."

Ben winced. "I'm really sorry. I shouldn't have—"

"No. Don't be silly. I get it." She didn't like it. But she understood. He was trying to do the right thing for Astrid, just like he always did. And she couldn't promise that Astrid would never be hurt if they started openly dating. Not when everything seemed so uncertain. Not when she didn't even know what she would do when the shelter closed.

But a little voice inside her whispered that if he had wanted her enough it wouldn't have mattered. If he had wanted to take a flying leap with her, she would have done it and not worried about the consequences. She would have rushed in with her heart open wide, but he didn't feel it. A person couldn't fall in love alone.

"Friends?" He opened his arms.

"Of course." She hugged him, not squeezing too tight, trying not to breathe in his scent. Friendly.

Friends wasn't so bad. She liked Ben, and he liked her. That was something, even if her chest ached.

Friends was fine.

Chapter Twenty-Eight

B en spent the next twenty-four hours assuring himself that he'd made the right decision. He'd talked to Ally. They'd firmly positioned themselves back in the Friend Zone. Which was exactly where they needed to be.

That afternoon, he drove Astrid up to the airport in Burlington to pick up his parents, trying—and failing—to steer the conversation away from the shelter.

Snow began to fall as they were driving back, giving them a convenient excuse for holing up inside for the rest of the night and watching the puffy white flakes cover the town. Over his dad's pancakes in the morning, Astrid chattered incessantly to her grandparents about the shelter and Ally, until his parents were both stealing glances at him and asking when they could all go over to Furry Friends. The snowfall had continued overnight, and there was a good fourteen inches on everything, so Ben escaped outside to shovel the driveway and clear his head.

He wanted to text Ally. To commiserate with her

about the frustrations of family and the fact that the entire freaking town was speculating about them—but he couldn't do that.

It wasn't that he regretted the kiss. He just didn't want anything getting blown out of proportion, and the second the town found out about them, it would've been like being strapped to a freight train, completely out of their control. He had to think of Astrid, didn't he? Ally wasn't sure she was staying, and this was the smart move— so why did the decision to keep his distance bother him so much?

Shoveling the driveway and the sidewalk in front of his house and Mrs. Fincher's place didn't take long. He was nearly done when his phone rang.

Ben stabbed his shovel into the snow so it stayed upright, stripped off his gloves, and rushed to unzip his jacket to get to the inner pocket before the phone stopped ringing. He didn't realize he was expecting to see Ally's name on the caller ID until he saw Deenie's instead.

Frowning, he connected the call before it could go to voice mail. "Hello?"

"Does the town have a snowblower?"

Ben snorted. "Hello to you, too."

Deenie's sigh was dramatic. "Hello. Merry Christmas. Yada yada. Does the town have a snowblower or not?"

"We do. For the sidewalks and the square—the areas the plows can't go."

"Can you send them over to Furry Friends? Ally's snowed in."

Ben frowned, leaning against the shovel handle. "They

have set routes, and with all the snow, it'll take them at least a day to finish them. What's wrong with Ally's snowblower?"

"Apparently it died," Deenie said. "I called this morning to see what time they were opening, and she said she wasn't sure they were today because the snowblower was busted and all the plow companies were booked, so she was just going to hunker down and watch *It's a Wonderful Life* and eat fruitcake until tomorrow when someone can dig them out, but it's only a few days till Christmas, which sounds like peak adoption time to me, and so I thought maybe the town could help them."

Ben frowned. He couldn't commandeer the town snowblowers, and shoveling the Gilmores' driveway was out of the question. Paul and Katie's driveway was barely long enough to fit his car, easily managed with a scoop shovel, but the Gilmores' stretched half the length of a football field at least.

They'd said they were just friends—but friends helped each other out, didn't they?

"I don't have a snowblower, but I know someone who does. Let me get back to you."

Deenie promised to keep working the problem from her end, and Ben pocketed his phone.

He put the shovel in the tiny garage, which was so cluttered with yard equipment there was no room for his car, and jogged to the front door, dusting the snow off his gloves. A plan rolled around in his head, taking shape as he moved. A *friendly* plan. Something he would do for anyone he knew who was snowed in.

Ben shoved open the front door, knocking his boots against the doorframe to shake off the snow but not stopping to take them off.

His mother appeared in the doorway to the kitchen. "That was quick. Astrid was just telling us about the brownies you made for the Christmas fair. We were thinking we might whip up a batch today."

"Great idea. Are you guys good with her for a while? I need to run take care of something."

His mother blinked in surprise. "Of course. We're happy to watch her."

"Great. Thanks. Have fun." He grabbed his keys and was out the door again before his mother could close her mouth, jogging toward his car.

Ben didn't bother ringing the bell. He knew the way. He let himself into the massive glass foyer of the house, walking through the echoing quiet of the first floor to the office at the back, where he knew he would find his target hunched over his computer.

"You know, some people take time off around the holidays," he commented, leaning against the doorjamb.

"Jesus!" Connor spun, half launching himself out of the chair. "What the hell?"

Ben smiled, just as amused to startle the shit out of Connor as he had been when he and Levi and Mac started doing it to distract Connor when he was moping after Monica left. "If you had a dog, people couldn't sneak up on you."

"Most people knock." Connor stood, gripping the back of his chair. "What are you doing here?"

"You said I could borrow your snowblower whenever I wanted."

"Yeah, but I didn't think you'd actually take me up on it. You never ask anyone for anything."

Ben shoved away from the door frame. "I don't have to borrow it. I can go…"

"No. I'll get you the keys." Connor was already moving past him toward the kitchen, and Ben quickly texted Deenie. "Why do you need a snowblower? Your driveway's microscopic. Is it for some town thing?"

"Something like that." At Connor's look, he pocketed his phone and explained. "Ally's is busted, so I'm going to head over and dig her out."

Connor froze with the snowblower key in his hand. "Ally, huh?"

"Don't start. I'm being neighborly."

"You know, I'm feeling incredibly neighborly. I should help, too. Take some time off for the holiday. Like you were saying. 'Tis the season to check out this shelter chick everyone's been talking about."

"Or you could stay out of it."

"Where's the fun in that?"

"If you come to the shelter, I'm siccing the Gilmores on you. You'll end up walking out with a dog."

Connor rolled his eyes. "You aren't going to let this dog thing go, are you?"

"It's hard to give up an idea when you're as right as I am." He'd been only half joking about Connor needing a dog before. They didn't talk about it, but Connor had been all work and no sense of humor since Monica left. He spent entirely too much time in that home office, and right now Ben would try anything to get him back in the land of the living—even a dog.

Connor snorted and tossed him the snowblower key. "I'm only going to see this girl you're definitely not going all sappy for."

"If you say so." His phone buzzed, and he pulled it out to check Deenie's exclamation point–filled reply. He grinned, spinning the key ring on his finger as he eyed Connor. "Do you still have that ladder?"

Connor arched a brow. "What kind of driveway is this?"

"Why stop at a driveway?"

Chapter Twenty-Nine

George Bailey raced through Bedford Falls, shouting the names of his loved ones as Gramps snored on the recliner with Copper curled up in his lap. Gram hummed to herself, darting in and out of the room like a whirling dervish, a woman on some unknown Christmas mission. Ally sat on the floor, wrapping the present she'd picked up for Deenie, watching television and listening to Colby's snores harmonizing with her grandfather's. It wasn't such a bad way to spend a December afternoon.

Out in the kennels, the dogs barked. Colby's snore cut off, and he lifted his massive head before yawning hugely and flopping back onto his dog bed with a sigh. Gramps shifted in his recliner, grunting softly and scratching Copper's belly to cover the fact that he'd been sleeping through the movie. *It's a Wonderful Life* went to commercial, but out in the kennels, the barking only became more frantic.

"What are they going on about?" Ally muttered, climbing to her feet to go investigate.

"Probably a moose," Gramps commented without stirring from his recliner as she passed.

"Probably," she agreed.

It sounded like the dogs greeting some new arrival to the shelter, but there was over a foot of fresh snow in the driveway to keep any visitors from making it up to see them—at least until tomorrow afternoon, when she was on the standby list for a local plowing company.

Since it might be a moose—or worse, a bear—she made a detour through the kitchen for a pot and a metal spoon to bang against each other to hopefully scare them away—though if the dogs weren't scaring whatever it was, she didn't know how she was going to.

She shoved her feet into her boots, shrugged on her coat—and heard what sounded like a helicopter approaching. The engine roar grew louder by the second.

Ally stepped out onto the front porch, and her jaw dropped at the sight that greeted her.

It wasn't a helicopter.

A riding snowblower rolled up the driveway, throwing snow through the air to its left in a high, white arc. The arc of snow blocked her view of the driver, but she saw Deenie over by the kennels, knee-deep in snow and directing a small army of townspeople with shovels. She saw Astrid and Kimber, as well as Elinor and a couple of other families who had adopted dogs in the last three weeks.

It had worn Ally out clearing a one-person-wide path from the house to the shelter this morning so she could take care of the dogs, but now a dozen hands were at work on the problem, widening the path and clearing the area in front of the barn, where another group of townspeople appeared to be setting up a ladder and holding strands of dangling icicle lights.

Ally felt a presence at her shoulder and glanced over to see Gram at her side, not even wearing a coat. "Did you do this? Is this what you've been bustling around all morning putting into motion?"

"Don't look at me," her grandmother said.

Gramps appeared behind his wife, putting her fluffy down coat over her shoulders. He looked past Ally and jutted his chin. "I'm pretty sure it was him."

Ally turned back, looking where her grandfather indicated, where the riding snowblower had turned and the arching white snow was no longer blocking her view of the driver as he made his way up the driveway again, widening the swath of clear space he'd already made. Ben looked up from his position at the steering wheel and grinned, lifting one hand in a wave, and the sight hit Ally right in the heart.

He'd brought the cavalry.

When he got closer, Ben shut off the snowblower's noisy engine and leapt off it, his legs sinking knee-deep into the unplowed snow between him and the cleared path. "I heard you were snowed in," he called as he trudged toward her, kicking snow everywhere.

Ally came down the steps to meet him, belatedly realizing she was still holding a pot and a metal serving spoon when Ben glanced down at them.

"Cooking something?"

"I thought you were a moose," she explained inanely.

He nodded, swiping off his hat and dusting the loose snow off it. "I get that a lot."

She laughed, a sharp, startled burst of sound. "How did you...I thought you were with your parents..."

"Oh, they're here," he assured her, nodding toward a couple bundled up in winter gear who were organizing strands of lights for the team currently climbing the ladders up to the barn's eaves. "Deenie called me."

"I can't believe you arranged all this."

"I can't take credit. It was all Deenie's idea. Except the lights. Those were me. And now, if you'll excuse me..." He jammed his hat back on his head. "I've got a job to finish."

He tromped back the way he'd come, climbing back onto the snowblower and firing up the noisy machine as Ally watched. She looked around, taking in all the townspeople pitching in. Her grandparents had retreated back inside—probably to properly put on their winter gear so they didn't miss the fun, but Ally didn't move, even when her fingers started to feel stiff from the cold where she was gripping the pot and the spoon.

This. This was what she wanted. To be part of a community that rallied together.

She'd created a bubble around herself when her parents died, putting distance between herself and the world, because when she let people get too close, she was afraid she would get hurt. They'd been her whole world, and she'd shut off a part of herself when she lost them.

Her loneliness hadn't been about New York. Or working too hard and traveling too much. It had been about *her*. That's why her loneliness hadn't been magically cured when she moved to Pine Hollow. Even when she came here, she was still in that bubble. She wasn't reaching out to see who was reaching back. She was hiding here. Behind the dogs. Behind her grandparents. Behind her camera.

But she hadn't hidden with Ben. And then she'd met Deenie, and somehow things had changed. The town saw her—and she didn't need to hide anymore. She was right where she belonged.

Deenie bounced over, beaming at her. "Were you surprised? We wanted you to be surprised. I love surprises."

Ally grinned. "I think it's safe to say I was surprised." She lifted the pot and spoon. "I was coming to scare off the moose."

Deenie snorted. "Honey, you need something bigger than that for a moose." She thumped onto the porch, her feet hitting each step in a rapid-patter succession. "Did you see that application that came in for JoJo?"

Ally cringed. One of the seniors from the Estates had fallen in love with little JoJo. She hadn't known how to break it to Deenie, but she'd forgotten she'd given her access to the shelter email account. "I did. I'm sorry."

"Don't be. I want her to go to a good home. Especially because I can't keep her."

Ally wanted to find some way for Deenie to end up with the little dog, but she could definitely empathize with wanting things she couldn't have. It wasn't just Ben. They hadn't had any luck with grants or alternate funding, and the dogs were all getting adopted. The shelter was really going to close. And then what would she do? She'd been so busy worrying about the dogs she hadn't let herself think about the future, but now it was all she could think of. She wanted to stay, but how would she make a living in Pine Hollow?

"Are we cooking?" Elinor asked, appearing at the porch rail with Harry straining at the end of her leash.

Ally flushed, realizing she was still clutching the pot and spoon, and ducked inside to get rid of them while Deenie explained. When she returned Elinor was on the porch, Harry seated beside her, though the Aussie instantly popped up when she saw Ally.

"How's she settling in?" Ally asked, crouching to greet the dog who wriggled with excitement.

"Good. Though I think I'm going to be taking her to Burlington for training classes sooner rather than later. She's the sweetest, cuddliest dog in the world, but I wasn't prepared for an escape artist of her caliber. I'll need to keep her entertained while I'm at work. But we'll figure it out."

The engine of the snowblower cut out again, and Ally instantly turned toward the sound, her gaze finding Ben. He leapt off the machine, greeting a tall man in a tailored winter coat and clapping him on the back. Ben indicated the porch and the two men started toward them. Ally instinctively straightened.

"She still in denial about that?" Elinor asked Deenie under her breath.

"Apparently," Deenie muttered back.

Ally shushed them, coming to her feet as Ben approached with the man she'd now identified as Connor, the trash-talking poker buddy she'd met at the tree lighting.

"Hey," Ben called as they reached the steps. "Connor

here is thinking about getting a dog. He'd like to meet Maximus."

"Maximus?" Deenie spoke before Ally could, skepticism ringing in her tone as she eyed Connor from his expensive leather gloves to his perfectly polished boots. "He's a lot of dog."

Connor eyed Deenie—with the glitter on her face and the hot pink earmuffs—just as skeptically. "Are you implying I can't handle a lot of dog?"

Deenie met his gaze without flinching and smiled sweetly. "Yes?"

Ally stepped forward before Deenie could antagonize him into retreat. "I'll take you to meet him."

"No, I got this," Deenie assured her, already bounding off the porch. "Come on, Princeton."

"I went to Yale, actually," Connor corrected her, falling into step beside her as they made their way toward the kennels. "If you're going to imply I'm a snob, at least get it right."

"Should I go supervise?" Ally asked, frowning after them.

"They'll be fine," Ben assured her. "Deenie's tough."

"It isn't Deenie I'd be worried about," Elinor commented dryly, before glancing pointedly past Ally. "Oh gosh, it looks like my light-untangling skills are needed at the barn. Have fun, you two." She trotted down the porch steps with Harry, leaving Ally alone with Ben.

Or as alone as they could be while standing on a porch in full view of all their neighbors.

The driveway was free of snow—and cars, since everyone had parked down on the street to leave room for the snowblower to maneuver. The paths around the shelter were rapidly being cleared—and the kids had already disappeared inside, no doubt to play with the remaining dogs. With the snow mostly taken care of, most of the adults were now clustered around the barn, staring up at the eaves and offering unsolicited advice to the lucky folks at the tops of the ladders. Her grandparents had joined the kibitzers, smiling and chatting with their neighbors.

"Is this all okay?" Ben asked, coming to stand beside her at the rail. "We pretty much invaded."

"Okay?" Ally looked up at him. The flying snow from the snowblower still clung to his shoulders and dampened his eyelashes and beard, making them look even darker. "I feel like George Bailey."

Ben frowned. "I don't know what that means."

"We were just watching *It's a Wonderful Life*. And I know this is going to sound *so* cheesy, but I feel exactly like George Bailey when the whole town comes together to save the savings and loan."

Ben winced. "Okay, don't hate me, but I barely remember that movie."

"Seriously?" she squeaked. "It's a Christmas classic."

He shook his head. "All I've got is something about pulling down the moon."

Ally smiled. Right now, she felt pretty confident he could have pulled down the moon for her. "If you're only going to remember one part, that's not a bad one." Over at the barn, one of the ladders wobbled and everyone gasped before it was quickly stabilized. Ben tensed at her side, then slowly relaxed. "What are your favorite

Christmas movies?" she asked to distract him from worrying about everyone else.

"Astrid loves *Elf*," he said without taking his eyes off the light-hangers.

"I asked about *your* favorites." At her side, a stillness seemed to fall over Ben. "You don't have to think of her first every single time, you know."

"It's habit," he admitted. Then, after a short pause. *"Scrooged."*

A surprised laugh popped out of her. "With Bill Murray?"

"That and *Die Hard*. Those are the real Christmas classics."

She couldn't seem to stop giggling. "Very sentimental."

He shrugged, grinning. "I'm a softie."

"I've noticed."

His eyes twinkled down at her, and the world faded away as their gazes caught and held. Her breath went short with the possibility. The same possibility that felt like it had been building since the second they met.

"Ben..." she whispered.

But as soon as she started to lean toward him, lifting her hand in preparation for putting it on his firm, snow-coated arm, a cheer went up from the barn group, and Ben leaned away, his attention moving back to the shelter where icicle lights now dangled from the eaves.

"Who wants cocoa?" Gram called, waving everyone back toward the house.

Ally's hand fell back to the porch railing as Ben cleared his throat. "Sounds like it's time for hot chocolate."

Chapter Thirty

Somewhere between snowplowing and cocoa, it turned into a party. The Gilmore living room was crowded with revelers. Kimber and Astrid played with the dogs while Deenie and Elinor sang Christmas carols in harmony, and everyone drank as much cocoa as they could hold.

Ben sipped peppermint cocoa and watched his parents trading stories of past Christmases with their old neighbors. This hadn't been what he'd intended when he'd asked Deenie if she knew anyone who had some extra Christmas lights lying around. He hadn't expected a party, but Astrid had already declared that this was the *best* Christmas tradition yet, and they had to do it every year.

It was tempting.

Ben glanced over at where Ally was doubled over laughing as Deenie and Elinor improvised additional lyrics to "Grandma Got Run Over by a Reindeer."

A lot of things were tempting.

He'd almost kissed her on the porch. Right in front of his parents, Astrid, and half the town.

That would have been a huge mistake.

Astrid was already so attached to her. The second he gave any hint that they were together, Astrid would latch on to that—the whole town would. Railroading them toward love. Which was the last thing he needed.

He liked Ally. But she wasn't necessarily staying in Pine Hollow, and even if she did, he didn't know if this was forever.

He needed to do everything he could to protect Astrid. To keep his love life separate from her so she wouldn't be affected if things went down in flames.

So he was avoiding standing too close to Ally. Or even within ten feet. He couldn't be reckless. Not with Astrid in the picture.

"Ally seems nice."

Ben hadn't noticed his mother creeping up at his side, or he would have made more of an effort to keep his eyes off Ally. He pointedly looked toward Astrid. "Don't," he murmured to his mother. "The entire town is speculating. I don't need you doing it, too."

"We all just want you to be happy," his mother said, the words a gentle scold.

"I am," he insisted.

And the crazy thing was...he really was. Not just keeping it together. Not just getting through the season. Not just having momentary flashes of joy to punctuate his base state of overworked panic. He was actually happy. He still had more things to do than hours in the day to do them, but somehow everything seemed a little more manageable now. Or maybe it was simply that he was learning not to sweat the small stuff so much.

Astrid was happy. She was healthy. If the other parents at her school thought he was too much of a snowplow parent or not enough of one or whatever it was parents thought about one another, they weren't going to pass around a petition to have her removed from his care. He hadn't even had that dream recently—the one with the clipboard-wielding social worker who appeared to tell him he had officially failed Katie and Paul's memory.

"Have I told you how proud I am of you lately?"

Ben met his mother's eyes, startled by the words. He'd needed someone to tell him he was doing a good job for so long—and no one but Ally had seemed to see how badly he needed that. Or maybe he just hadn't been able to hear it from anyone else. Maybe he hadn't been listening.

"I don't know," he admitted. "I'm not sure I would have heard you."

Sadness shifted in his mother's gaze, and he knew she was thinking of Katie. Of Paul and the fact that they should be here now. Ben slipped his arm around his mother's shoulders, tugging her against his side in a one-armed hug.

"Your father and I have been thinking of spending more time up here. He's ready to retire, and I thought I might cut back to half time so we could be around more. Help more."

Three weeks ago, Ben might only have heard his mother saying she didn't think he could do this on his own, but now he saw the cautious hope in her eyes—

like she wanted so badly to help but worried he would be upset by her offer.

"Astrid would love to see more of you," he said.

Relief flashed across her face. "Yeah?"

"I would, too."

His mother sniffled, her eyes glistening. "Well. Good."

Connor stepped in front of them, a giant mug of cocoa gripped in one large hand. "I'm getting a dog," he declared forcefully.

Ben blinked. "You are." The statement was half question.

"Maximus is perfect," Connor declared. "You can't break into my house anymore if I have the world's biggest, loudest guard dog."

"If you want to call it breaking and entering, you probably shouldn't have given me the door code."

His mother chuckled. "You boys have been bickering since you were five years old." She lifted her empty cocoa mug. "I need a refill." She gave Ben a squeeze before releasing him, her smile a little extra sappy as she moved away.

"Poker tomorrow night?" Connor asked. "I'll host. Your folks can have some valuable bonding time with Astrid and you can get drunker than Mac for a change."

Ben cursed softly. "I forgot it was Wednesday. I'm supposed to go to the pageant rehearsal in the afternoon, and you know how those things go. We'll probably be there all night."

Connor arched a brow. "You're doing the pageant now?"

"Some of the dogs are going to be in it. The ones we haven't found homes for yet. Partridge and Peanut—"

"Say no more. You should have just told me Ally was going to be there."

Ben worked his jaw. "It isn't like that." He actually did need to tell her about the rehearsal. He'd only gotten the text back from the committee chair half an hour ago.

"Sure it isn't," Connor teased. "So next week…"

"Poker Wednesday. Absolutely."

"You know we don't have to do poker," Connor suggested. "Just say the word, and we'd all show up to do this for you."

"This?"

"Barn raising. Or, in your case, kitchen remodeling. Or putting up walls in your basement so Mac doesn't scream at the spiders every week."

Ben frowned. "I don't think—"

"Elinor said something about your two-year plan. To fix up the place and move out. We kind of figured you didn't want to change anything, but if you want to get that stuff done, you know you don't have to do it alone, right?"

Something caught in his throat, but Ben kept his smile dry. "I always figured you were too pretty for manual labor."

"Oh, I am," Connor assured him. "But I have no problem putting Levi and Mac to work. I excel as a supervisor."

"I'll keep that in mind."

"See that you do." Connor moved to join the group

around the piano and Ben hung back, the offer shifting around in his thoughts.

For once asking for help didn't feel like admitting defeat. When had that happened? Sometime between the tree lighting and the bake sale?

As Ben watched, Ally bent down to say something to Deenie and then separated from the group, moving toward the back of the house. He needed to talk to her about the pageant, and if he did it where everyone could see, it would only stoke the rumors.

He glanced around, but no one seemed to be paying any attention to him, so he slipped away, trailing her down the hall away from the noise of the party. The hallway emptied into a room that looked like an artist studio, and Ben stopped on the threshold. Ally bent over a desk at the far end of the room, but she turned to face him, her camera in her hands.

"Hey." She lifted the camera. "I left this on the charger back here. You okay?"

"Yeah, I just…" Now that they were alone together, this felt entirely too intimate. "I talked to the pageant committee and they love the idea of adding the dogs. All we need to do is bring them by tomorrow afternoon for the final rehearsal, and they'll fit them in."

Her smile lit her face. "That's great. Thank you."

He hesitated. "You know I—the other night, it wasn't that I didn't want…"

"I understand," she murmured, closing the distance between them.

He couldn't take his eyes off her. Just like always seemed to happen when they were alone together, he couldn't seem to remember any of the reasons he shouldn't want her.

"I wanted to thank you. For today."

Her eyebrows arched high. "You're the one who brought the cavalry and dug us out."

"Yeah, but you..." She'd made it special. She'd made it feel like Christmas.

Ally smiled, tipping her head to study him. "Are you still convinced you'd be a terrible mayor?"

"What does that have to do with anything?"

"You love this town—even when it drives you crazy. You moved back here. You make time for the people even when you feel like you have no time for yourself, because it matters to you. You don't have to be mayor or councilman or any of it. You can just be Astrid's dad. But I think you might miss being the one everyone needs to keep this town running."

"But I'm not."

"Aren't you?"

The song drifting down the hallway changed and Ally went still, turning her face toward the sound, her eyes going distant.

"Ally?" he asked, speaking softly. "You okay?"

"Yeah..." She shook her head as "I'll Be Home for Christmas" piped softly into the room. "This was my mom's favorite Christmas song. My dad used to put it on for her, and they'd just sway in front of the fireplace." She focused on him, her eyes nearly black in the low light. "You still don't believe in signs, do you?"

"They're growing on me," he admitted, the words barely audible as he shuffled one step forward and placed his hand on her hip. "But the way you talk about signs, it seems like they're just a way of giving yourself permission to do what you want to do anyway."

"Maybe." Ally's smile was small and private, her lashes shuttering her eyes as she shifted her camera out of the way, setting it on the craft table near the door, and erased the last of the space between them. One of her hands rested gently on his upper arm, and he caught her other one at her side, slowly bringing it up to rest against his chest. The top of her head barely came to his chin and she swayed closer still, resting her cheek over his heart.

His heart seemed to slow and race at the same time, a thick, heavy beat, as if they shared one pulse, passing it back and forth between them wherever she pressed against him.

He knew this song, he must have heard it a million times, but he didn't think he'd ever hear it again without remembering this moment, the way the entire world seemed to fade away until it was just the two of them and the dreamy promise the lyrics wove around them.

When the song ended, Ally was slow to pull away, her chin tucked down so he couldn't see her face. "Feels like home every time I hear it," she murmured.

He cleared his throat roughly. "It's a great song."

She nodded toward the hallway, reaching for her camera. "We should probably..."

"Yeah." But he wasn't ready for her to leave yet. Wasn't ready to go back to the party where he had to pretend he didn't want to touch her. "Ally..."

She looked up then, meeting his eyes for the first time since they'd fallen together into the song. "Yes?"

He couldn't kiss her. Not here. He'd already been foolish, dancing with her where anyone could walk down the hall and see them.

They stared into one another's eyes a beat too long and then Ben forced himself to look away. "Nothing." He shook off the moment. "Why don't you head back first?" he suggested. "I'll follow in a few minutes."

She nodded. "All right. See ya later, Ben."

"See ya, Ally."

He waited until she was gone, trying to figure out what they'd just agreed to in all the unspoken messages that had seemed to fly between them. He didn't like unspoken things. He liked having everything laid out in black and white, making sure everyone was on the same page, but he hadn't wanted things to be clear because he didn't want this thing between them to end. Even if he knew he was playing with fire.

Turned out, he liked fire.

And maybe he didn't have to get burned. Ally had shown him that he didn't have to give up himself to be a good guardian to Astrid.

But if he tried to add one more thing to his life, would it upset the balance he'd found? Could he really have something more with Ally? Because he was starting to realize that was what he really wanted for Christmas.

Today had been almost perfect. Christmas carols and laughter and cocoa and community. And then that dance with Ben in Gram's studio...

It didn't get any better than that, and Ally wasn't ready for it to end. She didn't want everyone to head home. Or maybe she just didn't want one particular family to head out. One particular man.

She stood on the porch in her jacket, saying good-bye to everyone as they made their way back down the freshly cleared driveway. Deenie and Elinor walked arm in arm toward town, still singing Christmas carols. Music drifted out of the house as Ben made a production of zipping his coat, taking his time as he lingered beside her on the porch.

"It was great seeing you again, Ally," Connor said loudly beside her, shooting Ben a look she couldn't interpret. "Let me know when you process that application for Maximus."

"I will," Ally assured him. He'd already completed and submitted his application, but she was a little wary of his enthusiasm. Once Connor was out of earshot, jogging to catch up with Elinor and Deenie, she turned toward Ben. "I'm not sure that's the best fit. Maximus is quite a handful."

"Don't underestimate Connor's stubbornness," Ben advised, pulling on his hat.

"You're sure Deenie didn't just goad him into it?"

"That might have had something to do with it," Ben conceded. "But Connor's a good guy. And he needs something in his life right now. Maximus could be just the thing." He tugged on his gloves, looking up toward the barn where the twinkle lights gleamed in the darkening twilight. "The lights look good."

She followed his gaze. "They do."

"I'm just glad I didn't have to do them."

Her gaze snapped back to his. "You are? You seemed so gung ho the other night."

"I might have a tiny little problem with heights," he admitted.

Ally's jaw dropped. "Wait. You're afraid of heights, and you were going to climb up to the top of that barn to put up my Christmas lights just so you wouldn't owe me for doing laundry over here?"

"Never underestimate my stubbornness, either." He met her eyes. "You wanted lights. I wasn't going to let a little thing like crippling fear of plummeting to my death stop me."

She pressed her lips together, trying to fight the smile that felt like it was radiating out of her soul. Never underestimate his stubbornness... or his kindness. How could everyone in town not see what a prince this man was?

She wanted to kiss him, to throw her arms around him and pay no attention to who might be looking, but the front door opened behind them and more people spilled out onto the porch.

Ben shifted away. "I should get Astrid and my folks home." His eyes met hers and he lowered his chin a notch. "Ally."

"Ben." Her voice came out breathless, everything in her tight with awareness.

He slid past her, gently brushing her arm, then moved down the steps, off to gather up Astrid from where she'd disappeared into the kennels again to visit the dogs.

"It was very nice to meet you, dear."

Ally jumped, turning guiltily to face Ben's mother. "And you, too."

Mrs. West paused, looking toward the barn where Astrid had emerged to meet Ben. "Thank you," she murmured after a moment.

"Oh. For...?"

Ben's mother studied her, her gaze intent. "I don't know what's going on between you two or isn't, but you're good for him."

"Oh, I...I don't know that—"

Mrs. West met her eyes, Ben's knowing winter-blue gaze coming at her from the smaller woman's round face. "Ben isn't always an easy person to help. They can say whatever they want about nature versus nurture, but that boy was born wanting to do everything himself. I still remember when he was a toddler, and the only thing we could ever get him to say was, 'Me do it!' He never wanted anyone to help him. Not even us. But with you...I haven't seen him this relaxed in years."

"I don't think I did anything—"

"You don't have to think it," his mother said calmly. "But thank you all the same."

Ben crunched across the snow-covered gravel toward them. "What's all this?" he called when he reached the bottom of the steps.

"Nothing you need to concern yourself with," his mother said with a flip of her scarf, grinning at Ally. "Good night, Miss Gilmore."

"Good night, Mrs. West."

"Rachel. Please. You and I are going to be friends."

Ben was still frowning when his mother descended

the steps and linked her arm through his. His father emerged from the house a moment later.

Ally stood on the porch, waving the last of their guests goodbye and trying to hold on to this moment. This feeling. Trying not to think about the future. Just looking up at the lights on the barn eaves and feeling like she was in exactly the place she was meant to be.

Chapter Thirty-One

December twenty-third dawned crisp and cold, with a brisk wind that picked up the top layer of snow and blew it into slopes against the sides of buildings and fences all around Pine Hollow. The snow had all been blown off the trees, but the sloping drifts made all the edges seem like they'd been rounded off the buildings. Ally wanted to grab her camera and head into town as soon as the sun was up, but she detoured via the barn, which seemed to echo with empty pens even as the remaining dogs greeted her.

Once Connor claimed Maximus and the newly christened Hemingway went home with Mr. Blake, it would only be Partridge, Peanut, and Dolce and her puppies.

That afternoon she and the unclaimed dogs were due at the community theater for the final rehearsal of the Christmas pageant, but until then she had time—to clear her head and come up with a plan.

She had to find some way to keep the shelter open. She finally knew what she wanted. She knew where she wanted to be, but she needed income. She might be able to line up a few freelance jobs remotely, but her career would undoubtedly take a hit if she stayed in Pine Hollow. Could she make ends meet with a part-time local job that still left her time to help out at the shelter? Provided she could find some way to keep the shelter open.

Once the dogs were all fed and cuddled, she picked up Peanut. The tiny chihuahua still hadn't found his people and seemed especially lonely since his pen-mates had been adopted, so she tucked him into a little sling inside her jacket and carried him with her as she headed into town.

Ally had struggled with what to get her grandparents this year, but when she'd tried to think of the perfect gift for Ben and Astrid, the answer had been obvious.

All the photos in their house were of Astrid with her parents, before Ben had come to live with her. Over the last couple of weeks, Ally had managed to capture several great candids of Astrid and Ben together—at the Christmas Fair and the senior center—but the real gem had been yesterday when she'd gotten a picture of Astrid and Ben and Ben's parents all laughing together. She planned to blow up black-and-white versions of the photos and frame them, but she didn't have any spare frames.

So she ducked her head against the icy breeze and hurried toward the small shop Gram had told her about on Maple Street. It was more arts and craft supplies than frames, but as soon as Ally stepped through the door to the chime of bells and the familiar smell of developing chemicals, she knew she was home.

"Come on in and have a look around!" a raspy female voice called from the back. "I'll be right out."

Ally made her way through the clutter of the store until she spotted a table overflowing with mismatched frames of reclaimed wood. Some were rough and jagged, others smooth and polished, but each had been made with care and an artistic eye.

"You finding everything all right?"

Ally looked up as a woman came out of a back room. She had to be in her seventies, with a shock of white hair sticking straight up in spikes, glasses an inch thick, and tattoos running up and down her arms.

"These are gorgeous," Ally said, holding up one of the smoothly polished driftwood frames. "Did you make them?"

"Mm-hmm." The woman's gaze flicked down to the camera tucked into the crook of Ally's arm. "You Rita's granddaughter?"

"Ally Gilmore." She extended a hand. "Are you Peg?"

A leathery hand gripped hers. "That's me."

A tiny nose poked out of Ally's coat, and Peg's eyes widened behind her thick glasses. "And who's this?"

"This is Peanut. Sorry, I should have asked—is it all right if I have him in here?"

"I don't have many rules here. Peanut's as welcome as you are." She extended a hand for the tiny pup to sniff. "Do you think he'll let me hold him while you pick out what you want?"

"One way to find out." Ally gently lifted Peanut from his sling and settled him onto Peg's palms. The scent of developing chemicals drifted off her skin. "You have a darkroom back there?"

Peg's eyebrows popped up as she tucked Peanut safely

against her chest. "That I do. You're welcome to use it if you like. Most kids your age are all about the digital."

"Digital's convenient, but I like both. There's something more real somehow about watching a picture develop."

Peg grinned. "Woman after my own heart. I'm not much of a photographer, but I play around with it from time to time. My problem is I can never stick to one medium. That's how I ended up with this shop." Keeping Peanut tucked snug against her chest with one tattooed arm, she spread the other to indicate the whole shop. "Behold, all my many hobbies."

Ally took it all in—everything from paints to stained glass, clay sculptures and wood sculptures and blown glass ornaments. "It's incredible."

"No need to butter me up. I know you're a real artist. Rita's shown me some of your stuff."

"The photography's just a job," she hedged, suddenly self-conscious.

Peg snorted. "I think we both know that's not true. A passion is a passion. You ever think about showing some of your stuff at the farmer's market? During the winter we only have 'em once a month at the community center, and they've been canceled since the roof caved in, but I hear they're gonna be fixing it soon, so we should be up and running before long. Give ya a deal on my frames if you wanna use 'em to showcase your work at my booth."

"That sounds like I'd be getting the better end of that deal. Discounted frames and a spot at the farmer's market?"

"You forget. I've seen your stuff. I'll sell more of my frames with your stuff in 'em than I'd ever sell on my own, and people will come to look at your pictures and buy my knickknacks. Win-win." She shrugged. "Besides, it'll be fun."

Ally studied Peg. "Did my grandmother put you up to this?"

"Rita?" Peg snorted. "Nah. She brags on you, but that woman doesn't have a business-minded bone in her body. She wouldn't think of it." She cuddled Peanut a little higher, tucking his silky head beneath her chin. "Just consider it. Let me know if you're interested."

"I will," Ally promised. It was a good offer, one she would absolutely take Peg up on if she stayed, but selling a few photos wasn't going to keep her solvent.

"You could even bring some of these little guys."

Ally smiled at the offer to include the dogs—but she had to find a way to keep the shelter open first.

"So how many of those frames you need?"

She'd planned to get three for Astrid and Ben.

She bought a dozen.

Ally walked back home with a bulging canvas bag banging against her leg, her camera in the crook of her arm, and Peanut once again tucked into his sling inside her jacket. She was halfway back when her phone binged in her pocket. She paused in front of the bakery, smiling to herself as she remembered the first time she'd seen Ben—glowering at her over his coffee-stained shirt—and stepped to one side to set down the frames and check her phone.

She expected a text from Deenie or her grandparents,

or maybe Ben, but it was an email, not a text. Ally started to put her phone away when the subject line caught her eye.

Interview with the Spectrum Group.

She sucked in a breath.

The job she'd applied for before she left New York. Good benefits, good pay, but more importantly, that company was a team. A family. That's what all their employees said about working there. It was why she'd wanted the job. Seeing the same people every day, being part of a community like that. No more travel. No more building connections with people she never saw again.

Two months ago, the position with Spectrum had been her dream job—and even now her heart rate was accelerating as she thought about meeting with them.

But the truth rang inside her like a gong.

She didn't want that life anymore. Her dreams had changed. She wanted Pine Hollow. She wanted the shelter. She wanted *him*.

She was in love with Ben West.

The future was still so unsure here, but she couldn't imagine walking away from this.

"Did your jacket just whimper?"

Ally yanked her gaze off the phone to lock on the two women who had just exited the bakery. One was tall and dark-haired, and the other cradled an adorable little French bulldog in her arms. Spotting the dog—and a likely forever-mom for Peanut—she slapped on her brightest smile. "Possibly." She opened her jacket to reveal Peanut in his sling.

The women moved closer, their faces softening as

everyone's did when they saw Peanut. "That is the tiniest dog I have ever seen. Is he a puppy?"

"Nope, he's about ten years old. And up for adoption if you're interested."

The dark-haired woman's eyes were such a pale brown they were nearly gold, and they widened, locking onto Ally's. "So you're the one I've been hearing about."

"I am?" Ally asked.

"You run the shelter, right? I'm Isabelle Scott."

Her smile was so open and welcoming it took Ally a good thirty seconds to place the name. "You..."

"Used to be engaged to Ben West. Yeah. That's me."

Before Ally could figure out what people had been telling Ben's ex about her and what one was supposed to say to the ex-fiancée of the man she was falling for, the other woman gave a little squeak of excitement.

"Wait, you work at the shelter? So you must know who's been doing those cute little photos for the Twelve Dogs of Christmas emails. I am *in love* with them."

"Thank you." Ally gestured with the camera in her left hand. "I took them."

"Oh my goodness, darling, you are so talented. I'm Kaitlyn Murray, and this is Romeo." She indicated the little Frenchie in her arms, who snorted his own greeting. "I take pictures of Romeo for his Instagram, but they never look as good as yours. What do you charge? Because whatever it is, I. Will. Pay it."

Ally's eyes widened. "Charge?"

"Kaitlyn is obsessed with Romeo," Isabelle interjected wryly, her eyes glinting with humor.

"He's an *influencer*," Kaitlyn insisted, before her gaze

landed back on Ally. "Do you have a studio set up here? Or do you take the photos off-site? This time of year, I'm sure you're swamped with all the people who want Christmas cards with their babies, but it is *so* sweet that you're doing the charity stuff for the shelter, too. I'm sure you're booked past Christmas, but whenever you can fit us in—and of course I would tag you. Do you have Instagram? You must, right?"

Ally had been caught off guard, but she rallied quickly, a smile spreading across her face. "You know, I'm still getting the business set up here in Pine Hollow. I've been working out of New York for the last several years, and this is a new location. Doing the photos for Furry Friends was a good way to promote the shelter—such a good cause—and also show people what I can do."

"Oh my goodness." Kaitlyn beamed. "So smart. I should have known you were a pro opening a new location. I mean those photos. Gorge."

"So you're moving up here?" Isabelle asked. "I've heard all sorts of conflicting reports."

Ally flushed, reminded that this was Ben's ex. She didn't really know the details of how things had ended between them. Only that it had coincided with him gaining custody of Astrid. Did Isabelle want him back? Was that why she was back here? He was the king of mixed messages—was it possible he wanted that, too? "I don't know what you've heard, but Ben and I aren't..."

"Oh, honey, no. I'm not jealous. That was two years ago, and it's probably good we figured out we weren't a match when we did. I won't pretend I wasn't pissed at him for à while, but now I just want him to be happy.

If you make him happy—if he actually lets you—more power to you."

She wasn't sure how to react to being given the blessing to date a man who might not actually want to date her. Sure, she might have feelings for him, but that had to go both ways.

"We're just friends," she insisted. *For now.* "So you're back in Pine Hollow..."

"Just for the holidays. My family's here, and I never miss it. Will we see you at the pageant tomorrow?"

"Yes?" She meant it to sound definitive, but it came out as more of a question.

Isabelle smiled. "Excellent." She nudged Kaitlyn. "We should probably get going." She lifted up the box she was holding. "My siblings are waiting for these pastries, and if I don't get back with them soon there could be open warfare."

Kaitlyn whipped out a business card with Romeo's wrinkly face on it. "Here's all of Romeo's information. Whenever you can fit us in."

Ally accepted the card, trying to restrain her unprofessional glee. "I'll look at my schedule."

She had a feeling a slot might magically open up next week, just as soon as she had a chance to set up a proper studio, as opposed to the makeshift ones she'd been using for the dogs. There was that empty storeroom. Or she could take over one of the empty guest rooms in the farmhouse.

"Merry Christmas!" Kaitlyn and Isabelle called, and Ally echoed them, biting her lip and trying not to bounce.

She caught a few townspeople watching her and was sure the interaction with Ben's ex would be all over town before nightfall, but she couldn't make herself care. She had a *plan*.

This could work. And once she had the studio set up, she could use it for human portraits, too. Headshots for local actors and models, family portraits...the possibilities were endless.

Kaitlyn might be the same woman who Instagrammed her children's lunches at Astrid's school, but Ally wasn't about to hold that against her, since she'd just given her the epiphany of her life.

It felt like a sign. The universe telling her she could stay in Pine Hollow. With her grandparents, her new friends...and Ben.

She began walking quickly back toward Furry Friends, excitement hurrying her steps as her thoughts churned.

Why limit it to photography?

She couldn't believe she hadn't thought of this before.

What if the shelter wasn't just a shelter? What if they didn't have to rely on the town for their funding because they were pulling in a profit from pet photography and training classes? Yesterday Elinor had complained that the closest obedience trainers and doggie day cares were in Burlington. What if Ally arranged for someone to come out to the shelter once a week to teach all the local pet owners? What if they provided boarding and doggie day care services when the runs weren't full of rescues?

She didn't dare tell her grandparents yet. She didn't want to get their hopes up before she'd worked out all the details, but her own hopes were sky high.

She needed to tell Ben.

She rounded a corner, nearly bumping into a slow-moving couple shuffling along the sidewalk with a pair of slow-moving dogs.

"Mr. and Mrs. Johnson!"

"Well, if it isn't the young Miss Gilmore."

Ally smiled, crouching down awkwardly with her burdens to greet Fred and Ginger. "I didn't expect to see you. How are you enjoying Fred and Ginger?"

"They are a delight." Mrs. Johnson beamed. "We were just discussing what we could bring to the shelter as a thank-you present."

"Giving them a good home is the best thank-you I could ask for." Ally straightened from her crouch, noticing the Johnsons were holding hands again.

"Where's your young man this morning?" Mr. Johnson asked.

Ally flushed. "He isn't my young man." But she wanted him to be. Her gaze flicked down to those linked hands. "How did you know you wanted to spend the rest of your lives together?"

Mr. Johnson smiled. "I felt like I'd won the jackpot. Like I was pulling one over on fate because I got to be with Verna."

"And I felt the exact same way. I was so sure I was the lucky one."

"That's the ticket. When you both think you're getting the better end of the deal," her husband added. "When you can't believe you got so lucky."

"Of course, I still want to throttle him half the time because he's a doddering old man who can't seem to stop sitting on his glasses, and those things are *expensive,*" Mrs. Johnson fussed, and her husband smiled.

"You thinking about your young man?" he asked.

"We're just friends," Ally repeated.

Mrs. Johnson beamed. "That's the best kind of person to fall in love with."

Her husband winked. "Just some unsolicited advice from a nosy old couple."

They continued on their way, and Ally stared after them, nerves and excitement warring inside her. Ben had thrown on the brakes again and again. He didn't want the town talking about them. He didn't want Astrid getting invested. But he'd never said he didn't want *her.*

Ally had never been able to picture a future with Matthew, but when she closed her eyes and thought of front porches and dogs, Ben and Astrid were always there with her in her mind's eye. He would be a partner. He was the one she could imagine holding hands with when they were both ninety and she was probably blind as a bat.

And now she had a plan, a way to make that vision of the future come true. She'd never gone after what she wanted because she hadn't *known* what she wanted, but now...

If there was ever a time to go after what you wanted most in the world, wasn't it Christmas? Wasn't this the season of miracles? She'd found her place in the town. But she wanted more. She wanted Ben.

Energy coursed through her. She had a rehearsal to get to.

Chapter Thirty-Two

The backstage area of the Pine Hollow Community Theater was a maze of props for various shows. Astrid had met Ally at the stage door and taken Peanut and Partridge to the pageant directors to be introduced to the actors who would be handling them for their moment in the spotlight. Deenie was already here with Maximus—who had yet to be picked up by Connor, so Deenie declared he would make the perfect ass for the nativity. Maximus, not Connor.

Ben had apparently been conscripted to fix some snafu with the lighting system backstage, but Ally had yet to find him. She could hear the actors rehearsing onstage, loudly projecting their Christmas cheer, but as she navigated the maze backstage, all she saw were the darkened shapes of prop tables and curtains and what looked like a giant gilded throne—but turned out to be nothing more than painted Styrofoam when she ran her fingers over it.

"Ben?" she called softly, pulling back a heavy velvet curtain to reveal another heavy velvet curtain.

The sound of a muttered curse lured her past a court-room set. Ally veered around a stack of chairs and finally spotted her target standing in front of a lighting panel with a flashlight clenched between his teeth, his shoulders bunched as he worked.

"I see they put you to work."

Ben straightened, took the flashlight out of his mouth, and grimaced. "This is why I learned years ago to avoid the pageant at all costs. Something always goes wrong at the last minute, and I always seem to be the one who has to fix it."

Ally stepped closer, frowning at the lighting panel. "Do you know anything about theatrical lights?"

"Not a thing. But apparently 'IT' means I must be good at everything to do with electricity or technology."

"That's quite a skill set."

"Unfortunately, I think I actually found the problem, and since I fixed it, I'll only reinforce this misguided belief that they should ask me to fix things." He flicked something closed on the lighting panel and turned off the flashlight, pocketing it. "The dogs here? Astrid was bouncing off the walls waiting for you."

"I couldn't find parking." The community theater was like Grand Central Station this afternoon. "But she's got Partridge and Peanut now."

"Partridge still hasn't been claimed?" Ben gathered up the tools she hadn't noticed at his feet.

"I'm shocked, too." She was making small talk. Chit-chatting with him. This wasn't why she'd sought him out. He started to move back toward the stage, and Ally put out a hand. "Ben..."

He paused, his eyebrows going up. The light was dim back here, but she could still clearly see the question in his eyes. "Yeah?"

"I..." She had a million things she wanted to say to him, but all the words were jumbled up in her head, refusing to sort themselves out.

"Is everything okay?"

"See, the thing is...I..." She looked up at him, his brow wrinkled in a frown as he waited for her to finish. Carolers belted "We Wish You a Merry Christmas" from the stage, demanding a figgy pudding *right now*— which had to be the rudest Christmas carol in the history of Christmas carols, but suddenly she understood their impatience as a reckless impulse surged through her.

"I'm crazy about you," she blurted—and once the words started, she couldn't seem to stop them. "And Astrid. And I know we agreed that we were going to do the friends thing, because of Astrid and the town, but everyone thinks we're dating anyway, and I don't want to tell people that we aren't anymore, because I want to. I want to stay. I want to be with you. I even have a plan— to take photos of dogs and offer training and provide services so Furry Friends doesn't have to rely on the town for funding. I haven't thought it all through yet, but I want to try, and you aren't saying anything, which is making me really nervous, but hopefully you feel lucky like I feel lucky, because I want you on the front porch with me—" She couldn't seem to stop speaking. The words spilled out of her mouth without any forethought or direction from her brain—but luckily Ben knew how to stop them.

He stepped forward, closing the distance between them—and both of his hands cupped her face, tipping it up to him as his lips landed firm and smooth and perfect on hers. She gripped his forearms, going up on her tiptoes, relief pouring through her.

And then his arms were closing around her, drawing her tight against his body until her toes lifted right off the ground. Ally arched into him, flush against him, and that dizzy relief was chased by a searing, heady heat as Ben tilted his head, fitting his mouth so perfectly to hers.

This. No more will-they-or-won't-they. They *would.* Oh her sainted aunt, would they *ever.*

Ally clung to his sweater, his warmth folding around her, his tongue teasing and tangling with hers, and the rightness of the moment sank into her skin. It was like a cog that had been slightly out of alignment for years had finally clicked into place, and the satisfaction of it settled into her soul. Family, community, love, all the missing pieces interlocking like some kind of Christmas miracle—

"Uncle Ben?" called a high voice nearby.

Ben jerked his lips from hers and whirled, dropping Ally back on her feet so fast she was still steadying herself when one of the heavy velvet curtains was yanked in front of her.

"I'll be right there, Astrid!" Ben called from the other side of the curtain.

Ally stared at the heavy red velvet. Had he seriously just shoved her behind a curtain?

"There you are," Astrid spoke nearby, her voice muffled by the velvet. "Have you seen Ally?"

"I was working on the lights," Ben said quickly, dodging the question. "I think I've got 'em going now. I just need to check one more thing, and I'll be right out."

"Okay." Astrid's footsteps retreated, but Ally barely heard them. She was too busy replaying the last thirty seconds in her mind.

She'd told Ben she wanted to be with him, and he'd started kissing her, and then he'd literally *shoved her behind a curtain* so Astrid wouldn't see that they were together. He hadn't just tried to keep Astrid from seeing them actively kissing; he'd flat-out panicked at the idea of his niece seeing them standing next to each other, and his reaction had been to get rid of the evidence as fast as possible—i.e., get rid of Ally.

Not exactly the actions of a man wildly in love. Unease shifted inside her chest, along with something darker.

The curtain yanked back, and Ben raked a hand through his hair. "That was close."

Ally's jaw worked, but no words came out. She couldn't seem to quite put into words what felt so wrong about the last two minutes, because suddenly everything felt wrong, like something slimy had crawled over her skin. "Did you just hide me?"

"Astrid was coming. It was instinct."

"To hide me," she repeated. "Your instinct was to hide me."

Ben's brows pulled into a frown. "Obviously we don't want her to see this."

"Obviously..." Ally echoed, though it was anything but obvious to her. Did he mean the public displays of affection? Or was the "this" he was trying to keep from Astrid even broader than that?

He answered her questions before she could ask them. "I'm sorry. I thought we were on the same page. We still have to be careful..."

Ally frowned, the realization of how different their expectations were sinking down to the marrow of her bones. She'd thought they'd cleared the last hurdle once she told him she was staying. She'd thought this was it. She looked up at him, her brows knit together. Did he think she didn't mean it? Didn't he understand what she was saying?

"I got an email for an interview this morning," she explained. "The one I was waiting for. The job that was my dream job a month ago—"

His expression locked down, somehow pulling away from her without moving. "Are you taking it?"

"No, that's my point. I didn't even really consider it— I didn't open it—because this is what I want. Not New York. Pine Hollow and you and Astrid. But you have to want it, too."

"I do," he insisted. "I just don't want Astrid getting attached before we know what this is. I have to be careful."

Ally nodded, but she wasn't sure what she was agreeing to, her thoughts still spinning.

Back when she'd been dating Matthew, she'd always let him dictate their relationship. She'd gone along with his wishes. She'd never asked for what she wanted, because she'd never *known* what she wanted. But this was different. This hurt.

She'd been looking for a partner, that person who would stick with her for sixty-five years and still want to hold her hand, and Ben was hiding her behind curtains. He was hedging his bets. She knew better than most that the future wasn't guaranteed, but she wanted someone at her side who at least wanted to *try*. The cog shivered out of place, cracking under the strain.

"I've been falling by myself, haven't I?" she whispered. Ben wasn't looking for a partner. He always wanted to do things himself. She'd done it again. She'd been lonely and desperate and latched on to someone who didn't want what she wanted. Who didn't want *her*. "You were never going to let me in."

Ben raked a hand through his hair, wondering how he'd gone from the best damn kiss of his life to a conversation spinning out of control in the space of less than five minutes. "It isn't about that," he argued, the words sharpened by the unfairness of the accusation. He'd already let her in. Farther than just about anyone in his life. "It's about Astrid."

"No." She kept shaking her head. "Don't blame this on her. You're the one who has this unrealistic idea of who you need to be for her. And *you* are the one too scared to let anything you can't control into your life. But you miss out on *living* when you do that. You don't need a huge yard to have a dog. Just like you don't need a guarantee that we'll last forever before you let yourself go on a date. Astrid is a smart kid. She understands. And if we don't work out, yes, I'm sure she'll be disappointed, but kissing someone isn't a binding lifelong contract, and I'm pretty sure she gets that." Ally folded her arms tightly. "*You* are making this choice."

"I'm not making any choice. I just think it doesn't hurt to be cautious." If she gave up her dream job for him and things didn't turn out the way she wanted, she would resent him forever. "Maybe you should do that interview in New York."

"That isn't what I want," Ally snapped. "Haven't you been listening?"

"Of course I have—"

She talked over him. "I want to run the shelter. I want to feel like I'm doing something good by taking care of the dogs and finding them homes. I want to feel like I'm making people a little less disconnected and lonely. I only told you about that interview because I was trying to show you that I want *this*, so why are you so determined to push me away?"

"That isn't what I'm doing—"

"I want a partner. I want someone to be all in—but you've never been all in. You've been hanging back and protecting yourself and thinking of all the reasons we might break up down the line and how awful it would be if it fell apart, so you never let yourself go there with me. It *is* better to have loved and lost, but you won't let yourself."

Irritation flashed through him. She was looking at him like he was being selfish when everything he did was for everyone else. "I'm putting Astrid first," he snapped. "I have to think of her needs before mine, and she needs consistency. She needs people who are going to be there for her."

"And I won't? Haven't I been there for her? Haven't I done everything I can to show you that I care about you? That I want this? But you can't let people in, can you? You use Astrid as an excuse, but she's not the one building walls around herself and trying to do it all alone. It doesn't make you weak to need people, Ben. It doesn't make you any less a man. It just makes you human. And maybe a little less likely to drive yourself into an early grave. You can't do everything yourself. No one can. Even if you feel like that's what your sister asked you to do."

"Don't bring her into this."

"She's already in this. She's the Ghost of Christmas Past, Ebenezer. And you're making yourself crazy trying to live up to this sainted image you've created of who she would have been if she'd lived."

"That metaphor doesn't even make any sense."

"I know!" Ally fisted her hands against her scalp. "I just...I'm in love with you, Ben."

The words hit him like an arctic blast, flash-freezing something deep inside him with terror. But she wasn't done.

She dropped her hands, palms open. "I am so unbelievably crazy about you—and about Astrid. I *want* this. For years I told myself I didn't know what I wanted, because I was afraid I would never get it. That sense of home. Feeling like I fit somewhere, like I belong with someone.

I want that with you—but what do you want? Not what you think is best for Astrid, or what you think you have to do, or ought to want—what do you *want*?"

Frustration flashed through him at the impossible question. "I don't know! It doesn't matter!"

"Yes, it does! Because I am done being in relationships just because I'm scared of being alone. I won't be your secret. You can't just put me in one box and Astrid and the rest of your life in another. Hiding me behind curtains when I'm not convenient. I want someone who feels like he's lucky to have me. I want in. I want in your life and I want you in mine. But if I can't have that...I don't know if I can do this."

"Ally..."

"I'm sorry. I...I have to go."

"Ally." Ben put out a hand to stop her, but Ally was already weaving through the props backstage, rushing away from him, and he could only stand there helpless and watch her walk away. He couldn't chase her. Someone would see. Astrid might see. He was lucky they hadn't already been spotted.

What she wanted...

She was being unreasonable. Asking something of him he couldn't give.

She made it sound like it was a choice, but he had to think of Astrid. He had to protect her. And if protecting her from a broken heart meant protecting his own, that was just the way it was. The entire path of his life had changed two years ago, and there was no changing it back.

Chapter Thirty-Three

Ally rushed toward the exit, a nauseating cocktail of frustration and mortification burning a hole in her stomach lining. She'd put it all on the line. Everything she'd felt had spilled out of her, and his face had looked like it was carved from stone as he stared down at her, growing more and more distant and closed off.

A group of townspeople was doing some kind of dance number on the stage as she found a short set of stairs leading down to a red exit sign. Thank God Astrid didn't see her.

Ally burst out into the theater's tiny parking lot, the sunlight reflecting off snow in a blinding glare and stopping her in her tracks. Somehow in the dark recesses of the theater she'd forgotten it was still daylight.

"Ally, hey!" A few feet away, Deenie held Partridge's leash while he froze, mid-squat.

Partridge, who adored Ben just as hopelessly as she did. And now she was comparing her unrequited feelings to a dog who was ninety percent drool. Wonderful.

"What's up?" Deenie asked, when Partridge was done doing his business, walking him back toward the door. "Do they need us back inside?"

"I told him how I feel about him."

"Ben?" A grin split across Deenie's face. "About time! I was starting to think we were going to have to get you guys a how-to manual so you'd know what to do." Then she seemed to notice that Ally wasn't returning her smile. Deenie's shiny expression sagged. "Oh no..."

Ally pressed her lips together, unbelievably grateful she didn't have to explain. "I have to get out of here for a minute. Do you mind looking after the dogs—"

"Do you want me to bring them back to the shelter when they're done?" Deenie asked, going above and beyond.

"I can't ask to spend your entire afternoon—"

"Are you kidding? I'd be here anyway. Have you seen the makeup department? *So* much glitter."

"Thank you," Ally whispered, catching Deenie's hand. Deenie opened her mouth as if she would say more, but the door opened behind Ally and someone called out that they were ready for Partridge. Deenie squeezed her hand. As she dropped it, a bright smile fell into place over her concern, and she and Partridge charged inside.

Ally moved quickly across the microscopic parking area—only to find her car completely blocked in. Because of course it was. The theater was on the absolute opposite side of town from the shelter, but it was a gorgeous December afternoon, and Ally barely felt the cold. Frustration and disappointment fueled her steps, and she found herself moving faster and faster, the ground disappearing beneath her feet.

Everyone had warned her that Ben never let people in. That he was more Scrooge than George Bailey. She'd *known*, but she'd been so sure he would be different for her. God, what a horrible romantic cliché.

All this time she'd been wrong. All those moments when she'd thought they were speaking the same language, he'd been mentally buying her train ticket back to New York, keeping her at a safe distance.

Ally knew she was spiraling, her thoughts spinning further and further away from logic, but she couldn't seem to stop reliving that moment when he'd shoved her away from him and hid her from Astrid. Not that she'd wanted to be caught making out with Astrid's uncle beneath a fake lamppost, but he could have at least held her hand. Was that so much to ask for? A man who wanted to hold her hand?

Aggravation made the twenty-five-minute walk feel like a matter of seconds. She strode up her grandparents' driveway, heading straight for the farmhouse. There were no dogs left in the kennels anyway.

Up the porch steps and in through the front door without breaking stride, Ally stripped off her winter gear with quick, impatient movements as her grandmother looked up from the present she'd been wrapping at the breakfast table and her grandfather snorted, coming awake in his recliner.

"Back already?" Gram asked. "That pageant committee must have finally listened to all the complaints about the eight-hour rehearsals."

"The rehearsal's still going. I left the dogs with Deenie." And the car. She'd left the car too. She'd have to go back for it. And the dogs. God, what had she been thinking? But then, she hadn't been. She'd just needed to escape.

"Did something happen?" her grandfather asked.

Had something happened? *I told Ben I loved him. I kissed him. He hid me behind a curtain.* God, had she actually told him she loved him? The words all blurred together in her mind. She hadn't actually said that, had she? Reality seemed to be tightening its grip on her and suddenly the full impact of the last hour was setting in.

"I . . ." What had happened? "I had a fight with Ben."

"Oh no." Gram put down the scissors, coming around the table. "What happened?"

"I told him I was invited to interview for a job in New York—my dream job—but I didn't want to do it because my dreams had changed. I want to stay here. Run the shelter with you guys. Maybe add some pet photography services or training classes so Furry Friends becomes a hub for all things canine in Pine Hollow. But Ben just wanted me to go back to New York."

"Oh dear." Her grandparents exchanged an unreadable look. "Maybe you should consider taking the interview."

Ally went still with one hand still resting on the coat she'd been hanging up. "What? Why . . ." Realization landed like a stone on her chest. "You're waiting for me to leave, too?"

"No, honey, of course not. Not *waiting*. We're so happy you're here."

But they exchanged a look, and suddenly Ally had a feeling she was missing a giant piece right at the center of the puzzle. "What aren't you telling me?"

Gramps sat up, shoving down the footrest of the recliner. "We want you to stay with us just as long as you need to in order to get back on your feet."

The Johnsons had said her grandparents would be moving out to the Estates in the new year. She'd been so sure the older couple was confused. Her grandmother had said time and again that she would sooner die than move to an old folks' home. The Johnsons had it wrong. They'd misinterpreted the fact that her grandparents were out at the Estates visiting their friends all the time. They practically lived out there.

They practically lived out there.

"You're moving out to the Estates, aren't you?"

They exchanged another look. Copper scrambled out of the way as Gramps rose from the recliner, one hand resting on the back. "We did put down a deposit on one of the places out there, but that was before you said you were coming up here."

Ally turned to her grandmother in shock. "You said you never wanted to live someplace like that. When the Kennedys first moved up there, you said they'd have to take you straight from this house to the cemetery. That you'd rather die than live someplace where they cut your food for you."

"Well, you know they don't actually cut your food—it's really a nice place. I had no idea how many amenities—and your grandfather loves the poker tournaments. All his friends from the Elks are up there now."

"You were going to sell this place?"

"Well, we wanted to have a bit of work done after we moved out. Darleen, who runs the real estate office, said we'd get a better price if we updated some, but we didn't want to do any big renovations while we were still living here. Lilian suggested we should try to get on one of those *Property Brothers* shows. Have them pretty it up for us."

Lilian. Darleen. The Johnsons. Everyone had known. Everyone but her.

Another piece of the puzzle clicked into place. "That's why they cut our funding. They knew you were planning to sell the shelter anyway. The whole town knew—"

"Well, not the whole town," Gramps argued. "We only told a handful of people."

And word had spread. The way it always did in Pine Hollow. She was the one who'd been out of the loop. Because she didn't really belong here. She was a tourist. An outsider.

"When are you moving?"

"See, that's the thing," Gram said eagerly. "They'll hold our spot for us for as long as we want, so you can take all the time you need to get back on your feet. We don't want you feeling rushed at all. We love having you here, Ally."

But they'd never realized she wanted to stay. "I thought...you never said anything about me going back to New York."

"Well, of course not. We didn't want you to think we didn't want you here or that we were pressuring you to go back before you were ready. We assumed you'd make the decision when it was right for you. Maybe after Christmas."

Ally stared at her grandmother.

The entire time she'd thought she was helping her grandparents, they'd been waiting for her to leave so they could get on with their lives. She'd thought they needed her.

"I have to...I need to think." She reached for her coat again, shoving her feet back into her boots.

"Ally?" Worry warbled in Gram's voice.

"It's all right," Ally assured her—though no words had ever felt further from the truth. It felt like everything was falling apart. Everything she'd been so certain was falling into place.

Suddenly all signs were pointing away from Pine Hollow.

This wasn't her home. This wasn't where she belonged. It was her grandparents' place, and she was just a parasite on their lives. The connections she'd built in the community were gossamer thin—and only because of Gram and Gramps and Ben and the shelter. But if the shelter was closing, if all the dogs were gone, would Deenie even come by? Her grandparents were selling their house. Where would she even live?

"I'm sorry," she said, grabbing her scarf and hat. "I'm sorry about all of this."

"Ally..." Her grandfather spoke her name, and Colby lifted his head curiously, but she was already moving back out into the icy December afternoon.

She'd come here to escape her isolation, but now she felt more alone than ever. Before, at least she'd had the dream—the vision of the front porch in that distant future, but now even that felt like it was out of reach. Like she'd always been fooling herself to think she would get it. And it was time to face reality.

Chapter Thirty-Four

Ben wasn't in the holiday mood. He emerged from backstage to give the pageant committee the go-ahead to try the lights again. When the stage brightened like the sun, a cheer went up from the entire group, but Ben couldn't even crack a smile. He scanned the house of the theater instead, looking for Astrid, wondering how quickly they could get out of here.

He didn't see Astrid, but Partridge did spot him. The bulldog immediately started trying to drag Deenie up the aisle to get to Ben, his low, bulky body straining against his harness. Deenie gave Ben a long look, not smiling for perhaps the first time in recorded history.

She knew.

Shame tried to rise up, though he'd done *nothing wrong*. He hadn't led Ally on. He'd told her from the beginning that Astrid was his priority. He was doing the right thing, damn it.

Which didn't explain why he felt like the lowest kind of amoeba when Deenie turned and muttered, "Come on, Partridge." The bulldog whined, but reluctantly let himself be guided away.

"Where's Ally?"

"Astrid! Jeez!" Ben put a hand to his chest, turning to where his niece had snuck up on him in stealth mode. She stood at his side, cuddling the teacup-sized Peanut against her chest.

"Aunt Elinor says you jump like that because you're wound too tight, and if you relaxed a little more you wouldn't be so startled all the time."

"That's very helpful of Aunt Elinor," Ben grumped.

"Have you seen Ally?" Astrid repeated. "Every-one thought she was looking for you, but no one has seen her."

"I don't know where she is." He carefully avoided mentioning that he had seen her. And kissed her. And hid her behind a curtain so Astrid wouldn't see her. "Maybe she left."

"Without the dogs?" Astrid gave him a baffled look.

"I'm sure she'll be back for the dogs."

Astrid studied him, her ten-year-old eyes seeing far more than he would like them to. "You should have kissed her under the mistletoe when you had the chance."

Ben nearly choked on his tongue. "Excuse me?"

"The mistletoe? In the gazebo?" Astrid explained patiently. "I thought if you would just kiss Ally maybe you wouldn't be so stressed all the time. And we could get a dog. That's why Kimber and I set it up."

Ben gaped at his niece. He'd thought she was hoping for him to fall for Ally—it hadn't occurred to him she was actively scheming to throw them together. "Were you really trying to match me up with Ally so you can have a dog?"

"No. Mostly I've been trying to get you together with Ally because I like her. And you don't seem happy."

The words hit him in the gut. "Astrid. I'm happy. I love you, and I'm very happy."

"You have been since we met Ally," she pointed out. "Before that Kimber didn't want to come to our house because you were grumpy all the time. I told her you weren't really mad, that that was just, like, how you are sometimes, but she was scared of you."

Jesus. He'd thought Elinor was exaggerating when she told him he was frightening children, but Astrid's best friend had been afraid to come to their house. "I'm sorry, Astrid. I'll do better."

"You do great, Uncle Ben." She reached out to pat him on the arm like one of the residents at the Estates might. "I just want you to be happy."

"I am happy. I swear, kiddo, I'm happy."

"But you haven't seen Ally?"

There it was, that shame crawling up the back of his neck again. "Not in the last few minutes."

Astrid nodded and headed off, apparently in search of the shelter owner. Ben scanned the theater, looking for her as well. He didn't know what he would say to her, but he needed to see her—if only to convince himself that she wasn't still upset, that she would forgive him for that stupid moment backstage.

"Benjamin West."

Speaking of awkward moments. Ben silently groaned as he recognized that voice, turning to face the woman he'd once thought he was going to marry. "Isabelle. Merry Christmas."

"Merry Christmas," she echoed, reaching up to give him a hug—the kind that was more distant shoulder patting than body contact, so at least he knew they were on the same page about not wanting to rekindle anything this holiday season. "I met that girl you're dating this morning," Isabelle commented as she stepped back to a comfortable distance.

"We aren't dating," Ben insisted, the words coming out more harshly than he'd intended.

Isabelle studied him and closed her eyes briefly on a soft groaning, "Oh, Ben."

"What?" he snapped as the carolers onstage began belting out "We Wish You a Merry Christmas" again. "You want to tell me how to live my life? Because you have the moral high ground? You left the second things got hard."

"Wow. That's some revisionist history," Isabelle said, and he took a strange kind of satisfaction from the edge in her voice. "I stayed for months—through the funeral and probate and you being an absolute jerk to me whenever I tried to help. You were so freaking territorial. Anytime I wanted to do something for Astrid, it was like I had to figure out how to do an end run around an NFL lineman to even get to her."

"That isn't—"

"You got *mad* at me for picking her up from school."

"Without telling me!"

"Your phone died! I texted you!" Isabelle shouted— and heads turned in their direction, but she didn't notice.

Or she didn't care, on too much of a roll. "It wasn't my fault you didn't charge your damn phone—"

"I was worried. I didn't know where Astrid was—"

"For like two seconds! Until someone told you I'd picked her up—but apparently that was a crime against humanity, and it was my fault. *Everything* was my fault. Every time I tried to help, you *blamed* me." She stopped, sucking in a breath and seeming to notice that the carolers had gone quiet. "Sorry," she said at a softer volume. "I thought I was over this, but apparently I'm still angrier at you than I thought I was."

"I didn't realize you were angry," he admitted after a moment. He'd been so locked in his own grief then. Just trying to put one foot in front of the other and do the best thing for Astrid.

Isabelle laughed humorlessly. "You thought you were the only injured party, huh? Somehow I'm not surprised. You're a great guy, Ben. But you don't always make it easy on people who try to care about you."

"I never meant..."

"I know." She sighed, looking out over the theater, where everyone was studiously pretending they weren't listening. "I loved you, and I loved Astrid. I stuck around longer than I should have because I kept thinking you would see that I was there for you at some point and let me in. But you just kept pushing me away and insisting on doing everything yourself. You've always been like that, always trying to be this tower of strength for everyone else and never letting anyone do anything for you. I kept thinking it would get better when we got married, but I think it got worse when Katie..." She trailed off.

"I'm really sorry about Katie," she whispered, the words choked.

"Me too." He cleared his throat around the sudden thickness there. "And I'm sorry I put you in a box."

Isabelle's eyebrows arched with surprise. "That's actually a good way of putting it."

"Are you...okay?"

"I'm good," she assured him. "Great, actually. I have a job in Boston now. I love the city. I thought the traffic would drive me crazy, but the parks are incredible. It's good to be home, though. For Christmas." Her smile held a note of memory. "It's good to see you, Ben." She made a face. "Sorry I kind of went off on you."

"I think I'm actually glad you did. Though I don't want to consider what the gossip is going to be like tomorrow."

Isabelle grimaced. "Yeah. That's definitely one thing I don't miss." She glanced toward the stage, where the pageant coordinators were back to trying to direct the choir. "Sorry for the volume."

"You don't owe me any apologies. I deserved every decibel."

And it never did him any good to try to hide his personal life from the town anyway. He thought he'd been keeping it together, but Elinor and Astrid had apparently been talking about his Scrooginess and the fact that he was scaring her friends long before this Christmas. He thought he'd kept his feelings for Ally to himself, but everyone in town already thought they were dating. He'd hidden her behind a curtain so Astrid wouldn't see them together when Astrid had been conspiring to get them together under the mistletoe the whole time. No wonder he felt like he was tilting at windmills—he was trying to stop the flow of gossip in Pine Hollow, and that was a force that should come with a natural disaster label. Batten down the hatches, because you can't stop it no matter how you try.

"Bella! My scarf!" a young voice called impatiently.

Isabelle grinned. "That's my cue. Minnie's in the tableau this year and that makes me her wardrobe slave." She nodded toward one side of the stage where her youngest sister stood impatiently.

"She's gotten so tall."

"Right? Every time I go away for a month she grows another three inches. See ya round, Ben. Happy holidays."

He watched her go, everything she'd said sifting around in his brain, shining new light into the shadows of the past and making him see them in different ways. Maybe he had tried to control things too much, control the only things he'd felt like he had any control over in his life at that moment. Maybe—

"Ben! There you are! Do you think you could take a look at the sound system? I think there must be a faulty wire..."

Ben pushed the past out of his mind and focused on the present—and another minor pageant disaster to distract him from thinking about the moment backstage with Ally. She'd accused him of putting her in a box, but it was the only way he knew how to deal with all the things in his life that felt too big to manage—so he tucked all thoughts of her back into that box and went to work.

Chapter Thirty-Five

Ally texted Deenie as she was walking back to collect the car she'd left at the theater. Deenie had all the dogs outside and ready to go when Ally arrived, and helped her load them into the car without a single word about Ben. Ally pointedly avoided looking at Ben's car in the parking lot, focusing instead on the fact that her own was no longer blocked in and she could make a clean escape.

Though she should have known better than to think she would get away without a single word.

She'd just finished putting Maximus back in his run at Furry Friends and headed back out to get Partridge and Peanut when Deenie's powder-blue Bug pulled into the driveway. Colby stirred himself from his sprawl on the porch and padded over to greet the new arrivals as Deenie, Elinor, and the newly renamed Dora piled out.

"I come with reinforcements," Deenie announced.

Elinor held up a thermos. "She means eggnog."

"You guys don't have to be here," Ally protested, taking Peanut's tiny soft-sided carrier out of the front seat.

"Of course we do," Deenie declared, taking Peanut from her.

Dora/Harry dragged Elinor toward the shelter—apparently eager to get back to her old stomping grounds and see which smells had changed. Elinor stumbled along behind her, but made her sit before opening the door, clicking a tiny clicker attached to her wrist when she obeyed.

"I've been watching online training videos," she explained. "The next set of classes in Burlington doesn't start for weeks."

Ally wilted at the reminder of her plan to save the shelter with local classes. "Maybe you guys can get a group together and bring a trainer out to Pine Hollow."

Deenie's eyes lit. "You know, that's not a bad idea. We could host classes here—"

"No, we can't. Come on." Ally opened the door to the office, leading the others inside.

The office was tiny, not suited to three women and even more dogs, but it was the only place with seating besides the house, and she didn't want to be where her grandparents would hear her. Gram had moved Dolce and the puppies up to the house yesterday anyway, declaring they must be too lonely at the kennels now that so many of the other dogs were gone.

Elinor pulled a set of collapsible camping mugs from her bag. Deenie set Peanut's carrier on the floor and let the little guy out, while Dora leapt onto the loveseat beside Elinor. Ally took the seat behind the desk, accepting a mug of eggnog as Partridge sat on her foot and Colby came over to rest his giant head on her lap. She stroked Colby's silky ears, sighing as she stared around the room. She was going to miss this place.

She took a sip of eggnog—and nearly choked. She coughed, gripping her cup with both hands.

"Sorry, I should have warned you," Elinor said. "Magda's nog is like rocket fuel. Figured we could use it today."

"Why can't we host classes here?" Deenie asked, perching on the arm of the loveseat. "I love that idea. We could set up an agility course, bring in groomers—"

"I thought the same thing this morning," Ally admitted. Had that only been this morning? "I had this whole plan to save Furry Friends with a pet photography business and doggie day care, but it turns out I'm the only one who wanted it saved. My grandparents are going to sell the place and move out to the Estates. I can't afford to buy the house and all the land from them, and if the dogs are all gone and they don't need me, what's the point of staying? I even got an invitation to interview for my dream job in New York. It's obvious. The universe is telling me I should go back."

"Stress brain," Elinor declared, shaking her head. "That's your fear talking."

"That's my practicality talking," Ally corrected. "I don't belong here. Maybe I never did."

Deenie shifted on the arm of the couch. "Is this about Ben?"

"No." And it wasn't. Not entirely. "It's my grand-parents. And the shelter. And...my parents." She looked down into the creamy depths of the eggnog, as if it could solve all her problems. She'd been looking for that connection, that sense of family ever since she lost them. She was so scared of being alone, of losing her connection to the last family she had, but staying up here wasn't really an option. "The thing with Ben...it's just another thing. Another reason to leave. What is there for me here?"

"You've got me," Deenie said.

"And me," Elinor added.

Colby woofed.

"Colby clearly likes it here, too." Deenie grinned. "Those sound like some very compelling reasons to stay."

"But you aren't staying, are you?"

Deenie hesitated, drawing in a breath. "Probably not," she admitted. "Not forever anyway. You wanna run away to Rome? That's what I do whenever things aren't going my way."

Elinor looked at her. "Sometimes I think you're crazy, and then you say something like that, and I start to wonder if I'm the crazy one. We should all run away to Rome."

Ally smiled, not entirely sure they weren't serious. "I don't know what to do. I came here to figure out my life, and now I'm more confused than ever."

"Ben's an idiot," Elinor declared. "But I really do think he cares about you. I've never seen him look at anyone the way he looks at you."

"Does it matter how he feels if he won't let me into his life?"

They all fell silent at that one—a puzzle too complex for any of them.

"I wanted him to want this," Ally admitted, "but he was never really in."

"I hope you stay," Elinor said finally. "You have a place here, Ally Gilmore."

She wanted to believe it. But her place here was only temporary.

Ben had the mother of all headaches by the time he and Astrid finally escaped from the pageant rehearsal and were on their way home. He'd bitten the head off more than one volunteer and undoubtedly earned his Scrooge-ish reputation a dozen times over, but echoes of his conversation with Ally kept whispering in the back of his mind.

He felt like he was screwing up again. That all-too-familiar feeling that he was letting someone down plagued him all afternoon. Why did Ally have to ask for more than he could give her? Didn't she see that he wanted to be with her, but he couldn't just rush into things? They'd only known each other a few weeks. He needed to get his life in order before there was room in it for anyone else. He had a *plan*, and if she'd just listen to him—but she hadn't. And he was glowering at picturesque Pine Hollow as he drove home.

"Can we watch *Muppet Christmas Carol*?" Astrid

asked as she clambered out of the car, oblivious to the jabs of pain digging into his cranium.

"After dinner." They stripped off their winter gear, calling hellos to his parents in the kitchen. Ben headed back to the mudroom to put away the toolbox he'd brought—and drew up short at the foreign object sitting where his broken washing machine was supposed to be.

It gleamed bright white, shiny and new, with a big red bow stuck to the top.

Ben stared at the washing machine, irrational anger bubbling up inside him. "What did you do?" he barked.

He heard his family behind him in the hall and turned. His parents beamed. "Merry Christmas!" they shouted in unison.

"Where's our washing machine?" he demanded. "I was going to get it fixed."

"We wanted to do this for you." His father stepped forward, still smiling.

"Your father even fixed that stair today," his mother added helpfully.

Ben bristled.

They were trying to help. He knew they were trying to help. But it was back, that voice whispering that he'd failed, that he hadn't been up to his responsibilities, and he couldn't seem to temper the sharpness of his voice.

"I would have done it." He didn't need people swooping into his life and doing things for him. He would fix up the house. He would prove he could do this. Always so much to prove.

"We know." His mother's expression was cautious now.

He was being an ass. He could hear Ally's voice telling him it wasn't weakness to accept help. That he was the only one who thought he had anything to prove—but that feeling was back. That feeling that he was failing Katie and Paul and everyone could see it.

"Uncle Ben?"

He looked down into Astrid's concerned face and forced himself to take a breath. "Thank you."

The words weren't smooth, but his mother smiled. "You're welcome. Come on, Astrid. Some new presents for you under the tree."

Astrid rushed to investigate and Ben hung back, his father lingering with him.

"You all right?" his father asked, his gaze seeing far too much.

"I saw Isabelle today," Ben said after a moment—because it was easier than admitting he might have screwed things up with Ally and the regret was eating away at his insides.

His dad lifted his eyebrows. "Did you?"

He met his father's eyes. "She said I make it hard for people to care about me."

His father smiled. "It's not exactly a secret. Katie was the only one you would ever let help you."

Ben stared at the new washing machine. He'd never meant to push anyone away or make it hard for them to help him. He'd just known that he had responsibilities. That some things were up to him, and he couldn't foist them off onto anyone else. He had to make sure everything got done. But with Katie...

He didn't know why it had always been so easy to

let her take the reins, but it had. Maybe because for as long as he could remember, she just took them. She was the big sister. It was her job. She never *let* him push her away or try to do it without her. She was simply there. And God, he missed that. He missed her. He missed the seamless way she slipped herself into his life and made him laugh when he wanted to bristle. There was never going to be a time when he didn't have a hole in his life where she was supposed to be, but he had to learn to let someone else in. Someone besides Astrid. He couldn't put that on her. He needed...

He needed a partner.

A vision of Ally filled his mind.

"If it helps, you've been getting better," his father said. "Your mother and I've talked about it. How you've asked us to do things, and then you went and borrowed that snowblower from Connor. Astrid said you even asked Elinor to watch her a few times in the last few weeks."

For Ally. It had all been for Ally. Astrid wanted him to be happy and thought he had been since he'd met Ally. His parents wanted him to learn to accept help, and he had since he met Ally. The entire town wanted him to lighten up and be less of a Scrooge... enter Ally.

He'd only stopped feeling like he was drowning when Ally crashed into his life. In a matter of weeks she'd become one of his best friends, but she was more than that. She'd changed him, cracked open the calcified parts of his heart and let light in again. For the last two years he'd been burrowing down, building walls around himself, and becoming more and more of a Scrooge. Ally had slammed into him and changed all that.

He'd been playing it safe for so long—trying to control everything, trying to manage his life and his responsibilities, never wanting to take anything else on. But life wasn't about safe. Real life happened when you stopped trying to control everything and took a leap. Like getting a dog, even knowing Astrid might not always be the one to feed it and it might chew his slippers.

Or falling for Ally.

He'd tried to control everything and compartmentalize it all until he'd nearly lost her—he could have already lost her. He'd told her to take that job and go back to New York.

Ben met his father's eyes, urgency suddenly spiking through his veins. "I need to go. Can you...?"

Understanding kindled in his father's eyes. "Of course."

"Thanks."

Now he just had to figure out what he was going to say.

The dog shelter and farmhouse were both dark as Ben pulled to a stop in the driveway, realizing once again that he should have called or texted first. He threw the car into park, pulled out his phone and stared at it, trying to think of the right thing to say. Ally had always magically shown up when he was here—one of her signs from the universe maybe—but this time the door to the farmhouse stayed firmly shut.

Finally, Ben typed, *Can we talk?* and sent the text.

Three little dots appeared. Then disappeared again. Then reappeared.

Impatience finally spurred him to add *I'm in the driveway.*

The dots disappeared.

The front door opened.

Ben climbed quickly out of his car. He jogged up the front porch steps. Ally stood half behind the door, peering through the opening—and making no move to let him in. The house behind her was dark and silent.

"I should've brought coffee. That's our traditional peace offering, right?"

Ally didn't crack a smile. "Ben..."

"I'm sorry. I don't want you to go back to New York." There. He'd said it. That was good enough, right?

Ally sighed—not a dreamy, loving sigh, but one filled with exhaustion. "It's no use. My grandparents are selling the place and moving out to the Estates. I can't afford to keep the shelter open, and I'm not needed here."

Something went still inside him. He hadn't really thought she might leave. Even when he'd been bracing for it, the idea of her not being here hadn't been real. "But the town needs you." *I need you.*

"No, they don't. Most of this town doesn't even know who I am. I don't belong here. I'm just a tourist with a big camera, like you said the first day we met."

"Ally..."

"This was just a break from my regular life. A chance to try out how the other half lives, and now the signs are all pointing me back to New York."

"The signs only give you permission to do what you already want to do," he reminded her. "Are you sure you want to run?"

Fire flashed in her eyes, reminding him of the first time they'd met. "I *want* someone who isn't afraid to kiss me in the town square. And I'm not going to find that here. Am I?"

Her dark eyes were uncompromising, and the words he needed to say froze in his suddenly paralyzed throat. She wanted him to say it. She'd asked him earlier what he wanted, and he'd said it didn't matter—because it was easier than asking for what he wanted and not getting it. It was easier than taking the risk.

He'd lived the last two years feeling like all his choices had already been decided for him. Doing the best he could with the hand he'd been dealt. He wasn't sure he knew how to do anything else. How did he change the habits of a lifetime? How did he show her he wanted to?

He hesitated too long, and resignation filled Ally's face. "Never mind. It wouldn't matter anyway. Good night, Ben. Merry Christmas."

The door shut, and Ben stared at it for a solid minute before retreating to his car.

He didn't remember the drive home, too deeply embedded in his thoughts. He was parked in the tiny driveway before he was even aware of the fact that he was behind the wheel. He turned off the engine, the car clicking softly as it cooled.

He'd screwed up. Again. He needed to show Ally what she meant to him and to the town. He needed to do it in a way that *proved* he was all in. He needed to leap—and not look for the safety net. He needed to *show* her all the things he hadn't been able to say.

Ben pulled out his phone as he climbed out of the car, moving quickly.

He had a lot to do.

And he was going to need a lot of help.

Chapter Thirty-Six

Ally descended the farmhouse stairs on the morning before Christmas, the treads creaking beneath her slippers. She let Colby and Partridge out to pee, watching them sniffing around the yard from the warmth of the kitchen as she brewed the first pot of coffee. Usually Gram and Gramps were up before she was—they'd always been early risers, but lately they'd turned it into a competitive sport, in bed by nine and up again by four thirty.

This morning, however, they must have slept in, because Ally was alone in the kitchen, watching the water dripping off the eaves in steady streams, melting their hopes for a white Christmas by the second. It had warmed up overnight and the forty-degree weather outside was already revealing patches of brown beneath the white on the driveway.

Colby snuffled at the door, and Ally opened it to let him back in, Partridge waddling in his shadow. She hadn't had the heart to return Partridge to his run last night. He'd looked at her with those big puppy-dog eyes, and she hadn't been able to resist. Suddenly all the rules about not getting too attached didn't seem to matter so much anymore. Not when the shelter was about to close, and she was going to be going who-knew-where to do who-knew-what with her life. Maybe she *should* adopt Partridge. Though finding a place that allowed multiple dogs in the city might be harder.

Colby was used to the routine at Furry Friends. He'd always stayed here with her grandparents when she had to travel for work and couldn't bring him, but he was too big to stay at the Estates. She wouldn't be able to afford to travel as much—which meant she really needed that job with the Spectrum Group. But she was still having a hard time getting excited about it. Even knowing it was what she should do.

Ben coming by last night, telling her that he didn't want her to go to New York, but still not actually saying he wanted to be with her . . . it had just confirmed that she needed to go. He was the king of mixed messages, and it would be far too easy to let him back into her heart— but she didn't have a future here.

Ally poured her coffee, adding liberal doses of cream and sugar, and wandered into the living area to turn on the Christmas tree lights. The rest of the first floor was still dark, and she settled onto the couch with her mug in her hands and two warm dogs lying against her ankles.

She didn't know how long she sat there, staring at the Christmas tree, each ornament a memory. The unicorn her mother got when they took that trip up to the Corning glass factory. The Santa beneath a palm tree from the one time they'd spent Christmas at a resort in the Bahamas and decided that Christmas in a hotel room without a Christmas tree just didn't feel the same. And older ornaments. Ornaments she'd seen her entire life that her dad would tell stories about as he put them on Gram and Gramps's tree.

Her parents were here, in this space. Maybe that was part of why the idea of her grandparents selling and moving out to the Estates had hit her so hard. These creaking old walls had memories. Her father had grown up here. Her parents had driven her up here every Thanksgiving weekend to put up the tree and again on Christmas morning. When this place wasn't home anymore, would anywhere be?

The stairs groaned, and Ally watched her grandmother emerge onto the first floor, moving slowly pre-coffee. "Morning, sweetheart."

"Morning, Gram."

Her grandmother padded softly across the hardwood, touching the table as she passed it. Her mug was exactly where she left it every night after cleaning it, and she pulled it forward, resting the lip of the coffee pot against it as she poured.

Ally watched her, her chest squeezing tight. She got so mad at her grandmother for not being careful. She just hated to see her getting older, creeping closer to that time when Gram and Gramps would be gone, too. When she would be the last one who remembered anything about their Christmas traditions.

Gram joined her in the living area, setting down her coffee and collapsing onto her chair with a soft sigh. Ally let the silence settle around them, let her grandmother sip her coffee and stare at the tree until she couldn't wait any longer.

"I'm sorry I overreacted yesterday."

Her grandmother looked in her direction. "I'm not sure you did. Your grandfather and I have been talking. We should have told you about the Estates from the start. We just didn't want you to feel pressured to leave because you knew we were heading out there."

"I should have been more up front with you, too," Ally admitted. "I was so lonely in New York, and I think part of me hoped I'd just fit here like a missing puzzle piece. I'd get to see more of you guys, and I wouldn't have to worry about you up here on your own trying to take care of the dogs and do everything yourselves."

"We could both do better on the communication." Gram glanced at her over her coffee. "You were lonely?"

"Not all the time, but yeah. There was this one day— I'd had the worst day. Just . . . everything had gone wrong. I don't even remember what all happened, but my train wasn't running and I had to walk in the rain and my umbrella broke and all I was thinking about was getting home and walking Colby and then taking a hot shower. I was in such a hurry when I got there—I grabbed Colby, rushed him out to pee, and it wasn't until I was bringing him back that I realized I'd locked my keys inside the apartment. I didn't have a roommate, and the super took forever to respond to anything, and I didn't know my neighbors because I was never there. I didn't have anyone I could call. No one I'd given a spare key. No one who would let me crash at their place until I could get back into mine. I was *stuck*, and I realized as I'm sitting there, cold and wet, with poor Colby just as cold and wet, that I didn't have anyone. Pine Hollow was so different from New York. I thought...I wanted this to be where I fit, but you shouldn't be stuck in this house just because your granddaughter is lonely." Emotion choked her and she stared at the tree until she could speak again.

"I know you worry about us," Gram said softly in the silence. "But we worry about you, too. When your parents...when we lost them, I watched you pull away, hiding behind your camera. At first I was glad you had something that gave you comfort, but then it seemed like a barrier you put between yourself and anything that felt too raw. Look, but don't touch. We were so glad you came home this Christmas. So glad you put your camera down and laughed while you were here." Her grandmother cleared her throat. "I didn't realize you and Ben were...*romantic*."

"You didn't?" Ally asked, a surprised laugh washing away some of the emotion clogging her throat. "You must be the only one in town."

"He's a good boy," Gram commented.

"He hid me behind a curtain. Literally. You can't go into a relationship trying to pretend it isn't happening."

"No," Gram agreed. "But I can understand wanting to keep things private, especially when you're still figuring them out. The last time one of his relationships blew up, the whole town speculated about it. Maybe cut him a little slack?"

She had a point—and Ben did have a very good

reason to want to keep things private—but it still stung. "He was always trying to keep me at a distance."

"Maybe," Gram admitted. "Or maybe you were so scared he didn't want you that you saw him pushing you away whether he meant it or not." Copper came charging down the stairs, a harbinger of the arrival of her grandfather, who they both heard thumping around on the floor above. Ally started to stand to let Copper out, but her grandmother waved her back to her chair. She rose, padding to the kitchen and opening the side door. "You could fit here, Ally. If that's what you want. And that has nothing to do with Ben West. Home isn't some magical place. It's a choice."

It was a nice sentiment, but if her grandparents sold the shelter and moved out to the Estates, she would have no job, no place to live, and no prospects beyond a spot in a booth at a farmer's market that wasn't even going to be operational until the town managed to fix that roof. She couldn't very well run the pet mecca she'd envisioned without the shelter.

But Gram was right about one thing, whether or not she belonged in Pine Hollow had nothing to do with Ben West.

"I should get the dogs ready for the pageant tonight." She stood as her grandfather clumped down the stairs and Partridge scrambled to his feet at her side, gazing up at her adoringly. "We gotta see if we can find Partridge a home, don't we, buddy? Though maybe I should adopt him. What do you think, Partridge? You wanna be mine?"

"Oh, sweetheart, I forgot to tell you," Gram called

from the kitchen as she poured another cup of coffee for Gramps. "We got an application for Partridge."

"We did?" Ally had left her phone upstairs on her charger, but she'd checked it when she woke up. No new emails to the shelter account. And no texts from Ben.

"It came in last night. To my email."

"You have an email?"

"My texty-thing. On the phone."

Ally frowned, even more confused. "Someone texted you an application?"

"I'm taking care of it," her grandmother insisted. "We did do this for twenty years before you got here."

"Okay," Ally conceded, suddenly back on the verge of tears.

She'd been so stupidly fixated on the idea that Ben would come around and adopt Partridge. She'd seen him sneaking the bulldog treats. She'd known he had a soft spot for him. But a lot of things she'd wanted to happen this Christmas looked like they were nothing more than holiday wishes.

The presents she'd wrapped for Ben and Astrid still sat on the sideboard as she passed. She still wanted them to have those pictures, those memories, but would it be weird to give them to them now?

Still wearing her pajamas, Ally shoved her feet into her boots and grabbed her coat, holding the door open for Colby and Partridge as she headed toward the shelter to say good morning to the other dogs, even if it was starting to feel like goodbye.

Chapter Thirty-Seven

Organizing an impromptu fundraiser on less than twenty-four hours' notice was, unsurprisingly, incredibly challenging. Ben stood backstage, going over his checklist one last time as the audience for the Christmas pageant filled the seats, and the noise on the other side of the curtain grew. His plan to rally the town and surprise Ally with a fundraiser to save the shelter was actually coming together. But there was still one last piece to the puzzle, and it was the piece he was the most worried about—how Ally would react.

Ben didn't usually do things he couldn't control, but he was about to now.

Astrid sat nearby with Partridge, who looked completely ridiculous in his top hat and bow tie, but seemed very proud of his ensemble. Ben had put in an application last night to adopt the bulldog—through Mrs. Gilmore, since he'd wanted to surprise Ally—though now, as the moment for the big reveal grew closer, he was seriously starting to wonder if surprise had been the best way to go. He'd thought a big public spectacle would prove to her that he was invested, that he wasn't going to try to put her in a box or hide her. But now it seemed like a really good way to set himself up for public rejection. A rejection he might deserve.

Astrid still didn't know he'd put in the application for Partridge. He'd wanted the dog to be a Christmas surprise…and he hadn't been entirely sure he'd be approved. The application was much more in depth than he'd expected, forcing him to think about all the responsibilities pet ownership entailed, but instead of overwhelming him, having it all laid out like that had made it seem more manageable.

If only everything in life came with a checklist.

"Ben? It's time."

Ben swallowed down a sudden rush of nerves. *Now or never.* He nodded to Gayle Danvers, the chief pageant organizer, who was all smiles now that she was helping him with his big romantic gesture—as if she hadn't called him a Grinch in the middle of the bakery only a few weeks ago.

"Thank you, Mrs. Danvers. I know you didn't have to do this."

Her snow-white brows arched high. "Are you kidding? I don't know what this town would do without you. This is the least we can do."

He blinked, too startled by her comment to reply before she had disappeared around the curtain.

Astrid handed him Partridge's leash and gave him a double thumbs-up. "Good luck," she whispered as a hush began to fall on the other side of the curtain. They must be dimming the house lights. Ben took his position center stage. Partridge waddled at his side and sat on his foot when he stopped, snorting softly.

He heard Gayle's heels click out to the center of the stage on the other side of the curtain and held his breath as she began her intro.

"Welcome, Pine Holloweens, to the twenty-second annual Pine Hollow Christmas Pageant! Merry Christmas!" Scattered applause and responses of Merry Christmas greeted her. "We're so delighted to have a pageant for you this year that is bigger and better than ever, but before we get started, we have a special announcement from our very own town councilman, Ben West! Let's hear it for Ben!"

Applause erupted as the curtain whisked back and a spotlight landed on him. Ben flinched at the unexpected sound, squinting against the bright light. He'd known, in theory, that he would be doing this in front of the whole town, but he hadn't really thought about the fact that they would be clapping and listening and *watching*.

"Say something," Astrid hissed from the wings, and he realized he'd been standing silent for too long. Partridge tipped over, his bulk landing against Ben's shins and grounding him in the present.

Ben lifted the microphone.

"Merry Christmas," he began. "As many of you know, in order to repair the roof on the community center, the town recently had to cut funding for the Furry Friends Animal Rescue, which led to the Pine Hollow community coming together to find homes for all of the dogs at the shelter." He cleared his throat. "But I've recently come to realize how vital the Furry Friends rescue is to our community and how great a loss it would be to Pine Hollow...and to me...if it were to close for good."

He squinted past the spotlight shining in his eyes. Expectant faces stared up at him from the front row—and Ally stared back at him from the third row with questions all over her face.

Ben extended a hand. "Um, Ally, do you think you could come up here?"

Ally glanced back and forth to her grandparents, who were seated on either side of her. At their urging, she climbed to her feet, edging along the row until she reached the aisle.

"I know many of you have met Ally Gilmore in the last few weeks and seen what an asset she is to our community," Ben said as Ally approached the steps up to the stage. "It seemed like it was the least we could do to try to help her keep the shelter open." Ally climbed up to the stage, and Ben came downstage to meet her, Partridge waddling at his side. "So tonight, we aren't just having our usual pageant. The twenty-second annual Pine Hollow Christmas Pageant is now the First Annual Pine Hollow Christmas Pageant and Furry Friends Fundraiser."

Ally froze, staring at him with wide eyes. He caught her hand to keep her from retreating as a ripple went through the audience.

"Tonight, thanks to generous donations from local businesses, a number of unique Pine Hollow experiences will be up for auction on the town website. We have a fully catered event from the Cup, a three-tiered pastry tower from Magda's Bakery, a princess party from Deenie Mitchell, as well as private ski lessons, a year's worth of snowplowing, and many more incredible opportunities. Bid early, bid often, and be generous. We want to keep Furry Friends open for as long as we can, so this is the one time no one will be annoyed with you for being on your phone in the middle of the pageant." A ripple of laughter went through the crowd. "We'll have some of our donors up here throughout the night to tell you about the prizes you can win. All auctions close at midnight."

Ben's gaze dropped to where he was holding Ally's hand. *Now for the hard part.*

He could have ended right there. He could have urged her offstage and said the rest in private, but tonight he had something to prove. He knew the town was watching, but he didn't look at them. He looked right into Ally's eyes and nervously cleared his throat, the sound loud through the microphone he still clutched in a death grip.

"For the last few weeks—" Ben broke off, starting again. "I know I'm not the easiest guy to—uh. Crap." He'd practiced this in his head. He had the words, but now they were all jumbled up.

"What are you doing?" she whispered.

She looked so gorgeous. Dark curls knotted on top of her head like they had been the first time she'd stormed into town hall. A red Christmas dress hugged her curves, but it was her eyes that killed him. The dark brown depths watched him warily, as if afraid he was going to hurt her—and he never wanted to hurt her again.

"I love you," he blurted loudly into the microphone.

The audience gasped, including Ally, and words began spilling out of Ben's mouth.

"You make everything that overwhelms me feel manageable because I know we can do it together, but that isn't why I want you—not just because you make it easier...Crap, I'm doing this wrong....I want to share *things* with you. Everything. With you. I...You." He forced himself to breathe. His face felt like it was swelling. Was it possible to go into anaphylactic shock from nerves? "This is all for you. Because you *do* have a place here—whether it's with me or not, but I really want it to be with me. I'm sorry. So sorry. About everything. I know I'm not exactly a catch. I know I'd be getting the better end of the bargain, and you have no reason—" He was going to asphyxiate. He was going to pass out from panic. That was dignified.

"Ben," she whispered, and he focused on her eyes. The warm, crinkling humor in them grounded him.

"I'm messing this up," he whispered back. "Save me?"

Ally stared up at the man of her dreams, trying not to laugh as he bumbled his way like a wrecking ball through his big romantic moment—but she wouldn't have had it any other way. Ben always wanted everyone to see the poised version, the perfect version. He was annoyed by his flaws and his vulnerabilities. But he was throwing them open to her and everyone who loved him tonight.

She could feel the audience's eyes on them. His parents, her grandparents, Deenie and Connor and Elinor and the mayor and her wife. The whole town was here. And he was holding her hand, onstage, in public. But he hadn't stopped there. Ben West didn't do anything by half measures.

His face was also turning a concerning purple color.

Ally stepped forward, closing the distance between them before the man she loved passed out in front of the entire town. "*I'm* the lucky one. I'm crazy about you, Ebenezer West," she told him, close enough now that the microphone caught her words—and all their friends and neighbors sighed.

He grinned, his eyes dropping to her lips—

"Uncle Ben!" A hiss from the wings stopped him. They both looked over to where Astrid stood offstage, waving something that looked like a hobo stick. Ally frowned, but Ben just grinned.

"Right. Sorry. *Now.*" Ben gave Astrid a nod and she marched onto the stage, carrying a long pole—with a cluster of mistletoe tied to the end. She angled the bough so it dangled directly above their heads, fighting a smile.

"I screwed up the mistletoe thing before." Ben looked down at Ally with a crooked grin. "Wanna try again?"

The smile on her face must have been brighter than the spotlight. She felt like she was glowing, radiating happiness out of every pore. She gripped his lapels, tugging him down to her as she went up on her toes. "Absolutely."

Ben pulled her snug against him and smiled through the hoots and calls of encouragement from the audience— one of which sounded distinctly like Deenie. Ally was smiling so hugely she wasn't sure she'd be able to stop long enough to kiss him. He hesitated with his smile about an inch from hers and slowly slid one hand along the side of her face, threading his fingers into her hair, and the rest of the world faded away. It was just him, and her, and the mistletoe. Ally wet her lower lip and Ben's gaze tracked the movement. Then he was closing that last inch.

Her breath suspended, his lips touched hers, and she was home.

Choirs began singing "I'll Be Home for Christmas" in her head—and it wasn't until moments later when Ben lifted his head that she realized they were singing in real life too. She was home. The people of Pine Hollow were cheering. The mayor shouted, "Best Christmas pageant *ever*!" And Ben called, "Don't forget to bid on the auction items!" over the melee.

Then he kissed her again as her mother's favorite song played.

And Ally had to agree. Best Christmas ever.

Chapter Thirty-Eight

P artridge?!" A shriek of delight echoed off the rafters as Astrid flung herself at him. "Oh my goodness, thank you, Uncle Ben! Thank you, thank you, thank you! You are the best uncle ever in the history of uncles! And Ally!" Astrid pulled away from Ben to throw herself at Ally. "Thank you so much! I know you did this!"

"I can't take credit. This was all your uncle," Ally protested, but Astrid didn't hear her, too excited to be contained, already wrenching herself away and bounding across the room.

"Grandma! Grandpa! We're getting a dog!"

"I think she likes her present." Ally tucked herself against his side on the couch, grinning.

Christmas morning was in full swing. The Gilmores had arrived before dawn—which wasn't that early in northern Vermont, but it had still been dark out as Astrid rushed everyone into the living room, barely pausing to greet Colby, Partridge, and Copper in her excitement.

Astrid had torn through her presents, ricocheting from
elation to delight and back again—and that had been
before she realized her single greatest wish had been
granted. Partridge was here to stay.

Ben had wrapped a box with a note saying Astrid
could keep Partridge—since that seemed safer than
trying to put the bulldog in a box. He watched her
fling her arms around Partridge. It was hard to stand in
the way of that much happiness. He was going to have
his work cut out for him keeping her from adopting
an entire menagerie if she kept falling in love with the
dogs at the shelter—since he knew Astrid wasn't going
to stop volunteering now that Furry Friends would be
staying open.

Right on cue, the *Jaws* theme played in his pocket,
and Ben fished out his phone. This was one email to the
town account he wasn't dreading.

"Uh oh," Ally groaned, leaning close. "What is it this
time? It better be good for Christmas morning. Did Santa
break another roof that needs to be repaired?"

"Not that I know of." Ben angled his phone so she
could see the screen. "Connor just emailed me the final
tally from the fundraiser last night."

Ally peered at the numbers, her eyes going round.
"Ben…"

"What do you think? Wanna stick around for a while
and run the shelter?"

Ally met his eyes, her own misty. "You know I'm not
going anywhere."

They'd talked for hours last night—after he'd made a
spectacle of himself at the pageant, they'd snuck back-

stage and found a convenient curtain for both of them to hide behind.

They'd worked out a plan, which her grandparents had loved when they'd all discussed it over eggnog after the pageant. The money from the fundraiser would keep the shelter afloat until Ally could put the rest of her plans for turning Furry Friends into a Pine Hollow pet mecca into action. She would rent the farmhouse from her grandparents so they could still afford to move to the Estates right away. Deenie was even considering letting her sublet go and moving in with Ally.

And maybe down the road, when Ben finished his remodeling projects and he and Astrid were looking for more space...well. There was plenty of space at the farmhouse. But that was a possibility for another day.

Delia and her wife, Margaret, had stopped them after the pageant last night to put in an application for Peanut, so the shelter's population was down to Dolce and her unclaimed puppies, but with the money from the fundraiser, the shelter would be well funded for months to come and able to take in more dogs in need.

Ally had also told him about her plans to sell her photos at a local farmer's market, where he had no doubt they were going to be a huge hit. The photos she'd framed for him and Astrid were already perched on the bookcase on either side of a framed photo of Katie and Paul. He hadn't realized what a difference a few photos could make until he saw them and everything felt a little more right, a little more like home. The only thing that could have made them more perfect was if Ally was in them, too.

The photos were the best present he'd opened all day—though the Keurig "from Astrid," no doubt with her grandparents' financial assistance, had definitely come close.

As Astrid bounded around the room, Ally reached under the tree to snag a wrapped present about the size of a book before returning to his side on the couch.

"What's this?"

"I have one more present for you," she murmured, her voice low enough not to attract the attention of the rest of their families.

Ben frowned. "You already gave me the photos. You trying to show up my mug?"

His gift already paled in comparison to hers. He'd gotten her a coffee mug—a simple white mug with the outline of Vermont in black and the word "home" tucked inside a heart. He'd thought it was cute at the time, since coffee was sort of their thing, but that was before he'd teared up opening the pictures she'd framed of him and Astrid.

"I love my mug," she insisted. "And it isn't a competition. And even if it was, you would win because you saved the entire shelter." She shoved the present into his hands. "Just open it, Scrooge."

He laughed, tearing the paper, but when he pulled off the wrapping his smile froze in confusion. It was a snapshot in a small frame, but he couldn't figure out why she'd framed a blurry image of the top of a tree and a fraction of roof. It looked like a mistake. He met her eyes and found them sparkling at him.

"Remember when I was taking pictures of the square,

and I slammed into a certain grumpy Scrooge and spilled coffee all over him? Turns out my finger hit the shutter right as I hit you. *This*"—she pointed to the photo—"is the exact moment we met."

A startled laugh burst out of his mouth, and he pulled her close. "Best present ever."

"Me? Or the photo?"

"Guess." He drew her toward him.

When they finally broke apart, Ally was flushed. She leaned into his side, watching Astrid roll around on the floor with Partridge. "Now that you've saved the shelter and made Astrid's entire life by letting her have a dog and fixed the roof on the community center and given Pine Hollow a Christmas pageant they'll be talking about for years to come, what are you going to do for your next trick?"

"Take a nap?"

Ally arched a brow. "So no immediate plans to run for office?"

He groaned. "Delia got to you."

"She makes very good points. You would be amazing."

"I'm barely keeping it together as it is."

Ally rolled her eyes. "What fun is keeping it together? I'm gonna teach you to love the chaos, Ebenezer."

"Rescue dogs and Christmas pageants and all?"

"Absolutely."

Four weeks ago he would have protested. He would have fought against that vision of the future tooth and nail. Chaos would have been his nightmare, but now...

Christmas debris was everywhere. Ally curled against his side. Colby snored at their feet while Copper growled a piece of ribbon into submission. His parents were laughing at a story Ally's grandmother was telling, complete with exaggerated gestures. It was a loud, messy Christmas morning—and it was perfect.

"We'll see," he grumbled. He had a reputation as a Scrooge to protect, after all. It wouldn't do to give in too easily—even if he had already filled out the paperwork to be on the ballot.

Astrid bounced over, flinging herself beneath the tree in search of more presents.

"Now that you have a dog, I never have to give you another present ever again, right?" Ben teased her. "I seem to remember something about how you would never ask for anything ever again if you could just have a dog."

"I don't know," Astrid said from her position on the floor, slanting Ally a sideways look. "I wouldn't mind a little brother."

Ben groaned as Ally burst out laughing. "Slow down, kiddo," he advised. "Take the win."

But as Astrid dove back beneath the tree in search of more loot, he looked at Ally, tucked beneath his arm, her eyes glinting at him, full of humor. His heart squeezed—and a baby didn't sound like such a bad idea. More chaos. More responsibility. More on his already overflowing plate.

More joy. More laughter. More reasons for his heart to swell.

Ben smiled, his voice low, just for Ally's ears, "Maybe Christmas after next."

She laughed, but her eyes searched his and her smile grew still. "Maybe," she whispered back.

They'd figure it out as they went along, but right now, sitting in his house, with Partridge groaning and rolling onto his back with all four feet flung into the air and Colby snoring loudly, with his parents laughing and Ally's grandfather nodding off in his chair and Paul and Katie's picture smiling down at them all...right now Christmas was almost perfect.

Then he leaned down and kissed her. And it was.

Acknowledgments

Writing is a solitary endeavor, but no book makes it into the world without a team behind it, and that is truer for this book than most. Deepest thanks go to my amazing editor, Leah Hultenschmidt, who had the original idea for a small-town dog shelter Christmas book and then helped my first draft become exponentially better with her notes—while geeking out with me over David Tennant. Thank you for making this experience so wonderful—and thanks also to the rest of the team at Forever Books for welcoming me into the Forever family.

Also to my agent, Michelle Grajkowski, without whom I never would have had the chance to write the Pine Hollow series, thank you so much for your faith.

Huge thanks to my beta readers—Kali, Kris, and, of course, my mom—who read everything I write and are the best sounding boards in the world as I talk my way through revisions. (And to my dad, who listens even though he has no idea what I'm talking about.) You are saints. All of you.

Thank you also to my writer friends who talk me through plot holes, especially Kim Law. You're the best brainstorming partner I could ever ask for—and if we sometimes get sidetracked talking about *The Bachelor*, that's just part of our "process."

I also must thank the many dog shelter workers, volunteers, and fosters who so generously shared their stories with me as I was researching this book, especially those at Speak for the Unspoken. There are so many dogs out there in need of good homes, and these people work tirelessly to find each dog their forever home. They are absolute heroes.

And finally, I need to thank the canine inspirations for this book, the past and present fur babies I was lucky enough to love: Darby, Brady, and Byron. Bruno, Stinker, Tok, Shadow, and Lani. Biscuit, Jelly, Mia, Brianna, and Gracie. May we all be fortunate enough to have a pup wriggle their way into our hearts to stay.

About the Author

Contemporary romance author Lizzie Shane was born in Alaska and still calls the frozen north home, though she can frequently be found indulging her travel addiction. Thankfully, her laptop travels with her, and she has written her way through all fifty states and over fifty countries.

Lizzie has been honored to win the Golden Heart Award and HOLT Medallion, and has been named a finalist three times for Romance Writers of America's prestigious RITA Award®, but her main claim to fame is that she lost on *Jeopardy!* For more about Lizzie and her books, please visit www.lizzieshane.com.

Fall in love with these charming contemporary romances!

A VERY MERRY MATCH
by **Melinda Curtis**

Mary Margaret Sneed usually spends her holiday baking and caroling with her students. But this year, she's swapped shortbread and sleigh bells to take a second job—one she can never admit to when the town mayor starts courting her. Only the town's meddling matchmakers have determined there's nothing a little mistletoe can't fix . . . and if the Widows Club has its way, Mary Margaret and the mayor may just get the best Christmas gift of all this year. Includes a bonus story by Hope Ramsay!

THE TWELVE DOGS OF CHRISTMAS
by **Lizzie Shane**

Ally Gilmore has only four weeks to find homes for a dozen dogs in her family's rescue shelter. But when she confronts the Scroogey councilman who pulled their funding, Ally finds he's far more reasonable—and handsome—than she ever expected . . . especially after he promises to help her. As they spend more time together, the Pine Hollow gossip mill is convinced that the Grinch might show Ally that Pine Hollow is her home for more than just the holidays.

CHRISTMAS ON REINDEER ROAD
by Debbie Mason

After his wife died, Gabriel Buchanan left his job as a New York City homicide detective to focus on raising his three sons. But back in Highland Falls, he doesn't have to go looking for trouble. It finds him—in the form of Mallory Maitland, a beautiful neighbor struggling to raise her misbehaving stepsons. When they must work together to give their boys the Christmas their hearts desire, they may find that the best gift they can give them is a family together.

SEASON OF JOY
by Annie Rains

For single father Granger Fields, Christmas is his busiest—and most profitable—time of the year. But when a fire devastates his tree farm, Granger convinces free spirit Joy Benson to care for his daughters while he focuses on saving his business. Soon Joy's festive ideas and merrymaking convince Granger he needs a business partner. As crowds return to the farm, life with Joy begins to feel like home. Can Granger convince Joy that this is where she belongs? Includes a bonus story by Melinda Curtis!

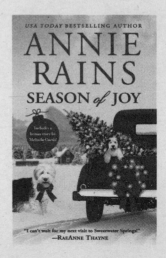

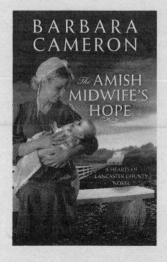

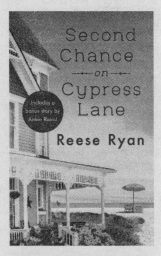

**SECOND CHANCE ON
CYPRESS LANE**
by Reese Ryan

Rising-star reporter Dakota Jones is
used to breaking the news, not making it. When a scandal costs her her
job, there's only one place she can go
to regroup. But her small South Car-
olina hometown comes with a major
catch: Dexter Roberts. The first man
to break Dakota's heart is suddenly
back in her life. She won't give him
another chance to hurt her, but she
can't help wondering what might
have been. Includes a bonus story by
Annie Rains!

FOREVER WITH YOU
by Barb Curtis

Leyna Milan knows family lega-
cies come with strings attached,
but she's determined to prove that
she can run her family's restaurant. Of course, Leyna never
expected that honoring her grandfather's wishes meant opening a
second location on her ex's
winery—or having to ignore Jay's
sexy grin and guard the heart he
shattered years before. But as they
work closely together, she begins
to discover that maybe first
love deserves a second chance…